AGAIN

GOODBYE AGAIN

Joseph Hone

>>>THE LILLIPUT PRESS >> DUBLIN

For Susie

First published 2011 by
THE LILLIPUT PRESS
62–63 Sitric Road, Arbour Hill
Dublin 7, Ireland
www.lilliputpress.ie

ISBN 978 1 84351 189 2

10 9 8 7 6 5 4 3 2 1

A CIP record for this title is available
from The British Library.

Set in 11 pt on 15.5 pt Caslon by Marsha Swan
Printed by Grafo in Spain

Engaging in denial and repression in order to save oneself the difficult task of integrating an experience into one's personality is of course by no means restricted to survivors. On the contrary, it is the most common reaction to the holocaust – to remember it as a historical fact, but to deny or repress its psychological impact, which would require a restructuring of one's personality and a different world view from that which one has heretofore embraced.

—Bruno Bettelheim, *Surviving the Holocaust*, 1986

Ben's Story

I saw the woman coming towards me at the reception in the big house at Killiney after my mother's funeral.

My heart missed a beat. It was Katie.

But it couldn't be her. Katie was dead. Yet how like her this woman was. The same measured, careful step, light on her feet, narrow shoulders. Same untended, short dark hair, flat-soled shoes, a casually unfashionable air. An impression of reserve: composed, decorous. Like Katie.

I was talking with the rabbi. My mother Sarah had been one of his congregation at the Adelaide Road Synagogue in Dublin. Now the woman hovered nearby.

I glanced at her again, uncertain. Perhaps it was the wine, promoting so strong a memory of Katie that I saw her now in any dark-haired woman, roughly the same looks, height and build. But no, this woman was so much like Katie – the same smallish height and build, the brown-green eyes, and the sharp cut of cheekbones, jawline, chin. Same compact body, where the shapes tended to be flat rather than curved, apart from the breasts, vaguely defined beneath a loose-fitting, navy-blue, silk blouse.

And more than the sum of all the parts – the same elusive ambiguous air: provocative yet guarded. A look that beckoned, but warned. 'My body perhaps, but you will never possess me.' It was as if Katie had been resurrected in a slightly altered physical state, but with a change of spirit and character, transformed into an easier, more available, less contrary person. A new Katie, who would wipe out the despair I felt in my loss of Katie herself – this new Katie, a wonderful gift, ready packaged, waiting for me a few yards away, a recompense.

My talk with the rabbi was interrupted by Sam McCartney offering condolences. McCartney was my mother's solicitor and now sole executor of her estate. Ageing, in his seventies, but still a big, pushy, florid-faced man, an old rugby hearty who had once played prop forward for Ireland. He usually sported a houndstooth tweed jacket, sometimes a scarlet waistcoat. Loudly dressed, loud-mouthed. Now he was more soberly garbed. A man I'd never liked. Over-friendly, tricky. And partly to blame for some of the problems in my early life, through his influence over my mother – agreement about my 'cheek' as he'd put it to her, in my declining sensible jobs in Dublin after I'd left school and wanted to be a painter.

So I had no qualms in cutting him and moving towards the woman. Close to her now, the resemblance was more pronounced. This woman and Katie were almost twins. Seeing my surprise, and thinking it due to her having broken up my talk with Sam McCartney, she was apologetic.

'I am sorry to interrupt. Forgive me.'

'No, not at all. I'd had my say there.' I couldn't take my eyes off her, so that I had to apologize in turn. 'Sorry … for staring.'

She made no acknowledgment of this. She seemed to have something more urgent in mind. 'I don't know quite where to begin,' she said quickly.

She must have been in her mid forties. Katie had been the same age. Had been? It was hard to think of her in the past tense. And I'd tried not to think of her this way for nearly a week.

'I'm sorry, Signor Contini,' the woman went on, 'I wanted to offer my sympathy on your mother's death, but didn't want to intrude at the service or cemetery.'

'No, no, that's quite all right.' With several drinks on board already I found my stride with her in a bright manner. 'Call me Ben. Certainly not "Signor", I'm only half-Italian and barely know the country. And of course I don't mind you coming here. My mother did have some friends of her own in Dublin. Though not many of this lot.' I waved my bandaged hand – I'd burnt it the week before – at the room. 'Half these dreadful businessmen and their pampered wives I don't know at all. And most of the other half I'd prefer not to know. Very few of them knew my mother anyway. She was something of a recluse. But you knew her, obviously.' I smiled. 'You were a friend of hers.'

'Well, no, actually. That's the problem.'

She frowned, at a loss, and I saw a sudden look of fear in her face, as if she was about to be confronted by some danger in the big drawing room. This was unlikely, filled as it was by some sixty respectable, boring and now discreetly convivial mourners, including a government minister, crowding out the dark-panelled, heavily carpeted space with its two great mock-Gothic mullioned windows looking out over Killiney Bay. It was a premonitory alarm, I decided. The rough outlines for a full portrait that would one day tell the whole sad story. I gazed at her now, as if appraising her for that very portrait.

'The problem?' I asked.

'Yes. You see, I didn't know your mother at all. Or your father. Never knew anything about your family until my father spoke to me about you this morning.'

'Your father?'

'Yes,' she rushed on, a memory of Middle Europe in her voice, firmer tones of America. 'He's very ill at home.'

'I'm sorry.'

'He's over eighty, and wanders. But he was quite clear this morning when he spoke to me about you and your family. He'd heard about your mother's death somehow, and he said to me, "You must go to Sarah Contini's funeral today, wife of old Luchino Contini. And speak to her son Ben. He'll be there. He'll explain everything. You must go and talk to him." So, you see, here I am.'

'Yes … there you are. And here am I.'

There was silence between us in the loud room, each of us gazing at the other uncertainly. The woman was clearly put out by the whole puzzling situation. For, equally clearly, she was a confident woman, keen to control things, to win. Just like Katie.

'I'm sorry. It must all sound rather crazy. You see, I've no idea …' She left the idea hanging in the air, even more put out by her failure to bring it to earth.

'Well, I wonder if you've made some mistake? If perhaps you misunderstood your father?'

She frowned again, bridling at this. 'No. No, certainly not. I heard him perfectly clearly. And he wasn't wandering at that point.' She looked at me dismissively, with rather the same air of smug detachment that Katie used to assume when she was in the wrong, and wouldn't admit it.

There was a chill impasse between us until, with a small sigh, she relented a fraction, but in a manner that suggested I was a tiresome child and she was only doing so because she was a guest in the house, and still needed to talk to me.

'The point is,' she said pedantically, 'I've no idea why my father said what he did. He didn't explain anymore: went all vague again … he's on morphine. But it seems clear he knew your parents well. Yet neither of my parents – my mother's dead – ever mentioned your parents to me, or you. So I don't know what he was getting at. Yet it was obviously important to him that I went to your mother's funeral, and met you.'

'Well, I've no idea why, either. Though, of course …' I saw my advantage here, but didn't press it in my tone. 'I might know your family, might know the connection, if you told me your family name. Your own name?'

The point struck home. She was put out again, and disliked the position even more this time. 'I'm sorry. I should have introduced myself at the start.' She was flustered. There was a scattiness about her that I liked, quite at odds with her previously controlled and schoolmistressy air. She had lost control for a moment.

'I'm … I'm Elsa Bergen, from further back up the hill, behind the Vico Road. Georgian house. We've lived there for years, since my parents came here from Austria as refugees after the war.'

'There's a connection, then. My father was a refugee as well. Luchino Mario Contini,' I said with something of a flourish. 'Italian-Jewish – he died here last year. And my mother was Dublin Jewish. But Bergen – that's not a Jewish name. Refugees from where?'

'Not Jewish, no. Catholic. My grandfather, then my father, they had an antiques shop in Vienna before the war. Mostly religious stuff – the family was very religious. But the shop was destroyed in the bombing there and most of his family killed. Except his wife, my mother, Anna, who died two years ago. My father was away in the German army during the war, and he survived as well. After the war, since they'd both hated the Nazis, and there was nothing left for them in Austria, they wanted a new life somewhere. They came to Dublin eventually, helped by the Quakers, and my father started another antiques and art shop here and bought the house in Killiney. I suppose you might describe my father as a "Good German".'

'You said he was Austrian.'

'More or less the same thing then, wasn't it?'

'Yes. You could say the same about my father. He was a "Good Jew" from what little I gathered of his life in Italy. But a stupid one. He and his family wouldn't deny their faith or hide during the war and decided to openly tough it out. They were very assimilated Jews. They never thought their Gentile chums, or their friends in the fascist militia, would get around to arresting and sending them off to the death camps. They were wrong. That's just what happened to them. In 1943, after Mussolini's government collapsed and the Germans took over in Italy, the SS and their Italian buddies started to hunt out the Jews seriously. They got my father and all his family, in Pisa where they lived, and north at Carrara, and packed them off to a camp for Italian Jews at Modena, and from there to Auschwitz. My father was the only one of his family to survive.'

'I'm sorry,' she said simply, eyes blinking. She touched her nose, unconsciously, then smoothed the minute crow's feet either side of her eyes. Mottled-green pupils set in wide white ovals, long dark eyebrows. Yes, mid forties, I thought. A little younger than me. Fresh, sober, sensible. No make-up or jewellery. A neat, sharply ridged nose, fine mouth, delicate lips, half-open, showing the pips of bright teeth, her mouth like a moist cut in an autumn fruit. Beautiful, in an open-air, the hell-with-fashion manner.

And then the sort of athletic body I liked, equally unfashionable in these anorexic times. The firm neck set on an unexpectedly short torso, well-set breasts, the narrowing waist running out to wide hips, a compact backside, the sense of sturdy legs below that. I'd like to have undressed her and started to paint her there and then.

'Yes …' I said, thinking. Then I pulled myself together and

shrugged. 'My father, his family – a sad story, among millions of other Jews. Though he soon recovered himself, did very well when he got to Dublin. Married my mother: she was from a rich Dublin Jewish family, bought this great mock baronial pile. All these terrible pictures …' I gestured round the room. 'That one, of my mother.' I pointed to a large, 1950s chocolate-box portrait over the fireplace of a youngish, somewhat plump woman, in pearls with permed hair, made to look exotic in a billowy eau-de-Nil tea gown.

'My father had that commissioned by some terrible Irish artist. And the rest …' I swung my arm further round the room. 'Russell Flint reproductions – *Persian Slave Market* and such like. And Alma-Tadema. There's one over there of his I particularly dislike.' I took her over to it. '*Egyptian Morning at the Baths*. But did you ever see a woman's nude body look like Russell Flint and Alma-Tadema has them? Quite sexless. A woman's body is full of awkward shapes and lengths, unexpected crevices and colours, flattish bits and slopes and little hillocks. That's where the beauty is. And the sexiness.' I turned and looked at her, nodding briefly, in open appreciation of the real thing.

She was put out by my gaze. 'Well, I'm very sorry about your father.' Wanting to change the subject even more, she continued, 'Was he a businessman?'

'Yes, but he was a civil engineer as well, before the war. He and his family owned the Contini marble quarries outside Pisa, and a larger quarry at Carrara, one of the famous white-marble quarries there. Mussolini was always wanting tons of stuff for his bloody great imperial buildings, so my father was exempted from military service, and that's what he made his business when he got over here to Dublin after the war: importing marble from Carrara, for fireplaces, floors, pillars, tables and tombstones. The lot. No artistic taste, but he knew about marble. That big fireplace he had made over there for example: hideous design, phoney Gothic with those simpering, half-clad maidens at either side – it's dreadful, but the marble's wonderful. Carrara Cremo. Pure, veinless white. Hard but smooth as soap. Run your hand over one of the girls – go on, try it – the marble is just like the inside of a real woman's thighs. Michelangelo used the same sort. Cut it himself from the same quarry in Carrara for his statue of David.' Now there's a realistic body for you! No coy underplaying of the muscles and genitals – the whole thing about to explode with power and sex.'

'Well, I'm glad your father was so successful when he came here.'

'Oh, he did very well when he met my mother. And you know what?' I drank again. 'She hasn't left me a penny! Just all these awful pictures. The house and the rest of her money all goes to a Dublin charity. A cruel, mean woman.'

'I see.' She was cool, clearly shocked that I should so openly disparage my mother.

'You'd understand my feelings if you knew how she treated me. I'm not trying to drown my sorrows for her, I can tell you. It's someone else who's just died on me. Rather knocked me out.'

'I'm sorry.' She made no further enquiries here. She fidgeted. She would have made her excuses and left, I'm sure, but for the unfinished business she had with me.

'So,' I said, 'it seems our parents knew each other. Both our fathers refugees from the Nazis, and our families living not half a mile apart here in Killiney. Yet you and I never met, know nothing of the other's family. Strange.'

'Yes.'

'I'm sure we'll find the connection.' I looked at her now without desire and a sober smile. 'Some simple explanation.'

She didn't return the smile.

'I'm sorry.' I put down my glass. The wine had brought me to the desired stage of forgetting Katie, or rather, it had brought me to the comforting belief that she was still alive and I was with her again. It was time to properly concern myself with this revenant. 'I'm sorry to have been abrupt about my mother. I loved my father, but not her. She disliked me and bullied him, and I hate funerals, except for this part of them, the wake – and I usually come to enjoy that too much. Listen, I'm sorrier still not to have offered you any refreshment: Miss? Mrs? Ms?' I looked towards the table where the drinks were, which I'd ordered from Mitchell's in Kildare Street – on my mother's account. 'Gin, whiskey? Wine?'

'"Miss" I suppose, if you have to put a handle to the name. But call me Elsa. Elsa Bergen, my family name. Though I am married, legally at least. Don't even know where he is now …' She stopped abruptly, annoyed at herself for disclosing too much personal information. 'I'm sorry. I don't know what I was on about. Yes, a glass of wine would be lovely.'

We pushed our way to the drinks table. I reflected on the rider she had added to her marriage. I turned to her. 'No need to be sorry, is there?' I asked.

'About what?'

'Your still being married. A common situation. Been mine, with my wife, for years.' I didn't add that this had been Katie's situation, too, married for almost as long, to a man who'd behaved badly to her and long separated without her ever bothering to divorce him. I just said, 'Divorce is such a bore, and so bad for the children. Who wants to put even more money in the hands of the bloody lawyers?'

'Yes.'

'Unless one wants to marry someone else.'

'Of course.'

Her face had brightened, perhaps at this idea of happy second chances. We'd got to the big table. 'There's some good red wine. A Châteauneuf, or even better, a white Châteauneuf.'

'A small glass of white would be lovely,' she said judiciously. I poured her a glass, another for myself. 'Canapés?' I asked. 'Awful word. Titbits is much better. Though you Americans say "tidbits". The old puritan ethic. But you're right, that was the original seventeenth-century spelling of the word in England.' I picked up a dish, then another. 'Some cheesy things, salami and anchovies, and olives. I love olives.' I offered her a bowl of big, purply black Greek olives.

'So do I!' She was suddenly excited, picking up one delicately, but unable to restrain the wolfing enthusiasm with which she ate it. 'Kalamata!' she said joyously, as if the Mediterranean fruit had released all her earlier inhibitions, her cagey, decorous formality. She was indecorous now, putting a hand almost roughly to her mouth, voiding the stone but not putting it aside, gazing at it as if it were a jewel discovered.

'I love olives.'

'Have another one.' I took one myself. She looked at me, startled, as if waking from another dream.

'No. No, I won't.' Controlled again, reverting to her earlier mood.

'Go on, for goodness sake, if you like them!'

She looked at me again, seeming to draw confidence and daring from my gaze. 'All right, I will!' She took another olive, then a third. 'I'm sorry to be greedy.'

'You're not. Expected thing to be at an Irish wake ... and thirsty.' I raised my glass. 'Happiness,' I said. 'I don't care for "Cheers" or "Your health". I'd prefer a good whack of happiness, whether I'm cheery or healthy or not.'

She raised her glass and took a fourth olive. Gorging on the juicy fruit, fingertips becoming purple, our rapport changed: we might have been old friends. People were pushing around us, chattering, she had to raise her voice. 'I do have some excuse, being greedy with the olives. I'm doing a book about them.'

'About olives?'

'Yes, olives and olive oil. The history and culture of the fruit, the different lands and landscapes which nurture it, its culinary, medicinal and other uses.'

'That sounds like the stuff they put inside the jacket.'

'Yes, it is. Just that.'

'Someone's actually going to publish it?'

'Yes, in New York. I've done several other books. I travel round different countries, meeting the chefs, the cooks, making notes. Then I write it all up when I get back. Travel, comment, cookbook.'

'Tremendous!' I meant it, but I could see she thought I was being ironic. 'Where do you get back to?'

'New York ... I have an apartment there. With frequent trips over here since my father became ill.'

'Well, we've all got to drop off the perch sometime. Make room for the rising generation. World's chock-a-block already, isn't it?'

I took another gulp of wine, swaying slightly. I realized she was astonished by this drunken, tactless comment. 'I'm sorry, I've been under the weather recently. Forgive me.'

I shepherded her away from the crowd round the drinks table, towards one of the big mullioned windows looking over the bay. We stood there silently, looking over the bright summer view, the unexpected clump of palm trees at the end of the garden, the crescent beach with its bathers and deckchairs to the left, the boathouse with my father's old motor cruiser, the *Sorrento*, inside to the right and the blue waters of the bay straight ahead.

'It's supposed to be like the Bay of Naples,' I remarked, quieter now, 'which is why my father wanted to live here. I've not seen the bay of Naples, but I bet the light would be quite different, and the colours. You'd get that whitish Mediterranean blue inshore, off the shallow rocks. Ultramarine, then deep Prussian-blue farther out. The headland over there – that'd be washed umber, a touch of bright ochre.'

'You're obviously a painter,' she said abruptly.

'Yes.'

'What sort?'

'Just paintings.' I continued to study the view. 'It's funny – your father and mine, if they were old friends – they might have stood here, right at this window, years ago, looking at exactly the same view. I wonder what they were talking about?' I turned and looked at her, blinking after the glare of sunlight coming off the water. 'Strange to think of one's parents, all the vast amount of things we don't know about them. What they did before we were born, and afterwards, when we weren't with them? It's the supreme egoism of children, isn't it, to think their parents only had a life when they were physically with them, playing or reading to them or whatever, when of course that was only the tip of the iceberg of their lives.'

'I suppose so.'

We looked out to sea, yachts and dinghies sailing over the choppy water, whitecaps riding further out in the bay. I turned to her again. 'So maybe there's no simple answer about why your father told you to come to the funeral, what it was that I was to "explain" to you. But we could work on it.'

'Yes, perhaps. We'll see.' She stalled. It was clear she didn't want to work on it, wanted to cut her losses and get away from me.

A big man, a building contractor, a client of my father, interrupted us then. 'Your dear good mother, Benjamin …' He grasped my hand for several minutes, maudlin, full of phoney commiseration and bonhomie.

After I'd done with him I looked round for Elsa. She'd gone. Just upped and left. We hadn't said goodbye, and there was still the mystery of our family connection to resolve. The way she resembled Katie – what did this mean? Was fate giving me a second chance? Did I want this? Katie had behaved appallingly and I surely didn't want a repetition of that.

I suddenly wanted this new woman Elsa – this Jekyll to Katie's Hyde. I'd contact her later – if I felt like it. Bloody rude of her, disappearing like that without a word. Just like Katie, I thought, so often vanishing in the middle of a meal or during an interval at the theatre. Contrary. I went back to the big table, refilled my glass, and set about provoking the other guests.

TWO ‹‹

Later, with all the convivial mourners gone, I stumbled around, alone in the drawing room, a little drunk.

Taking an opened bottle of the white Châteauneuf I moved about the house, from one overstuffed room to another. Mostly heavy Victorian furniture, but some fine Gothic revival pieces as well. My father had liked the style and collected it from various antique dealers. There were several original William Morris pieces: a dining table and chairs, an oak cupboard in the hall, a chest of drawers, cabinets and other pieces upstairs.

I swayed up the wide polished oak staircase to the bedrooms on the first floor and looked into the rooms – the guest rooms, my father's bedroom (in my memory my parents had always slept apart) where there was an extraordinary piece of furniture, a dressing-room toilet cabinet designed by William Burges, a splendidly quirky Victorian architect and furniture maker. The cabinet was delicately made, beautiful – largely done in pine, painted in red, yellow and black washes, with intricately worked brass fittings, cornerings and handles.

I opened it, displaying the rows of little drawers inside, pigeon-holes, a mirror, various clever places for toilet knick-knacks, a cupboard below containing a chamber-pot, washbowl and jug, all painted with garlands of bluebells and daisies.

I pulled out one of the little drawers. A cut-throat razor, a decayed shaving brush, an old bottle of Collis Browne's Tonic.

At the back of another drawer was a collection of small black-and-white photographs. My parents at the Dublin Horse Show years before. But then, beneath these, I came across something quite different. An older photograph. My father as a young man in an Italian army officer's uniform, smiling, pleased with himself. I'd not known my father had been in the army and thought he'd been exempted. Then I noticed the pith helmet and the Africans.

Of course. This was before the war, Mussolini's barbarous campaign in Abyssinia. My father had served out there, and here he was, at the head of a line of bedraggled, wounded and manacled Abyssinians. And my father holding the first of them, pulling him by a chain attached to his neck. I was surprised.

I went into my mother's big bedroom looking out over the bright, early-evening light on the bay. I sat down on the canopied four-poster bed. There was a formal studio portrait on a bureau nearby. My parents shortly after they'd married, sometime in the early fifties. They were smiling at each other. Not like later.

My father, small with darkly brilliantined hair, neat moustache, suave good looks, very Latin; almost a caricature of an Italian. His chest puffed out, with the same aggressive confidence of the earlier African photograph, but matured, diluted in this later portrait by his dark bedroom eyes, softened with intimations of passion, warmth, even nobility.

Cruelty and warmth. The photographs reflected the extremes in his character. He'd been a man of extraordinarily varied and unset-tled temperament. Quick to anger, with a ruthless edge to him, but then as quickly silent, as if stunned, when he became gentle and penitent, filled with tearful innocence.

His eyes in this photograph showed something else beyond the seductive Latin airs, the genial man about town with other Dublin businessmen, drinking gin and tonics in the old buttery bar downstairs in the Hibernian hotel. There were shadows in his eyes, the haunted look of a man who, at thirty, had seen and experienced the very worst in Auschwitz.

My mother, by contrast, showed a complete innocence in the studio photograph. A pleasant, round face, untouched by life. She was not like that later, when experience had laid hands on her. A face increasingly racked by pain and bitterness, vented often on me – I've never known why.

Taking the bottle I went up to the second floor where there was a long, glass-roofed landing with rooms to either side, guests' and maids' rooms years before. It was hot under the glass roof, where the sun had blazed down all through the long hot day. I sat on the floor, back against the wall, took the bottle, drank, closed my eyes and tried to laugh at my life.

I'd been a good all-round athlete at St Columba's College, my school up in the Dublin mountains: a first-team cricket and rugby player, and I became a quick hand at boxing too, as a middle-weight, taught by a burly cocksure ex-army sergeant, Johnny Branigan, who I had once surprised with a fast left hook to the jaw, stunning him for a moment, before he tried to do the same to me. After making a century in a cup match, I'd thought about becoming a professional cricketer with Middlesex. But when I was sixteen I fell in love with my father's motor cruiser, the *Sorrento*, still moored in the boathouse, crewing it with my father in all sorts of weather, up and down the Irish Sea. The passion I came to have for boats then, thinking I might join the British navy, until I got the recruiting brochure and application forms, and felt the cold shadows of hierarchy, duty, restrictions – not the freedom of the seas.

Eventually I realized I was best of all at painting and sculpting. A gift for drawing and colour, and handling clay. The art master at St Columba's encouraged me. So at sixteen I finally decided to be a painter. I remember the day in the art class when, annoyed at the general standard and leaning over a painting of mine, and in front of all the other boys, he said, 'Contini here, you'll never take a leaf out of his book. He has the gift, and you lot of pampered little jades don't.' The man was queer and fancied me as well as my work, but all the same he was probably right. I did have a gift. So I'd said to him, just to give cheek, 'Yes, Sir, I'm going to be a painter!' Then added for good measure, 'And a sculptor.' In fact, I was just an ambitious and aggressive schoolboy.

In any event my mother thought my being a serious painter was a hopeless idea, but my father encouraged me, paid my fees at the old College of Art in Kildare Street, and did the same later, financing me at the Beaux-Arts in Paris, where I studied painting and sculpture. My father was always keen for me to do well as an artist, and I liked him for that as much as anything. Now, thirty years later, I was still a painter – but blocked. Nothing decent done since the trouble with Katie brewed up two years ago. It used to be portraits and nudes, good stuff usually. Forceful, strong colours, the right lines and musculature. Paintings, and some commissioned sculpture, where there was nearly always more than the sum of the parts. That surprising extra – a hidden thought or sexiness in the sitter revealed, but in the art world now a painter scorned, with hardly a penny earned from my work in the last two years. I took another swig of the Châteauneuf.

I'd started out well enough after I'd left the Beaux-Arts, and stayed on in Paris. I'd soon come to sell my work well at a small Left Bank gallery. I'd begun painting in the manner of several artists.

Something of Utrillo, then Soutine, Modigliani. School of Paris style. Street scenes, portraits, nudes. Particularly nudes. I'd been fascinated by women's bodies ever since I was a child, about eleven, in bed with flu, and had a big Phaidon art book, *Modern Masterpieces*, which I'd found in the library. Halfway through there was an erotically reclining nude by Modigliani: it struck me with a blood-tingling sensation. I was startled by the provocative ease and availability of the woman, eavesdropping on her at a very private moment.

The picture stirred me sexually, so that I'd taken paper and traced it, my flu-fever seeming to increase the stimulation I took from it, copying it repeatedly, as if the better to possess every line and contour, every secret part of this marvellous woman. My mother found some of these tracings in my bed after I'd got up one day. She was shocked. 'What's the matter?' I'd challenged her. 'It's a modern masterpiece. It says so on the cover of the book.'

Later on in Paris the lines of my work became more rounded, the colours softer and more varied – Pissarro and Bonnard became the great influences. Pissarro for his street and river scenes, Bonnard for his nudes.

The way Bonnard handled the flickering points of light in a bathroom, on the tiles, a mirror, the bath water, on the skin of his wife immersed in the mottled, green-blue, seemingly molten liquid. There was a hidden sexuality in the colourings and the vague composition that made the woman seem ethereal and unavailable, all the more desired.

Portraits and nudes. The first became my bread and butter, the second my passion – when I returned to London in the seventies and married Angela – living in London near Primrose Hill, where the two children had been born, Molly and Beatrice, before the marriage started to disintegrate.

Angela had eventually taken up with an older married lover, an architect in Yorkshire, who wouldn't divorce and marry her. The usual story. She'd gone up to live near him in Yorkshire, where the two girls had gone to a Quaker boarding school that I'd paid for in those financially balmy years.

I rarely saw Angela now. Our relationship had drifted into indifference on her part and dulled incomprehension on mine. I'd never understood what she saw in the architect – a rather pompous, abrupt little man with a cracked front tooth, called Arthur. I always thought I had much more going for me.

I saw the two girls now and then: we were good, if rather distant friends. Molly, the elder at twenty and at university in Scotland, wants to be a forester. She has a boyfriend in the Highlands who works for the Forestry Commission. Beatty, two years younger, is still at the Quaker school doing A levels. Angela survives financially. A little money of her own and the lover subsidises her. Of course I should have divorced her years ago. She had behaved badly, running off like that with the shyster architect, but why divorce when no one else had come along whom I wanted to marry?

Until Katie, four years ago. I wanted to marry her all right. After three years of barely flawed happiness, I certainly wanted that. When I eventually asked her she said yes. The next day no, then finally chucked me, and then killed herself. Was it an accident? Perhaps the diary and scrapbook I found in her canvas bag will explain things. The bag she'd left last week, after I'd talked again about a proper future together, before she'd refused my offer and driven off without another word. A journal of some sort, when I'd looked at it briefly, but interleaved with dried wildflowers, Paris Metro tickets and the like from our country walks and trips abroad. An Album Consolatum, it might have been.

She'd had no need of this, I thought. She'd lived with me so tentatively and abandoned me so unexpectedly and completely a week before – why should she ever need to console herself for something she had never lost? She left me half an hour after we'd made love that summer afternoon – a last gift, and a permanent goodbye. I jumped into my old Bentley and followed her up the mile-long farm track that leads from my old barn in the Cotswolds to a small road at the top.

Near the top of the track I saw her car, rammed into the big beech tree in the flax field. By the time I got there the engine was on fire, flames licking up from the badly crushed bonnet. I thought she was dead, slumped over the wheel, the rim pressed into her chest. She wasn't dead. She pulled herself back and opened her eyes, and then the engine began to flame viciously, fire starting to engulf the car.

The windows were closed. 'Get out, for God's sake! Open the door, the windows!' She wouldn't. She sat there, immobile, her hair starting to singe, the body I had made love with half an hour before being consumed by fire, incarcerated in the steel oven of the car.

I pulled at the door handle. I couldn't open it. 'Open the door, Katie! Open, push it!'

She wouldn't, or couldn't. Instead she turned her head, and out of the pall of smoky fumes that were beginning to envelop her, she looked at me dismissively in that silent way she had of saying no. Elusive, unpossessed to the last. I kicked at the door like a madman. I didn't know if I was trying to save her or punish her, if I wanted her dead or alive, for I had come to hate her in these last years as much as I loved her.

I managed to get the door open at last and tugged at her, trying to drag her out, but she clung fiercely to the wheel, the flames leaping up from the dashboard, and my hair was beginning to singe. I had to retreat. 'Get out, Katie, for God's sake. Get out!' I screamed.

Then I heard a shout behind me. I turned. It was Tom Phillips, my farmer landlord who lived at the head of the track, running towards me.

'Quick!' I said when he reached me. I had to save her life, which was mine as well, I realized, for I loved her then without reserve, knowing there might be only seconds left to save us both.

Tom and I, diving into the smoke and fire, finally managed to drag her out of the car. We were too late. Her dark hair was gone and only the stubbled, sooty crown of her skull was left. She was half-naked, her clothes burnt away, some still burning. Patches of the skin on her face had peeled away, displaying little volcanoes of bubbling, bleeding red – the fatty flesh of her breasts and biceps blistering, suppurating. She fell out of the car into the flax field, like a collapsed scarecrow, still smoking. And my last sight of her, before I had to turn away, was her face among the crushed blue flax, a happy-anguished face, seeing all that was special there for an instant, that particular nose that had rubbed mine, the small mouth that had kissed, the eyes that had seen, ears that had heard – all her senses that I had shared, the whole life that I had loved burnt out of her. The ambulance came and took her away. Tom took me back to his house, where I called one of Katie's grooms at the riding school she owned, and told him what had happened – that Katie had been taken off to the hospital in Oxford. The groom, a taciturn fellow, barely responded, as if I'd just called to say she'd be late for tea. Since Katie hadn't any close relations, I told the groom to call her friend, Monika – the only friend of Katie's that I knew about – who lived next-door to the riding school. 'Ask Monika to go to the hospital, deal with things,' I told the man. Then I could speak no more. Katie was surely dead.

I stayed up at the farmhouse with Tom and his wife Margery. They gave me a tot of brandy and later a young policeman came to interview us. I told the man all that had happened, and Tom confirmed it. The policeman took our names and addresses, and Tom brought me back to my barn, where I started in on the drink; the last of some cooking brandy and a bottle of Bulgarian red, gone before Tom arrived down the lane again with a message from Sam

McCartney in Dublin. My mother had died that afternoon. Would I come straight over? Tom said he'd drive me to Birmingham Airport the next morning. I could think of nothing but Katie then, anguished, the pain only beginning.

'It must have been an accident,' I said to Tom. 'We'd had a row, so she drove away like fury, then skidded off the track and straight into that beech tree.'

'I don't know about an accident,' Tom said. 'The track is dead straight there, and firm. Nothing to skid on, and the beech tree is a good twenty yards off the track, the sun behind her, and the car almost new. You'd have to have had a real intention to drive into that tree.'

Maybe Tom was right. It hadn't been an accident. It was suicide. After all, I'd seen her face, entirely conscious, scorning fate, making her own funeral pyre. That would have been very like her. Why should she kill herself just because I'd asked her for a proper life together? That was hardly a killing matter. If it was suicide there must have been some other reason. Only one thing certain – Katie was gone and all I had of her now were definitive memories.

Even when she was alive they often seemed definitive, since latterly I never knew if I was going to see her again. After weeks without seeing her – my only contact just an evening phone call now and then, when I'd try, and usually fail, to get through to her from the phone box beside the pub I went to near Chipping Norton, she would turn up out of the blue for sex in the afternoon, or sometimes for the night, and then disappear for another few weeks or longer.

I'd learned to be without her in any real sense. I lived alone and tried to bury myself in my work, painting furiously, each canvas worse then the last, and working on a nude sculpture of her in red Cornish clay.

My last good painting was of Katie, done over two years before, during our good times. I'd painted her lying naked in the foreground of the hazy, mauve-blue flax-flowered field beyond my barn, at the end of the long track, in the middle of nowhere.

I'd sold the painting for £6000, surviving for the last few years on the £4000 or so – after my dealer's commission – that her naked body had fetched. The money was just enough for the rent, paint, canvases, smokes, drinks, food and petrol for the battered old green 1947 Bentley that I'd accepted instead of a fee for a portrait ten years before. I should have taken cash. I was running out of it even then, and I didn't have enough to pay the rent of the flat in Primrose Hill, so that after Angela left I abandoned the flat and looked for something in the country.

I found the old barn by chance, travelling the north Cotswolds one day. I'd stopped at a pub in Chipping Norton and asked the landlord if he knew of anywhere to rent, an old barn or outhouse, as a studio. It was market day. He pointed to a sharp-faced, bird-like little man in a cloth cap sitting with a large jolly woman in the corner. 'Ask him – Tom Phillips, local farmer. He might have something.' He did.

I paid him only a nominal rent of £20 a month for the barn. Tom just wanted me to legally occupy the building to keep one of his scheming daughters and her husband at bay, who had started to convert the barn, assuming, wrongly, that her father was leaving her the place. His daughter had already installed an open staircase, half an upper floor and two large skylights, which made a fine north-facing studio.

I lived downstairs in the long open space, the birds high above me. Several pairs of immigrant doves came and went over the seasons and years, nesting way up in the rafters, flapping and warbling urgently in the spring, chuckling softly on dark winter days, a chorus of quiet ease, their white droppings and feathers coming to litter the floor like a strange snowfall – rafters from which I'd hung a battered chandelier, an old theatrical prop, made of gilded papier-mâché, heavily baroque, which I'd found in the local dump.

Downstairs there was a huge open fireplace at one end, flagstones and bare stone walls. A divan bed, tattered carpets, a sofa with the stuffing leaking out, some old armchairs, tables and bookshelves that I'd picked up at local sales or from the rubbish tip. There was electricity but no telephone, plumbing or water. I had to go out the back to a hand pump for that. No lavatory either. I used the ancient privy in a rackety wooden shed behind the barn.

Everything was basic in the barn. That was the thrill of the place – that it wasn't a house, simply four bare walls and a roof, the long empty space downstairs a stage that I could make over entirely in my own images, moving the furniture about or just sitting there thinking of things, looking at the partly completed clay nude of Katie, drinking a glass or two of cheap Bulgarian red, listening to my Verdi CDs or an old Richard Tauber tape on my music centre and not worrying about the dirt. A roaring log fire in winter, cool within the great thick walls in summer. No sound but the wind in the corn, or the strange delicate swish of the breeze as it passed over the mauve-blue flax, moving across the hazy flowers in a long wave, the hand of God. Bright mornings of birdsong – crows in the beech trees, larks in the spring air. I love the place, though now and then I feel I could do with some company.

On winter Sundays I went up to the farmhouse and had elaborate teas with Tom and his wife Margery, the last of the old-fashioned farming people in the area. Great slices of breadcrumbed ham, cut from the bone, cold roast beef, horseradish sauce, Branston pickle, tomatoes and salad cream, all manoeuvred onto thick slices of fresh, crusty white bread, which Margery baked – the meal washed down with strong tea, laced with gin if you wanted it, for this was a traditional Sunday ritual of Tom's. Sometimes as a result of these great whacks of gin in the tea, and having picked up logs in the yard and put them in the boot of the Bentley, I would take off down the lane in splendid state, singing 'The Skye Boat Song' loudly, the car swinging madly in and out of the ruts. Yes, a mad life lost in the wolds, and a fine madness when Katie was there.

She'd come regularly to the barn and spend nights and most weekends during the first three years of our affair, and I'd painted her time and again, summer and winter, portraits, nudes, sitting, standing, lying out on the low divan, pushed near the big fire in winter, naked in the warmth, her skin with a reddish tinge, coloured by the glowing logs.

Then things changed for her at home, and she came less and less often to the barn, then hardly at all, and didn't care much to see me up at the stables either. I painted her only once after that, over a year ago, the nude of her lying at the edge of the flax field. After that she wouldn't be painted, and my painting went to pot. I practically gave it up.

I took some more Châteauneuf, rolled myself a cigarette. So much for my various careers. The long struggle for good work seemed to have ended here, where it had begun thirty years before – upstairs, further upstairs, in this house. There was another, narrow stairway at the end of the landing, leading up to the attics. I got up and made towards it, climbing the steep stairs, sweating.

I'd made a studio for myself in one of these attic rooms when I was eighteen and first studying art in Dublin. I'd fitted it out in all the traditional ways as I'd seen them then: an attic with a skylight giving north light, dark drapes, a raised 'throne', big easel, a high stool, but I'd abandoned the place a year later after a flaming row with my mother and left for Paris.

I suppose my stuff was still up here. Nobody ever went up to these rooms. I moved along the narrow corridor, passing rooms filled with old furniture and lumber, until I reached my old studio at the end. I pushed the door open. The early-evening sun streamed through the cobwebbed skylight. The place was filthy, dust motes rising as I trod the boards. The throne was gone, but everything else was still there, including a stack of my old canvases in the corner.

I sat up on the high stool, right under the skylight, the sun beating down on me, the little room right under the slates an oven after the long day's heat. I had another go at the wine, mopped my brow, and licked my salty lips.

My head started to swim.

Suddenly I was swaying, the stool tipping. I fell, sideways, smashing into the stack of old canvases against the wall, my head glancing off the stonework, stunned for a moment.

When I got my senses back my head was still swimming; my eyesight was blurred and my shoulder hurt. The room seemed almost in darkness now. I crouched up on all fours, trying to clear my head, looking at the wall where my old canvases lay scattered, some of the wooden stretchers broken. Gradually my vision cleared.

I got up and looked at the paintings. Only the stretchers of the front two or three were smashed. The other half-dozen oils at the back were all right. I picked through them. Tyro work, many of them nudes. Derivative, too influenced by Modigliani's nudes.

Then I saw the picture.

It was at the back of the stack, unharmed. A nude woman, not a large canvas. The first thing I knew was that, though it was much in the Modigliani style, I hadn't done it myself. The painting was far too good. The subtle colours of the woman's face a darkish peachy tone, with touches of coral and orange that seemed to glow in the slanting beams of sunlight.

The body done in pink, light umber, lemon yellow, sitting on the edge of a divan, set against a dark maroon background, so that the lines and contours of her flesh stood out, were all the more sensuously apparent, the body vibrant, seeming to come out of the canvas at me. There was a fine symmetry in the placing of her arms, making angled parallel lines across the upper body, one hand at her crotch, the other touching the end of a blue beaded necklace. A young, dark-haired woman with a sad, almost tortured face, head cast down, eyes half-closed, as if she had just been, or knew she was about to be, abandoned by the painter.

The composition, colouring, the woman herself – with her angular set of head, long neck, oval eyes, mask-like face, breasts splayed to either side of one forearm – the whole thing was wonderful. In the style of Modigliani, or a copy. Though if the latter, I'd never seen the original in any book or gallery.

Yet there was something about it that denied all fakery. I turned the picture over. It was stretched on an old pinewood frame, backed by decaying hessian, slightly torn at the bottom. I pulled the tear and saw how at some point the canvas had been reset over too small a stretcher, so that it rolled down and round the edge of the wood, leaving part of the picture invisible. I eased up more of the hessian backing, revealing the bottom edge of the inscription, quite clearly, scrawled in black paint. 'Amelie-Amedeo-Amore'.

Now I was almost certain this was the real thing. Amedeo Modigliani had been poet as well as painter, steeped in Italian classic literature, often quoting Dante, Petrarch, Virgil and Catullus to his friends in cafés or his models as he painted them. There was something in this simple inscription that absolutely reflected the style of the man.

I felt sober, the drink draining out of me. Yes, this must be the real thing, the finest Modigliani nude I'd ever seen. I couldn't take my eyes off this sad and erotic woman. I heard the telephone ring, faintly, far away downstairs. I let it ring, gazing at the woman.

Later, when I'd brought the painting down to the drawing room, setting it on the sofa, the phone rang again.

'I'm sorry to bother you again. It's me, Elsa Bergen. We met earlier this afternoon.'

'Yes, you disappeared suddenly. I was wondering where you'd got to.'

'I'm sorry, leaving in such a hurry. I had to go back home and see my father ...' She hesitated. 'He died. It was all rather quick. Thank God I got back in time. But before he died he asked me if I'd seen you, if you'd "explained" things to me. I said no, and he said, "You must go and see him again. He knows. He'll tell you." He died a few minutes later.'

'I'm so sorry.'

'Yes, well, you see,' she rushed on, 'there must really be something – some special connection between our two families, which we couldn't fathom, something we've missed. So I wanted to call, to see if we could meet again. Maybe tomorrow morning? About ten?'

'Yes, that's fine.'

What the hell is this all about, I wondered, after I'd put the phone down. If the matter between our families was so important why hadn't the old man told her about it there and then, before he died?

I brought the nude over to the big window that gave straight out into the pink-tinted waters of the bay. The sun was beginning to set. The painting, reflecting some of this light, shone with a strange bronze sheen, the woman seeming more alive than ever. I left her. It had been a long day and I'd drunk too much. I put the picture on a chair, flopped down on the big sofa and fell asleep.

I woke early next morning. Bright sunlight streamed through the big windows, illuminating the nude, propped on an armchair. I dragged myself off the sofa. I felt unsteady. Was this really an original Modigliani? I wasn't as sure now as I had been the previous evening.

I stared at her. It was an exceptionally erotic painting, even for Modigliani, and it must have been by him. Who could have faked so personal an effect of intimacy and reproach? Or invent such a simple inscription? A faker would simply have scrawled the artist's signature, if he'd bothered even with that, as Modigliani often hadn't.

'Amelie-Amedeo-Amore.'

There had been a deep mutual passion here, behind the words and in the painting. I was fascinated by this woman. Who was she? – this Amelie, painted seventy or more years before in Paris, hidden, forgotten in a Dublin attic, and now reborn.

It was only then, having established to my own satisfaction at least that this was an original, that other questions struck me. How had my father, a man of no real taste in art, least of all in modern art, come to possess such a picture? Why hide it, among my own poor imitations of Modigliani's works?

Still, one point was clear beyond dispute. The painting was mine now, since my father, on his death, had left me all the hopeless pictures in the house, along with his motor cruiser, my mother to have these for her lifetime before passing them on to me. So now, without her knowing it, she had bequeathed me the nude masterpiece as well. Splendid irony! She had denied me my inheritance in the house, leaving it to a Dublin charity, but now she had made me a millionaire several times over.

My mother hadn't trusted me in anything. First because of my insistence on taking up the dubious career of a painter, then, latterly at least, for my conspicuous lack of success in this, and finally for what she had always seen as my irresponsible, my 'bohemian' way of life.

She'd never seen how there was as much of the bourgeois in me as there was of the bohemian – the first characteristic having led to my unfortunate marriage, over twenty years before, to the essentially very conformist young woman I'd met when I first lived in London: Angela, daughter of a High Court judge.

Penniless twelve hours ago, I was rich beyond the dreams of avarice now. Amelie, at present prices, must be worth millions. Yet looking at the picture again I felt I never wanted to be parted from this woman. She struck me, in her face and shapes, her crown of dark hair, the sense of understanding and intelligence, her unafraid sexuality, to be the sort of woman who could be both wife and mistress.

The phone rang. It was Dermot O'Higgins, an antiques dealer with an engaging Dublin voice. He'd read of my mother's death in the paper and had heard from a friend in the trade that my father had collected fine Gothic-revival furniture. I might be interested in selling one or two of these pieces? They were likely to be valuable. Cash, of course. Perhaps he might come round later?

From where I stood by the telephone in the drawing room I could see out into the big hall and through the other door into the dining room – rooms with quite a bit of Gothic-revival furniture. I'd no right to sell any of it, but since I'd been left penniless, I would, without a qualm. Besides – and I looked over at the nude again – selling some of the furniture and getting a good stack of cash for it would be a first step in never having to part with this extraordinary woman.

'Yes, certainly,' I told the man. 'Come at 12.30, say? Don't think there's much of any great value here, but you're welcome to look.'

An hour later Elsa arrived.

We sat on the terrace in the sun, great rose bushes blooming around us. Mrs Mullins, who'd cooked for my parents and lived in the gate lodge with her husband Billy the gardener, had brought us coffee. Washed and shaved, with some breakfast, the hangover had gone and I felt quite spruce. Elsa, however, was no longer her controlled self. There were cracks in her decorum, a barely repressed fluster, her face drawn. Her father was dead and had left her with a mystery, probably something quite unpleasant, since he wasn't able to speak of it even on his deathbed.

I thought I saw the reason now for that look of premonitory alarm on Elsa's face at the reception. I'm half-Irish, half-Italian – and Jewish. I tend to believe in fate and precognition.

'What possible connection could there be?' she asked, sipping her coffee. She was wearing a stiff blue denim skirt, long pleats on either side, the material grating slightly, like the palm fronds in the breeze at the end of the garden, each time she moved her thighs.

'A connection between our fathers, obviously. Both refugees.'

'Your father never wanted to go back to Italy?'

'What for? All his family were dead. After the war he ended up in a British-controlled displaced persons camp in Austria, and after that, through the Irish Quakers, to Dublin, in 1946 or 1947 I think it was. That's really all I know. And the tattoo inside his forearm was, of course, his camp number. I remember first seeing it as a child, and thinking he'd written it there with a pen as a sort of game.'

She sipped her coffee, bending forward, so that the neckline of her blouse fell slightly open. 'Well, same as most of my parents' family – killed in the war one way or another. My parents didn't want to go on living in Vienna, and they finally managed to get emigration papers to Dublin, in about 1946 or 47. Must have got here about the same time as your father. So they couldn't have known each other in the war.'

'No.' I rolled a cigarette. 'They must have met in Dublin.'

'You see,' she said almost with enthusiasm, 'my father, and yours, really suffered in the war, and then led perfectly ordinary lives here. Your parents certainly did. I read the appreciation of your mother in *The Irish Times* – all those charities your parents were involved in. And my father was well respected, here in Killiney and at his antiques shop in Baggot Street.'

'Yes, blameless lives.' Then, thinking of the Modigliani nude, I asked, 'Did your father sell modern paintings in his shop as well as antique furniture and stuff?'

'Not original paintings, no, but he sold all sorts of reproductions and posters: Renaissance masterpieces right down to the Impressionists. You know the sort of thing. But the really valuable things he sold at the back of the shop. A private room, by appointment only. Rare old books in leather bindings, illuminated manuscripts, churchy things, just like he sold in his family shop in Vienna before the war. Altar triptychs, lovely little enamel miniatures of the Madonna and Child. He was very Catholic. That was one reason he wanted to come to Ireland.'

'Where did he get these things to sell?'

She was puzzled for a moment. 'Why, he went round country houses, I remember. He took me with him several times, and he bought things at auction, here and on the Continent – and in England, where I was sent to a boarding school when I was eleven, a dreadful place in Sussex. He came to see me sometimes …' She stopped, aware how she was embarking on the personal, and I had an inkling then of some family unhappiness in her life. 'Yes,' I said lightly, 'but how did your father start off here, in 1947? He must have been penniless.'

'I don't know exactly.' She was puzzled again, as if the question had never occurred to her. 'Well, he wouldn't have needed much, would he? A few things to sell initially, some money to rent the shop in Baggot Street. Not much.'

'A few things to sell, yes, but they were very expensive things by the sound of it. Illuminated manuscripts and so on. And your Georgian house? That wouldn't have come cheap, even in the 1940s.'

'I don't know.' She veered away from the subject.

There was silence in the sunshine. I poured some more coffee from the filter pot. 'Bewley's Finest Rich Roast Arabica,' I told her, sniffing my cup. 'I used to go to their Oriental Café in Grafton Street when I was art student here. One and nine pence for a whole pot with Marie biscuits, and you could sit there all morning reading or chatting, warm in the winter. It's still there.'

She was pensive. 'I went there too, as a child, with my mother. She liked it.'

'She was Austrian as well?'

'Yes, from Vienna, which was why she liked Bewley's. Only vaguely decent coffee in Dublin, she said.' She picked up her cup, pensive again.

Silence. I felt overwhelmingly sober and dull, but she became brisk, smoothing the denim skirt so that I saw the shape of her knees beneath the fabric.

'Well,' she said, 'We've talked again and there doesn't seem to be any new angles on how our fathers knew each other. Sorry to have wasted your time. You must have some clearing up to do. Big place.'

'You, too, I imagine.'

'Yes, the house is packed with stuff. No idea what to do with it. Anyway – nothing until after his funeral on Friday.'

'And the house itself? Is it yours now?'

'Yes, and I have to do something about that before I go back to New York.'

'You don't want to live there yourself? If it's Georgian, looking over the bay, it must be lovely.'

'It is, but I don't want to live there.' She stopped, ill at ease, and turned away. When she turned back, I looked straight into her green-blue eyes, smiling in a way that seemed to relax her.

'I'm sorry,' she said. 'Sometimes there was an uneasy air at home. My parents seemed difficult together sometimes.' She shrugged.

'I felt the same with my parents – they were unhappy, and my mother seemed to blame me for it. But obviously it must have been the war and Auschwitz. My father lost everything, like your parents did. More than enough to make one's parents difficult, between themselves, and with their children.'

She stood up quickly, back in her prim and preoccupied mode, as if she'd realized how she'd said too much. She wasn't going to ask me over to her house, I saw, or to her father's funeral. She'd done her business with me. There was no relevant connection between our families.

Yet I felt there was – there in her father's words to her on his deathbed. Those words had meant something crucial. The connection was lurking there, hidden in the past, just as the Modigliani nude had been hidden in the attic.

In any case I didn't want her to go. To keep her I had only one last card to play.

'There is one strange thing.' I came up behind her. 'Which may have some bearing on it all.'

She turned abruptly. 'Yes?'

'I found a painting here last night, hidden up in one of the attic rooms. A Modigliani nude. An original. I know his work well.'

She frowned. 'A copy, surely.'

'No. It's too personal. Everything is right about it. The colours, the line, the woman herself. I know it's an original. I'll show you.'

'Wait a moment – even if it is, how would this bear on the connection between our fathers?'

'The painting was hidden in an attic here. My father had no interest in modern art, nor my mother, but your father, you told me, did.'

'And?'

'It's possible your father came by this original Modigliani in some house in Dublin or in the country on one of his buying trips, or someone brought it into his shop, not knowing it was an original. And perhaps wanting money for his shop he sold it to my father, or gave it as security for a loan.'

'That's nonsense!' She interrupted me. 'My father would never have bought anything in an underhand way like that. He was absolutely honest.'

'So was my father!' I wasn't going to be put down. 'Upright, honest, God-fearing.'

'Yes, I'm sure he was.'

'Wait … I told you, we only really know our parents when they're with us. You can never be certain what people get up to when you're not with them.' I looked at her carefully. She seemed transfixed. 'Come and look at the painting.'

In the drawing room I lifted the painting from behind the sofa and rested it on a chair, in just the right light from the big windows. In the fine light its colours were all the more vivid and striking. Elsa stepped back, involuntarily, as if the nude woman had threatened her.

She was astonished. 'It's wonderful! Breathtaking … the woman … she springs out at you, as if she were alive.'

'Yes, just that.'

'You're right – it has absolutely the feel of an original.'

'If that's the case,' I said quickly, 'I wonder if the answer to the mystery of your father telling you to meet me, might lie right here in this painting?'

She turned to me with that look of premonitory alarm in her face again.

'Very fine. Very fine indeed,' Dermot O'Higgins added judiciously, inspecting the Burges toilet cabinet upstairs in my father's bedroom. A rotund, dapper little man in his forties, neatly dressed in an old-fashioned English manner, a light-beige summer suit, a vaguely regimental tie, red hanky in his breast pocket, brown brogues. Surprising, since his accent was pure Dublin. His face was pudgy and reddish, with a mole, like a beauty spot, on his cheek. He might have been a drinker, or queer. Or both. And he reeked of some lime-smelling aftershave lotion.

'I've only seen one other like it,' he continued. 'A wash-hand stand, belonged to Evelyn Waugh. Exhibited at the V&A some years ago. This is finer, more delicate.' Having opened the main doors, he fiddled with the various brass-handled drawers and cupboards, lovingly inspecting the flower-patterned chamber pot, the wash bowl and ewer. 'Superb, Mr Contini. Quite superb.' He sighed.

I was pleased with the way things were going.

'Of course,' he turned to me diffidently, 'I know something

of Burges's work. He sometimes included a secret recess or little drawer in such creations, for hiding jewellery or small valuables.'

'Did he indeed? In this, do you think?'

'Very possibly. May I?'

'Go ahead.'

'Yes, you see here …' He started to run his fingers over the wood inside. 'One can sometimes find the key to such drawers in the strips of inset wood which Burges used decoratively, but which also act as a release mechanism into these hiding places. These rosewood strips here …'

There were a dozen such inset strips of rosewood, an inch wide, six inches long, beneath the twelve pigeonholes for storing toilet knick-knacks inside. He pushed the end of each strip in turn, until one of them responded, the tip of his index finger pushing into a gap, as a small hinged drawer swivelled out in the shape of a half-circle.

Inside was a folded yellowing sheet of paper.

We both looked at it, saying nothing. I picked it out and opened it. There were two columns of writing, with numbers after the words, in Italian, my father's hand. 'It's some sort of inventory of my father's. Various paintings, objets d'art.'

'Paintings? Objets d'art? May I look at it?' I handed him the paper. 'Yes, indeed, great Renaissance paintings and antique ecclesiastical objects. Altar furniture, triptychs, chalices, reliquaries, illuminated manuscripts. That sort of thing,' he added easily, as if they were of little importance.

'Great Renaissance paintings?'

'Yes, here – this one.' He showed me the paper, pointing to a line halfway down the first column. "Czartoryski: *Portrait of a Young Man*" – that's by Raphael.'

'Raphael?' I was surprised. 'But that would be one of his great portraits.'

'Yes, indeed.'

'So, why would my father … it can't be an inventory of his things. He would never have had such a painting.'

'Well, not an inventory of works he owned, but perhaps a list of things, in museums, art galleries or churches that he saw, or wanted to see in Europe. In churches particularly, it seems. You see here, lower down? This group of objects, "the Wroclaw Chalice, the Poznan Bible, the Lubin Reliquary" – all from churches in Poland, it seems.'

'Valuable I suppose?'

'Oh, yes, very.'

'But those towns are all in Poland – not Italy.'

'Yes, but your father was a cultured man, I'm sure. He would have travelled about Europe.'

I looked at O'Higgins. His face was bland. 'No, my father wasn't a cultured man. He was a civil engineer and marble-quarry owner, and he wouldn't have travelled to Poland to look at a chalices and reliquaries.' I knew at once who had done this: Elsa's father, Joseph Bergen, with his religious antiques shop in Vienna selling just such churchy things, and the same sort of objects from a private room in Dublin after the war.

'No, well I couldn't say then. Just some list your father made.' O'Higgins looked bored. 'Though there is one interesting thing here, at the bottom.' He showed me the paper. 'This item – the only one, so far as I can see, which isn't medieval or Renaissance, indeed it's almost contemporary. Here,' he set his finger on the line, ' "Modigliani Nude?" Your father must have had an interest in modern art.'

I didn't say anything for a moment, I was so surprised. 'Well, possibly,' I said at last, making nothing of it, folding up the paper and putting it in my pocket. 'Anyway, shall we take a look round the other rooms?' We moved out of my father's bedroom and along the landing.

'I wonder if you knew …' I was going to ask O'Higgins if he knew Joseph Bergen and his back room in his antiques shop in Dublin. I stopped. Why would Bergen sell such things from a back room, by appointment only? Had he something to hide? At least one thing was obvious: here was a clear connection between my father and Joseph Bergen. Bergen had sold these things and my father had made a list of them, but why had my father made the list, and why had both men been so eager to keep the whole business hidden?

Was this a list of things that my father had somehow obtained illegally long ago, and which Bergen had sold in his Baggot Street shop? I would say no more to O'Higgins about it all. Instead I showed him some more furniture about the house, before returning to the drawing room. I offered him a drink.

'Thank you. Just a small one. I'm driving.'

I poured him a large one. 'Tonic, lemon, ice?'

'Thank you.' He eyed the glass approvingly, went over to the big window, looking out on the terrace, the rose garden, the bay beyond, sparkling blue in the sunlight. 'An amazing place you have here, Mr Contini. The view – superb!' He gazed at the view of Killiney bay with sad longing, like a picture at auction he couldn't afford. 'They say it's like the bay of Naples.'

'Yes, they do, and they're wrong. The colours would be quite different as well as the climate. And they'd speak Italian, with pasta and wine and fat waiters singing "Come Back to Sorrento". And pickpockets.'

'Well.' O'Higgins turned back and sat down, 'You're a painter yourself, of course.'

'Yes.'

'I don't know your work, I'm afraid.'

'No. I don't exhibit now.'

There was silence, until he leant forward confidingly, tumbler clasped in both hands between his knees. 'Forgive me for mentioning it, Mr Contini, but a friend in the trade … he knows something of your situation here, about your family. How you have, as it were, only habitation rights in the house here, can't sell it, or perhaps even things in it?'

'He knows that, does he?' I was genuinely surprised.

'Well, yes, he does. These things tend to get around, small place like Dublin.'

'I suppose so.'

'The point is, I can understand your need for discretion in the selling of any of this furniture.'

'Yes,' I agreed. I knew what he was getting at. 'Of course I can rely on your discretion as well so far as your buying the furniture from me,' I added sagely.

'Of course.'

I drank again, drew on my roll-up and looked at the man. A genial rogue. Of course they all were, these antique dealers.

Later, for some fine items of original William Morris Gothic-revival furniture, Mr O'Higgins handed me £4000 in crisp British £50 notes. After he'd left, with the furniture inside and on top of his Volvo estate, I poured myself another gin and tonic, then picked up the money, letting the wad of notes flick from my thumb. 'That's better,' I said, looking up at the wishy-washy portrait of my mother in her eau-de-Nil tea gown over the mantelpiece, with her permed hair and faint smile, her charitable smile. 'That's much better.' I raised my glass to her.

'What a day!' The June sun continued to beat down, a happy heatwave, and I was speaking to Elsa on the phone, two days later, after her father's funeral. 'Would you like to come out with me in my father's old motor cruiser? It's good fun,' I rushed on. 'Take your mind off things. We could go down the coast a bit, have a picnic lunch beyond Wicklow Head or somewhere. There's still some good titbits left from that reception, olives and cheese and things. Would you like to?' I paused, out of breath.

Silence at the other end. I was sure she was going to say no, but after a long pause she agreed to come, and I felt a surge of real happiness for the first time in many months.

The *Sorrento* was a fine old sixty-foot motor cruiser, pitch pine on oak, with a teak deck, built by Osbourne's in Southampton in the early 1950s. Four two-berth cabins, fore and aft, dining saloon, wheelhouse amidships, big twin GM diesels, capable of driving her at over twenty knots, sleek lines, a square stern, long rising fore-deck where the bows angled away sharply, radar and all the rest – she was a beautiful boat.

Billy Mullins, the gardener and odd-job man who had helped crew the boat in the old days had kept her in good trim since my father's death the year before. After a bit of tinkering about in the bowels that morning, both engines had fired, the exhausts uttering a throaty, burbling roar.

Elsa came aboard and ten minutes later the twin propellers bit into the water, leaving a trail of frothy foam behind us and we roared away, making out to sea into the glittering morning.

'No, I didn't know what to make of you.' Elsa spread the coarse pâté on a chunk of baguette, then took some salami and a wedge of Pont-L'Evêque. I poured us both a glass of iced Perrier water.

'You didn't know quite what to make of me? You didn't like me one bit. I was on the bottle.'

We'd anchored in a small inlet south of Wicklow Head. A steep cliff ran down to a small cove of jagged rocks where the green-blue swell lapped against jagged stone, swaying the boat gently, the water so clear that from the foredeck where we were eating we could see right down, fifteen feet or so, to the shingly barnacled stones, where fronds of dark seaweed moved.

I took some salami in my fingers, squeezed lemon on it, then paused. 'I like the taste of wine, and sometimes I can't stop.'

'And the effects?'

'The usual. Good and bad. One gets insights as well as headaches with a hangover.' I ate the salami. 'Doesn't everyone have an addiction? Not drink or drugs, but an addiction to being in control for example. Many people get a kick out of that.'

She ate an olive, silent, then nodded. 'I suppose so.'

'What's your addiction?'

'I knew you'd ask.' Her lips moved in the beginnings of a smile. 'I'd prepared an answer. Chocolate, I was going to say. In fact, I've so many addictions – the ones that don't usually show – I've lost count of them.'

'That's honest, at least. And that's the best and rarest addiction.'

'Is it?'

'It must be, because it scares the hell out of people more than any other addiction. You become a real pariah if you get a reputation for honesty with people. The thing is,' I leant forward, 'most people float on the quicksands by kidding themselves, and other people, that they're honest. Like hell they are. Just the opposite. They keep afloat on lies and smugness. Their hypocrisy!' I ended vehemently.

'It worries you, doesn't it? Honesty.'

'Yes.'

'You talk as if someone had been very dishonest with you.'

'My wife, among others.' I picked at the salami, gazing at it, without eating it. 'Sometimes I'd like to be just a very ordinary person, comfortably kept afloat by all sorts of lies and nonsense. If I'd been just an ordinary chap, with a spot of humility, I'd have gotten on better with people, been a bit more serene – though that usually means just suiting the other person. Instead I took to old cord suits, bright red scarves and wide black hats and became a bloody painter. Though I've more or less lost the knack.'

'Why? What happened?'

I wasn't going to tell her about Katie. 'Things sometimes just die on you.'

'I'm sorry.' She was genuinely sympathetic. 'So what do you want to do with your life now?'

'Oh, just a few simple things really. Get a bit of money together and my old Bentley and take off down the Rhône Valley – Dijon, Burgundy, High Provence. Never seen any of those places. There are many very ordinary things I'd like to do now. And be.'

She had relaxed as she listened to all this, dropping her shoulders, the drawn, wary look in her face disappearing, as if some burden had been lifted from her. Shading her eyes against the sun, she looked at me carefully.

'Yes, I know exactly what you mean. Your honesty addiction … mine as well.' Now she didn't mind talking about the personal, she wanted to. 'I can be outspoken and tyrannical sometimes. Most of all, like you, I can't stick the hypocrites, the people who lie to themselves and to me, and then make out they're in step, and you're not … the ones who won't risk admitting mistakes. They can't afford to be wrong, their sanity depends on it.'

I frowned. In what she'd just said, Elsa might have been describing Katie's characteristics and how she had promoted these with me.

'I've had just that happen with several people in my life,' I said. 'It's an old trick. People have to damn your own fairly honest character, so they can survive with their own pretty dishonest one. Then they can throw you overboard without a qualm and stay secure on their comfy, cagey raft of lies. I've sometimes felt I should have joined them there for an easier life.'

'No. You can't do that. It's no use trying to be an apple tree when you're a mulberry bush.'

There was silence, with the swell rocking the boat gently and the anchor chain grating softly against the stern.

'Listen.' She spoke up. 'You said you wanted to explore the Rhône Valley, and maybe on to Italy? I'm going down that way for this book on olives and oil. I was going anyway, before my father started sinking. We could go together?'

I considered the matter, unconcerned, as if she'd suggested we take a trip to the local supermarket.

'What would I do?'

'The Modigliani nude,' she said at once. 'You said it might be at the heart of the whole business, the connection between my father and yours.'

'Yes, I did. I do.'

'So maybe we could find out about it together? Who it belonged to originally, how it got to be hidden in your father's attic, and so on.'

She smiled. And so on, I thought. That was likely to be the real problem, but I wasn't going to turn down her suggestion on that account. 'Yes,' I said. 'Perhaps find out who the woman in the painting was. Though I don't know quite where one would start.'

'The archives in the Louvre? – or the Musée d'Orsay?'

That provocative smile again. Like Katie's, when she wanted me to do something with her. Paris, the Louvre, the Musée d'Orsay – that had been the first trip Katie and I had made abroad together, five years before, in early summer. And here was almost her double, beckoning me along the same path. Up the garden path? To a dead end? That's how it had ended with Katie.

Well, damn it, Katie was dead and Elsa was alive and I would go to Paris with her. So I said, 'Yes, start in Paris. I've an old friend there, an American art collector – Harry Broughton. Knows all about French paintings, painters, the Impressionists, and the School of Paris – Utrillo, Modigliani, Soutine, all those wild boys. He'd help.'

'So, it's an idea then?'

'It's a good idea.'

'You could take your stuff with you, and start painting again. You painters have portable easels, don't you? Parasols and so on?'

'Oh yes, and smocks and berets and we hit the absinthe and cut our ears off when things aren't going well.' Silence, until we both smiled. 'But yes, I could bring my stuff with me.'

'Plenty to paint, if you do the olive groves with me.'

'Trouble is, I tend to concentrate on the nude.'

'I see,' she said, nodding. 'Now it's clear. I thought you were just a lecher, the way you looked at me at the reception and when we had coffee.'

'I am, but I like to paint the women first.'

Again, I expected her disapproval. Instead, she kept looking at me, smiling slightly in the hot silence. 'Shall we swim?' she asked suddenly.

'I didn't bring a costume.'

'Nor did I. But it doesn't matter. No one's looking.'

We swam, just in our underwear, off the end of the boat, between the stern and the rocks, under the cliffs, in the deep blue water, with the seaweed swaying over the barnacles fifteen feet down. We dived, alternately, a froth of bubbles rising to the surface, shooting up like rockets from the depths into the bright heat.

Now I saw her body properly: the almost unnatural splay at her waist, fine rounded thighs, sturdy legs, small feet, the flash of flattened, water-soaked dark hair, glistening in the sun, as she shot up from the sea like a missile. Her body, as I'd thought, was very like Katie's.

Afterwards, both of us drying on the deck of the boat, flat out, eyes closed, she asked, 'That person you were talking about, who had to do you down so they could throw you overboard – I assume it was a woman. Your wife?'

'Yes, and another later woman, the most recent one.'

'I don't want to pry.'

'Why not? Supposed to be honest, aren't we?'

'I'm good at being honest about others, not so much with myself.' She stayed as she was, eyes closed, stretched out. 'It's a relief, hearing you talk like that,' she said. 'Because rather the same sort of thing happened to me.'

'Your husband?'

'No, that was something else, years ago. No, by a woman I loved, in New York.'

'I see.' I didn't see. I saw only disappointment and surprise. The last thing I'd have guessed of her. Yet maybe I should have seen it. There was a tomboyish air about her, like Katie, who had once told me she'd liked to have been a man.

'I'm sorry,' I said at last. 'It's tough, being given the boot by someone you love. Worse still when they invent reasons for it.'

'Well, that's reason enough for the chucking, isn't it? – that they have to invent an excuse for it, a lie, like we were saying, because there's usually some other reason in their lives. They usually chuck you for their own problems – not yours. That's what happened with me, though she prettied it up by saying that she had to be free of me, to live.' She paused, opening her eyes.

'My friend – the last woman I was with – wanted to be free of me, not to live,' I said.

'I don't follow.'

'A week ago, near my barn in the Cotswolds where I live, when we last saw each other, she dumped me, then drove away and killed herself.'

Elsa sat up, startled. 'She what?'

'Drove into a tree. The car caught fire, she wouldn't get out. Burnt herself alive.'

Elsa shook her head. 'God, I'm sorry – that's terrible. I still don't follow.'

'Nor do I.'

Elsa bowed her head, arms resting on her hunched-up knees. Her skin was dry now, and bronzed all over. I wanted to paint her. Looking at her, as she sat on the deck hunched up, in a graceful combination of angled and paralleled arms and legs, face hidden, head bowed between her knees, the crown of damp dark hair, all quite still, frozen in the sun – I wanted to paint her like she was now, there and the-+n.

The real inspiration in all my paint-and-turpentine business is this sense of excitement, in looking at a woman, and falling in love with her body, and knowing that whatever happens later, in loving or leaving, you're going to capture her body, its contours and colours, and the thoughts in her face, and all the sex you may or may not have shared with her – and all the details of her bones, all the shapes and slopes that you were closest to, most intimate and happy with, that the whole complex thrill, whatever the loss or gain in reality, will always be there on canvas, incorruptible.

Elsa stood up finally. She looked out to sea. 'Olives and the oil … It's lucky I write. And that you paint.'

'When I did paint. I think Katie – that was her name – was jealous of my painting. I sensed it, it was something she couldn't do, and wanted to do, and control, like everything else in her life.'

'I've wondered if that was Martha's problem too – my cook-books. She was younger than me, a successful attorney, but who came to think she should be writing smart-ass sexy novels about the law and the cops – but she never had that boring gift, and she knew it. So she took it out on me, and my cookbooks. But maybe I'm wrong about Martha being jealous of my work, and there's no accounting for it.'

Silence, until I said, 'There is accounting for it. There's account-ing for everything and everybody, if you work hard enough at it, in a book or a painting. Or at that Modigliani nude,' I added.

'Yes.' She seemed doubtful.

'Hey, you know something? We could go straight to Paris on this boat.'

'To Paris – how?'

'Down the Irish Sea here, and across the channel to Le Havre, then up the Seine to Paris.'

'Could we?' She was pleased, like a child.

'Of course we could! In this good weather, no trouble. Three or four days. She's a fast boat and I'm a good sailor. I was going to join the British navy once.'

'All right then, yes!' she said urgently, eyes glittering.

Standing up, semi-naked in the bright light, she dusted herself down, patting her bronzed thighs. It was strange how easy and informal she was, wearing hardly any clothes, with a man she barely knew; as if she'd known me for years and I was her lover.

Katie had been just the same, quite unashamed, from the word go. But then I had been her lover almost from the beginning, for she had made the running with me. I'd liked her – her reticence, her independent, secretive air, the original talk and dry wit. And I'd liked the look of her even more. The sense of a fine body, sturdy and sexy, beneath her clothes. I'd never thought to become her lover. She seemed too prim and proper for that. A decorous woman, polite, virtuous, honourable – and married.

How wrong even I can be about people.

About a month after we'd met, she said she'd been given two tickets for the little theatre in Chipping Norton, not far from the riding school and my old barn. Would I like to come with her? I picked her up in my car. On the way back afterwards, as if in a quite unconscious gesture, she'd put her hand on my knee. She said nothing, and I did nothing, until she'd said, 'There's a track off the road a mile ahead.' It was the track leading up to my barn. I turned into it, drove past the Phillip's farm, stopped the car, and kissed her chastely, her face faintly illuminated by the dashboard lights. She reached forward, holding me, wanting to kiss again, relaxed but with an eagerness I could feel all over her body. She took my hand, putting it on her knee, then lifted the hem of her skirt and placed my hand on her naked knee, encouraging it further, up her thigh, where soon I found she wasn't wearing any knickers. We'd made love, her skirt around her neck – passionate, furious, fulfilling – as if neither of us had had it in years, which was true.

I'd asked her if she was on the pill. 'Yes,' she said. 'I've been on it almost from the day we first met, wanting you to screw me, and wondering why the hell you wouldn't do anything about it.' The surprising sexual coarseness behind the prim-and-proper façade. I 'made love'. She 'screwed'. It was an exciting idea to begin with. I'd no idea of the price I'd have to pay for it in the end.

'Would you like to see the admiralty charts in the wheelhouse?' I asked Elsa, 'How we'll get to Paris?'

She nodded. I stood up. 'There is one thing, though, one obvious point,' I said, 'which we should think about before we go. If your father was able to tell you that you should meet me, that I would "explain" everything – why didn't he tell you what it was that I was to explain to you himself? He must have known the connection between him and my father. So why didn't he just tell you?'

'Yes, I've thought of that, and I don't know why.'

'If he didn't tell you, more than likely it was because it was something unpleasant.'

'But what, though? What?' She came towards me, anguished.

I was just going to tell her about the list of priceless pictures and objets d'art, the inventory I'd found in the Burges toilet cabinet, but something stopped me. It could wait until we got back to Killiney, or to Paris. She turned and started to get dressed, picking up her bits and pieces. I got dressed myself and we went into the wheelhouse to look at the charts.

'Ben,' she said, turning to me, suddenly alive and buoyant. 'It'll be great to go straight to Paris on this boat! No one will ever know, It'll be such a good secret.'

I didn't know what she meant, but was happy as she was with the idea, so I didn't ask.

I thought I was going to France to find out about the Modigliani nude, and have a good time with Elsa. I was kidding myself. I was going to Paris because of the life not lived with Katie – to try to live it with Elsa.

When we got back that evening, and Elsa had gone home, I felt sufficiently encouraged about things to get out Katie's journal.

I glanced through the pages. Quite a bit of it was about us, but whatever good thoughts she had written about us were usually cancelled at once by doubts, questions, criticisms, of herself, then latterly of me – these grim reflections set round the memorabilia of dead wild flowers, herbs and leaves picked up on our walks and trips. A collection of withered stalks and petals, which had punctuated the bright days of our affair, now interleaved with a text of despair.

I skipped through half a dozen pages before I began to read properly towards the end of the journal, a passage dated about two months before, in that fast, sprawling handwriting of hers that used to make my heart race, in earlier times when she had written to me; short notes saying something quite inconsequential, or that she loved me.

'Cheerfulness keeps breaking out!' He said to me after we'd made love last night. Again trying to persuade me of 'us', as a pair with a real future together, though I know how very far he is from being cheerful. The hurt to his idealism – I've felt it just as deeply as he has – in wanting to live, to be with, to marry me. This is greater than ever in him now, since he keeps it so firmly suppressed. In any case I want to stop his pain for ever. And mine. And the only way to do that is to stop 'us', so that I can't hurt him anymore –

knowing I can't properly love him now, that I've been pretending love with him, almost from the start. Pretending happiness. I know this now, because I'm with the only person I don't have to pretend with. With him there is a real me, which he evokes – a joyous, soaring, voyaging me…

I couldn't go on. I was sitting in the drawing room, looking out on the last of the evening light on the bay. Mrs Mullins had cleared away the funeral drinks long before. I went to look for them. After a whiskey I read the passage again. Katie had prided herself on her honesty, but she'd been honest only when it suited her, and she was certainly fooling herself here.

She'd loved me all right, fully and honestly, for three years. You can fake pleasure in the act of love, but not the look of love in a person's face. You can fake it in a letter, or in words, but not in a tone of voice, or in the eyes. I'd seen and heard her love in all these things, and I'd felt it just as much in bed with her, when she took my hand, falling asleep, fingers entwined. How her love was there even in sleep, when her body gravitated towards mine, loving me unconsciously, when she moved into my arms, hair askew.

As for her 'pretending happiness' with me on our trips away together – this was nonsense. She'd travelled joyously with me on scores of occasions, at home and abroad, in Paris, Ireland, and two years before in Italy, where I'd been teaching painting and sculpture in a summer art school in Carrara.

No, she hadn't faked anything with me in those first three years, I thought bitterly. Everything we'd done then had been genuine. Instead, two years ago, she'd started to drop me. When I asked her why all she would say was that I was 'difficult', or some other even vaguer criticism, as if to define it would be to expose the shallowness of her complaint.

Now I saw there was a reason. It was here in the second part of the passage I'd just read, in this 'only person I don't have to pretend with'. Well, surely this must be another man. But who? The only other man she ever went out with was her father.

Yes, her father, the Major. I'd had my suspicions there already – if only because Katie's sudden lack of interest in me had exactly coincided with her father's return home from his travels. Now in his mid seventies, he'd been an army officer, out in India originally, and then Germany, married and divorced a first wife, returned to England, retired early, bought the house and some land near Chipping Norton, in what became the riding school, and had then married Katie's mother. Ten years later he'd baled out and started his wanderings, in Scandinavia, the Middle East, back to India. Katie never seemed very clear about where he'd been, or what he'd been up to, except to comment on his interest in anthropology, ancient tribes or some such. Two years ago, feeling his age, I suppose, he'd returned to England, arriving out of the blue, just after we'd got back from the summer school in Carrara.

All this I learnt in an offhand way from Katie, and, in an even more offhand manner, that he'd been involved with half a dozen other women during his marriage to Katie's mother, who had died some years before I met Katie.

By the sound of him, I hadn't liked him. When I met him, as I did several times where he'd come to live again up at the riding school, I liked him even less. The feeling was mutual and the reason was obvious. I was Katie's lover, and he was jealous.

Short, with neatly cropped white hair, he had a broken nose, fierce blue eyes and tanned skin. He was dominant in an old-fashioned, British officer manner.

He was called Hector – and he often did just this, once expatiating to me for a whole half-hour in his crisply enunciated tones on the prehistory of the British race. I saw them one time. She'd met him in the car park of a pub on the road to Cheltenham, high up on the wolds, and they'd gone off with her dogs across the winter fields towards a rise in the land, an old hill fort or long barrow. He was talking animatedly, pointing out something to her, then climbing to the top of the mound, and gesticulating like a prophet, his hand roving round the big circle.

God knows what they were up to, but these meetings seemed innocent enough, at least in so far as his being 'another man' in her life.

But something disturbed me in their relationship, however, and that something, I felt, had taken Katie away from me, and now it seemed I was right. The evidence was here, in her journal, where he'd evoked her real self. Her father had died of a heart attack three months before, and although Katie had taken this in her usual unemotional way, it seemed to me now that her suicide had more to do with her father's death than with me.

The hell with all these lousy Katie mysteries for the moment. I called Harry Broughton in Paris that evening and told him my mother had died and that I'd be taking the boat over to Paris for a break in a few days' time, and that I'd see him when I got there. I didn't tell him that Elsa was coming with me. That could wait. I packed my bag, took some canvasses, paints, an easel, Katie's diary and the Modigliani nude.

On the uneventful voyage to France, to Le Havre and then up the Seine to Paris I saw I had a problem. If I was to keep any semblance of a natural order of things with Elsa, we were going to have to see him together. But Harry had met Katie several times and had two largish paintings of her in the big first-floor salon of his apartment in the house he owned in the Marais, a portrait and a nude, both of which he'd bought from me. So when Harry saw Elsa, and if Elsa saw the paintings of Katie, some awkward cats would be out of the bag.

Elsa, if she saw the pictures of her double on the wall, would really begin to wonder what the hell was going on. I had to tell Elsa about her resemblance to Katie before we met Harry, but I kept putting it off. There was comfort, and an excitement, in imagining Katie still alive in Elsa. I wanted first to talk to Harry alone, if I could. So I delayed matters, telling myself I'd explain everything to Elsa over a coffee on that first morning in Paris before we met him. In the event she stayed on the boat that morning, tired from the voyage over.

'You go and see your friend Harry on your own. I'm sure you have things to talk about. I can meet him later, get myself together meanwhile and meet you back at the boat when you're ready.'

'Okay. Give me an hour or so and I'll pick you up back here and we'll go have some lunch.'

I took the Modi nude, left the boat and walked up onto the quay of the Port de Plaisance where we'd moored. Harry's place, in the Marais, was just fifteen minutes away. I crossed over the Place, along the rue Saint Antoine, into the Marais, and along the rue des Rosiers in the heart of the old Jewish quarter. A big building, an abandoned red-brick hammam, the Turkish baths on one side, with Goldenberg's famous deli on the other. I gazed at the tremendous display in the window – the tart, spicy smells wafting out the doorway on the summer air. Rye, pumpernickel, unleavened loaves, salads and olives, hot pastrami, pickled herrings, coleslaw, herb feta cheeses: all that was Jewish and foody in the crowded street of bearded men in skull caps or black homburgs, with old kosher women and young Hebrew heartbreakers. Widow's weeds and miniskirts. The orthodox and unorthodox everywhere. I turned off the street and made for the old house on the Place du Marché St Catherine.

Harry was finishing a late breakfast when I arrived at his first-floor apartment. In his eighties, bare-chested, loosely swathed in a red silk dressing gown, white hair still thick. With his fierce old pugilist's face he looked like a retired boxer. He'd boxed for Columbia before the war, where he'd graduated in art history, a study he'd sometimes regretted later. 'Yeah,' he used to say, in his laconic New Yorker manner. 'I coulda made a better career as a middleweight. More money, and certainly less trouble, just to floor a man now and then, instead of fighting devious little shysters in the art business.'

He knew all the history in his field, and more than that: behind the bluff exterior, he had fine taste and an unerring feel for all that

was best in a painting, in the arts, architecture, in life itself. He'd
got a post with the Metropolitan Museum before the war. Then he
was drafted, and when the allies went into France after D-Day he'd
been among the first off the boats, as one of the US Army's Monu-
ments Officers, there with the troops to try to protect Europe's
cultural heritage from the general mayhem.

A man of many amiable parts, wearing his art learning so lightly
he sometimes seemed quite naked of it – just a culture-struck GI
who had stayed on in Paris after the war, living on his wits and his
charm and the kindness of good women.

He had never left France, but had taken up with and married
one good woman, Michele, now dead, with a son and a daughter I'd
met years before, both of them now married and married abroad.
I'd first met Harry in the early seventies at an exhibition of my
paintings at a Left Bank gallery. He'd bought several canvases
straightaway, and had compounded his enthusiasm for my work
by taking me out afterwards, celebrating his purchases, in a little
restaurant round the corner, La Tourelle. It was still there, and had
been my regular canteen with Katie whenever we'd come to the
city. Harry owned a lovely restored eighteenth-century house on
the small square of St Catherine. He had his apartment and leased
the other floors, with a fine Polish restaurant on the ground floor.
It seemed almost a sideline of his that he had made his fortune in
the ruck of the world's art market, buying and selling, gathering his
own fine collection in the process. Whenever I'd been with him he
never seemed to be doing anything so vulgar as dealing. He was
the old-style, cultured, American gentleman, interested in beautiful things, browsing in antique shops, art galleries, the flea market,
and something of a boulevardier after Michele died: theatres, the
opera, cinemas, cafés, restaurants – enjoying the city and its people.
I liked Harry. He was candid. He took risks. No cagey silences, lies
of omission, scheming compromise, comfy wallowing in the grey

areas, none of the conventional hypocrisies. He always played high odds, win or lose, like a Runyon gambler. He was a mulberry bush.

He was taking his breakfast in the big salon looking over the square, some of his pictures on the walls. The three marvellous canvases I remembered, the Utrillo street scene, *Porte des Lilas*, an early Soutine, *Paysan*, and a classic Renoir nude of a young woman, untitled. And my two paintings of Katie, away on another wall to the side.

Sitting down with a cup of coffee I told him about Elsa; how she was so like Katie – that she'd killed herself the week before, and how this other woman, who seemed Katie's double, had turned up out of the blue at my mother's funeral reception.

'Now wait a moment, Ben. You're going too fast. Rewind. What the hell's been going on?'

So I told Harry in more detail what had been going on for the past week, told him all I knew and all I didn't know.

'Okay, but why haven't you told this Elsa she looks just like Katie? It's quite a coincidence, but it happens. They say everyone has a double somewhere in the world. It's not an offence. So why hide it from her?'

'Seems more than a coincidence. It means something.'

'Bullshit! You're running that Jewish, Irish, Italian thing again. You look worried. You been up to something fishy?'

'No, but someone has. My father, and maybe Elsa … and her father. That's what I wanted to talk to you about.'

'You have doubts about this Elsa?'

I nodded. 'I don't know why. I always thought I was good at fathoming women.'

'In your paintings, yes. Reality's a different matter.'

'Thanks.'

I went over to one of the tall windows and gazed over the small cobbled square, the old market place, café chairs to one side, benches, some elderly women sitting in the sun, a youth in a reversed baseball cap, T-shirt and baggy trousers skimming round the square on roller blades, mobile phone in hand.

I moved about the room, on edge. 'It's not just Elsa I'm puzzled about.' I rolled a cigarette. 'There's quite a lot else. The parcel I have here.' I pointed to the Modigliani nude, bubble-wrapped, where I'd put it on the sofa.

'A canvas – one of yours?'

'No, I'll show you later. Since Elsa's not here, I want to show you something else, maybe more important, that she doesn't know about, but you might – tracing looted art, paintings and so on, that was another thing of yours, wasn't it?'

'Yes, many of the top Nazis were at it. We had to track the stuff down, all over, after the war. Why?'

'What do you make of this?' I handed him my father's art inventory. 'It turned up in a secret drawer in my father's bedroom. List of old paintings, bibles and things, which he wrote out years ago.'

Harry ran his eye quickly down the columns, then studied it more carefully. He looked up at me with surprise, almost alarm. 'What d'ya mean "old paintings and things"? Half these pictures are Renaissance masterpieces. This one particularly. The "Czartoryski Raphael: *Portrait of a Young Man*". Goddamnit, I know about these things all right. That Raphael was looted from the Czartoryski Palace outside Krakow early in the war by Dr Hans Frank and his SS friends. Frank was boss of the "General Government" in Poland, the southern section where they moved all the Polish Jews before they shipped them off to Auschwitz. Before Dr Frank shipped them off. Upwards of two million of them. Frank was one of the worst, a real cultured shit. Dürer, Goethe, Beethoven. Dr Hans Frank? You couldn't get worse. At least they strung him up after Nuremberg.'

'And the Raphael? Did they get that, too?'

'No, that's the point.' Harry stood up quickly, waving the paper about. 'None of the stuff on this list, so far as I know, ever turned up after the war, or since. All these things were looted from Jews, museums, churches and private art collections in Poland. Then, early '45, when they knew the game was up, with the Russians moving in from the east, they shipped most of the stuff out of Krakow into Austria and hid it in castle cellars, caves and salt mines. We found much of it, but not all of it ... and not this stuff.' He waved the inventory again, over with me by the window now, breathing quickly. 'Jesus, Ben – this list, why, this is all Frank's stuff and more, that was never found!' He scanned the list again. 'Raphael's greatest portrait ... the Dürer drawings ... the Wroclaw Chalice ... the Poznan Bible? Priceless!'

'So the only thing we don't know is how my father came to have a list of them.'

'No. That's a sticker.'

'I'll give you one reason – my father must have been involved in the looting of all these things, and so was Elsa Bergen's father, Joseph Bergen. He opened an antiques shop in Dublin, like his family had in Vienna before the war. What did he sell from a private room in the back of the shop? Churchy things, altar chalices, reliquaries, old bibles – and no doubt great Renaissance paintings as well.'

'You're kidding.'

'I'm not. You can see from the numbers after some of the objects on the list the year when they were sold and for how much. See? "49.50,000" and "52.100,000" and so on. Dollars or pounds. Many small fortunes back then.'

'But only about half of the items have numbers after them, and not the Raphael.'

'That's because they didn't get around to selling the rest, or didn't need to. The rest is still hidden somewhere.'

Silence. The sun moved up over the houses on the other side of the square, shining directly into the room, illuminating the nude of Katie on the far wall. I wandered over and looked at it. I used to phone her most early evenings, from the box outside my local pub near Chipping Norton: and even if I didn't get through, I knew she'd always be back at the house, having fed the horses and about to feed her dogs, so I could usually be sure to reach her later on the phone.

I found it difficult to grasp the fact now, that Katie wasn't available anymore at the end of a telephone.

I turned. 'I could do with a drink, Harry.'

'Sure, it's in the kitchen. What do you want? I'll join you. I've some good vodka in the fridge, the real thing, the Polish restaurant downstairs gets it for me.'

A few minutes later, glasses in hand, Harry raised his shot of cold vodka and tossed it back. 'Looted, sold, and some of it still hidden somewhere – yes, that could figure.'

'So my father and Elsa's must have been into some big Nazi art-looting business during the war. With Dr Frank and his pals. Must have been Nazis themselves.'

'Wait a minute, Ben, your father was a Jew. Sent to Auschwitz. He couldn't have been involved in any of this.'

'We'll come to that. But after the war these Nazis took gold out, maybe paintings, to support themselves.'

'Yes, to South America, most of them. Frank had a number of other Nazi friends in on the art-looting game then – including his SS sidekick in Krakow, Helmuth Pfaffenroth – another one of the worst, an obsessional Jew killer, couldn't get 'em into the gas showers quick enough.'

'All good friends of Dr Frank's. Among them my father, and Elsa's, who went to Ireland, where Elsa's father flogged all these paintings for the two of them in Dublin. Bergen was a Nazi, my father was involved with him and their clients were big crooks as well, and what they didn't sell is still hidden somewhere. That's the long and the short of it.'

Harry shook his head. 'Ben, it's only a theory about your father and Bergen. No real proof – just like your suspicions about Elsa. Why haven't you told her about this list?'

'I told you. There's something not quite straight about her. Why did her father tell her she had to meet me just before he died without telling her why? Well, maybe he did tell her why and she isn't telling me. Maybe she hopes we'll become chums, accomplices, lovers – whatever – and I'll lead her to the hidden loot.'

Harry frowned. 'Hardly lovers. You told me she liked women.'

'One woman.'

'Ben, you're suggesting far too big a business altogether.'

'Am I? You said the stuff on this list was priceless. Worth millions now, in the hands of some crooked dealers, or maybe some of the old Nazis, still looking for the stuff. That's big business surely?'

'I doubt it. No one could sell any of those paintings, the illuminated bibles or the Dürer drawings on the open market. They're all far too well known.'

'A private market, then. That happens – some crazy millionaire keeping the pictures in a secret room ...'

'No, Ben, that's a fantasy, got up by idle journalists.'

'May I?' I went and got another shot of vodka. I was annoyed with Harry. He'd changed tack completely, putting up obstacles to all my theories, which he continued to do when I returned.

'Whatever about your father or Elsa being involved, if you're right and the rest of this hoard is still hidden somewhere, and there are old or new Nazis looking for it – I'd keep out of it, Ben. I remember Dr Frank and his sort. Gave evidence against some of them at Nuremberg. With Nazis, old or new, you'd be playing with fire.'

'Yes, like Katie.' I drank the vodka.

'I don't follow?'

'Burning herself alive in that car.' I turned to Harry. 'When I saw Elsa, I thought this was the chance to make things right, all that I'd lost with Katie.'

Harry shook his head. 'You're the one who's difficult to fathom, Ben. Not your new girlfriend. For God's sake, you can't repeat the –'

'I don't want to repeat the past! Just the opposite. I want to make it work this time.' I finished the drink. 'I'd like to find a life with this new woman.' I was excited, breathing hard.

'Okay, but for one small problem – she's a lesbian.'

'She liked men once. She was married to one, she told me.'

Harry shook his big old boxer's head in disbelief. 'So you're betting on turning this woman round sexually – and then loving her only because she looks like Katie. You're nuts, Ben. Always crazy about women.'

'One woman.'

'Right, well then keep out of the way of the krauts, or maybe you won't be betting on any more women – ever.'

I turned to him. 'I'm surprised, from your point of view. Wouldn't you like to know where this art loot went to, where the rest of it must be hidden?'

'No. If the stuff still exists, let it rot,' he added with a touch of vehemence. 'Old stones – never found any good in turning 'em over.'

'But ...'

'Come on, Ben, stop fancying yourself as a Nazi hunter, pretending concern about things you know damn all about.' Harry was edgy, almost angry. I dropped the topic.

'Okay. Come and look at this other thing I brought over.' I unwrapped the Modigliani nude. 'Is it the real thing?'

Harry gazed at the nude for a minute, then looked up. 'Where in hell did you get this?'

'My father's house. Hidden in an attic, like the inventory. It's not a copy?'

He looked at it for another minute. 'No. No, it's the real thing. One of his finest.'

'Ever seen it before? Or know about it?'

'No. Never, and I know nothing about it, except it's from Modi's later period, that great year in Paris, 1916 and 17, when he did all those marvellous nudes, dozens of them. Who is she?'

' "Amelie".' I showed him the inscription on the turnover at the bottom of the canvas. "Amelie-Amedeo-Amore".'

'That's not an "A", it's an "E". And it's a last "a". You've got Modi's script wrong. That's "Emelia", Italian.'

'OK, so how did my father come by it? It's at the end of his inventory.'

'This must have been looted, too.'

'Yes, and that does interest me, because the woman interests me. Who is she? How did my father come by her? Why hide her up in the attic all these years? You think to find out would be to unearth something nasty under the woodpile?'

He nodded. 'You go ahead, turn over the woodpile. I'd take this woman as she is. A gift horse. Don't start looking at her teeth. Never does any good.'

It was Harry's turn now to pour himself another drink. He seemed unnerved. The past was hurting him in some way or other, that was understandable – his couldn't have been a pleasant past in Europe, during and just after the war. He drank his vodka quickly, then moved away, looking up at my nude of Katie on the far wall. He turned back.

'Yes, you've lost Katie, and your wife as I remember, and quite a few other women in between you told me of.'

'Yes, a whole gallery of women; but at least I still have them on canvas, back at the barn.'

'Better to have kept one or two in the flesh.'

'I always tried to keep them both ways. "Perfection of the work and of the life". Most of them ran out on me, like you said.' I rolled a cigarette, turning away.

'Ever strike you why?'

I turned back quickly. 'I was too much my own man. The mistake I made was in pointing out their faults now and then. That wasn't part of the deal for them. Now I just want the decent life. With this woman. Start over.'

'The life? What about your art?'

'Christ, Harry! I've not painted anything good in two years, and barely made a penny out of my "art" in twice as long. I'm just a piss-artist now, or very nearly.'

'Didn't think you'd throw in the towel so easily, Ben. You're good. Good as Modi in your way. Christ, sometimes I think – you and your nudes – that you are Modi, reincarnate! Just look at those pictures of Katie. Think I'd have them in the same room with the Soutine, Utrillo, the Renoir nude – if they weren't the best?' He turned to me. 'Know something? Do you good if this broad Elsa runs out on you. You're not cut out for the domestic life, and maybe you're right about her. Something fishy there. You should cut your losses, while you still have the chance.'

'You think I'm on a hiding to nothing with her?'

'Yes, but you'll always have your work. Maybe you should just cut out the women for a bit.'

'The women are my work, Harry. You know that. There wouldn't be any work, but for them.'

'You can't always afford them, and not this one. Not one with whom you're trying to relive the life you had with a dead woman. That's just obsessional.'

'All decent work is obsessional.'

He sighed. 'Ben, forget Katie. Most affairs go wrong in the end, unless you're both going some place serious with them. If you're not, they explode.'

'Wrong? It didn't go wrong between Katie and me! It went wrong because her father turned up out of the blue two years ago, came back home to roost. He'd left the last woman he'd been living with, having left others before that, but he was getting on. Decided to pack the women in for some home comforts. Katie's mother divorced him years ago, when Katie was a child. Lot of turbulence then, and a bad business for Katie, all kept under wraps behind the solid bourgeois façade. Anyway, Katie took up with him when he came back. That's what went wrong between us. She had no real time for me then, only for him.'

'Christ! She took up with him – that way?'

'I don't think so, since that was the only thing she kept with me – bed. She could never commit herself to a man, except her father, because she thought he'd abandoned her as a child – and that this was her fault because she'd been a bad girl – she always wanted him back, to make things up with him, to be loved by him again. The only intimacy she could give anyone else was in sex. It was the only thing that always tempted her back to me.'

Harry was silent for a moment.

Then he said, 'Okay, Ben. You may be right, but stop piling up the agony for yourself over her. Where she is now not even sex is going to tempt her back to you.'

'Okay, like I said, I'll tell Elsa about Katie. Forget how she might be "meant". See if I can make something with her, just as she is, for who she is.' I started to leave, then turned. 'Oh, something else.' I held up the Modi nude. 'Know anyone else in Paris who might know about the painting? Some expert? Or an old-timer who maybe knew Modi's friends?'

'No. No, I don't. All the Modi old-timers are dead. Besides, I can vouch for the authenticity of that painting as it stands, if you wanted to sell it. Worth upwards of fifteen million bucks, or more. Never have to worry about money again.'

Harry was playing the devil on a high hill.

'I don't want to sell it,' I said firmly. 'I want to find out who she is. How my father came by her. And why he had that list of looted art. I loved him. He was good to me. Now it turns out he may have been a Nazi art looter. I want to find out which man he was. And maybe this Modi nude is the key to the whole thing, which is why we came over here, to find out about her. Because Elsa's in the same boat. Was her father a Nazi art looter, too? She loved him as well.'

'So – several other father figures involved in all this. Yet you blame Katie for that.' He shrugged. 'Let the dead bury their dead.'

'I'd like to know the truth, one way or the other. Thought you would, too.'

He was suddenly roused. 'Some truths are better left hidden.'

'Yes, if you want them to fester, and end up having to take a leg off, instead of a finger. Unless you think my father was a Nazi art looter – or worse?'

'No, Goddamnit! He couldn't have been. Your father was a Jew who survived Auschwitz, and you can't get more Jewish than that. You're nuts, Ben.'

'Okay, maybe there's some innocent explanation for that list. Maybe not. I'd like to know, one way or the other, win or lose. Least I can do for him now – give him the justice of the truth.'

Harry didn't comment. He went to the window again, then turned around. 'Tell you what – like I said, I can sell that Modi nude for you tomorrow – ten, fifteen million dollars or more. Go back home, put it in some good securities, get yourself a decent place to live. And Elsa – you might get her then. Because I'll tell you one reason why you and Katie went wrong. You hadn't had a bean for most of the time you were with her. Penniless, and likely to stay that way. Still married, and living in a draughty barn in the boondocks with no heating, telephone or plumbing. Women like to take a bath now and then, you know. No future that way with you. Maybe you thought that didn't matter because you were so good in bed together and had such good times and jokes and trips abroad.'

'Don't those things matter plenty, Harry?'

'Yes, but with the bourgeois money matters more – more than the thirty-two positions, Groucho Marx and the leaning tower of Pisa. Money in the bank, Ben, and not on your mind – matters a helluva lot to them, because the old bourgeoisie are just in the business of survival now. And so are you. And that painting, "Emelia" – she's your meal-ticket. If you sell her, and drop all your other cockamamie theories and enquiries. If you don't, if you're so damned contrary as to want to go digging into her past, and your father's and Elsa's – well then, you'll deserve everything you'll probably get.'

He turned away, looking out the window. Then he turned back, almost petulant. 'Get Katie right out of your mind, too. Stop trying to figure out why she killed herself.'

'Why bring her up again?'

'Because you're still obsessed with her – and she's put you out of your right mind about things generally, made you crazy about all this Nazi art loot thing. Accept the fact she just chucked you. Accept that you crossed onto the wrong side of the tracks there, Ben, into that smart riding school of hers. And so did she, into a drafty barn, no plumbing, with a penniless married man, awash in turpentine, booze and dreams of good women. What future was there for her with you in your arty barn? Or was she to have you and your turps and booze and sex up at her riding school – and frighten the horses?'

'No, not necessarily.'

'Look, she saw all this – that she couldn't live with you on your "creative" terms, in her place – and she wasn't going to abandon the riding school and set up shop with you in your bohemian barn. So she retreated, started to drop you, and made up excuses; that you were difficult, unreasonable, childish, whatever.'

'Okay, but …'

'You know something else – you're better off without Katie. I knew her. She was an original and plenty attractive but ruthless behind the accommodating façade. Always thought she was right, especially when she was in the wrong. You blinded yourself to her faults. She probably took to you for the sex, Ben. That's what she really wanted from you: just a good screw now and then, no strings attached.'

'You make her out to be something of a bitch.'

'You said it, Ben, but you should have known something of all this, because it's in your two paintings of her, up there on the wall. In her eyes, expression – the hardness, arrogance, along with the sexiness, but you were besotted with her, so you wouldn't see this other side to her.'

I might have been angry by now, if there hadn't been some truth in all that Harry had said. 'No, it wasn't all just sex, Harry. You can tell.'

Harry nodded. 'Maybe, but I can tell you the real thing you and Katie were up to together, like all lovers in the end – the power play, the sexual politics that always sneaks in between the sheets. Control, Ben. You had it, you lost it. She had it then, but the only way she could really control things in the end was by chucking you and taking up with her father, if that makes you feel better.'

Harry moved away. I was surprised he'd brought Katie up again. He was hitting below the belt, clearly aiming to sink me on a personal level.

He came over to me, relaxed now, the honest broker. 'Well?' he asked. 'What about selling the picture? With a bit of money you could really concentrate on your work back home. Your problems would be over. I'm being absolutely straight with you.'

Harry wasn't being absolutely straight with me. He had some other reason, besides my art and my well being, for not wanting me to go on with my enquiries. So here he was offering me millions to produce work again, and to get rid of Elsa. All this was an offer he hoped I couldn't refuse.

'Okay,' I said, stalling. 'I'll consider selling the picture. Though if I did sell it, you'd need to produce the provenance, wouldn't you? What would you say? "Hidden in the attic of a house in Dublin, owned just after the war by a penniless Jew from Auschwitz." And there's the rub – it probably was owned by some Jew originally, who ended up in Auschwitz. Some rich Jew – and not my father.'

Harry said nothing, until he looked at me. 'Ben, don't mess with this business. Drop it. Drop Elsa. Drop it all. I'll sell that Modi for you. Take the money and run.'

'I told you – I'll consider it. I can't drop Elsa. I brought her over here. I'll go pick her up now, and you can meet her later, make up your own mind.'

I wrapped up the picture, said goodbye, went downstairs and walked back to the boat. And then I saw how my father had got all those pictures safely over to Dublin. The Carrara marble he'd shipped from Italy over the years, out of the Carrara port, the finer polished stuff protected in big wooden crates, landed at the Dublin docks, and never opened until they'd been trucked out to his marble works in the suburbs. He'd hidden the paintings in those unopened crates.

The jigsaw was beginning to fit, and the more the pieces came together the more I wondered about Elsa, the more I had doubts about Harry. He didn't want me to continue with my enquiries about the Nazi art-looting business, was willing to pay me off to see that I didn't – and had taken against Elsa. Why? Maybe because he'd been involved in a bit of art looting himself after the war.

Well, perhaps I was crazy, with all these intimations and theories. A dictatorial, difficult, penniless piss-artist – beyond the endurance of the best of women. A real loser. I could chuck it all, turn round, go back to Harry with the picture, let him sell it, and live happily ever after. But I couldn't do this, because I saw now what was 'meant' in all my intimations and theories. My whole life was at stake, as were the lives of my father and mother, and of Katie – and now it seemed of Elsa and Harry as well. They'd all been hiding something. That was the real reason I couldn't take the money and run, because if I didn't prove them all liars and deceivers I'd certainly be a loser. Deception was the great leveller for them all, but it wasn't my style.

SIX ‹‹

Elsa's Story

Coming up from the saloon to the wheelhouse, the sun in my eyes, I didn't see him at first. He was standing by the wheel, gun in hand, waiting for me. 'Don't shout.' The almost apologetic, American voice I remembered in my father's house in Dublin. Then, with sudden venom, 'We have to talk.'

It was the same man, in his thirties. You could see this in the tired skin, but at a glance he looked younger. The air of an eternal, book-swamped student, dazzled by ideas beyond his reach. A narrow, undernourished face, granny glasses, lank dark dandruffy hair, tired blue eyes, gazing through me as if at some ever-receding holy grail. Baggy white tracksuit bottoms, T-shirt and trainers all at least a size too big for him, so that the movement of his stick-like body and spindly legs inside the swathes of billowy material made him look grotesque. A thin man desperately trying to fill out a fat one. Every-thing was at odds, didn't match. He was piteous – and dangerous.

'It seems –' He hesitated, an actor unsure of his lines. 'Seems you thought you could give us the slip, coming over here on his boat like that.' I didn't reply. 'Didn't you?' He threatened me with the gun.

'It wasn't my idea. It was his. His boat.'

'Don't try to get away from us again. We'll find you … we have people everywhere. We're watching him right now. His bags and things. Where are they? I don't have much time.'

'Down in his cabin, beyond the saloon.'

He gestured me down the stairs, following me through the saloon and into Ben's cabin. He found his bag, started to go through it quickly. He came on a cloth-bound book, opened it, flicking through the pages. Some sort of journal, written in a scrawled hand, and a scrapbook, with dried leaves and wild flowers stuck between the pages. He stopped at a page. 'Well, at least you've got him that way. Sleeping with him already.'

I turned on him. 'I haven't been sleeping with him.'

He showed me the drawing. 'How did he get to draw you naked in bed like this then?' I saw the sheet of white paper, tipped into the scrapbook, a pen and ink drawing. It was me. I was mystified. The drawing showed me sleeping, naked, head on a pillow, my face in half-profile.

My spine prickled. It wasn't me. This was another woman, who looked just like me. Of course – it must have been Ben's dead girl-friend, Katie. It was her scrapbook, and Ben's drawing of her. I was looking at my double. A dead woman. I turned the pages casually while he carried on looking through the cabin, opening drawers, cupboards. I read a bit of the journal, near the end. 'I want to stop his pain, and mine, and the only way to do that is to stop "us".'

Why hadn't Ben told me Katie looked just like me? What the hell was he up to? I needed to know, and I needed some hard evidence, to confront him with. So I needed this drawing. When the guy wasn't looking I put it in my bag.

The man found nothing, or nothing he was looking for. 'I don't have time.' He turned, frustrated, mopping his brow in the heat. Then he smiled. 'He still has the painting, and that's what really counts.'

'Why don't you just take it off him then?'

'We may have to take it off him, but we want him to do the leg work on this job, lead us to the other paintings. We don't exist. Remember that. We – and you – we're here to follow him. So don't try to give us the slip again.' He was about to leave, then he turned. 'Maybe you've told him all about us and everything else already?'

'No, I haven't.'

'Well, don't. If he finds out we'll kill you, but as long as he fancies you – well, that'll make things easier for all of us.' He came towards me. 'Don't try to cut us out again. Remember what we did with your father in Dublin, when he wouldn't cooperate.'

'Thank God he died before …'

'No, you're wrong there. That was a misfortune – for both of you. My friends were overzealous. If your father had lived a bit longer he would have told us where the rest of those paintings are hidden, and you wouldn't have been involved, but your father also knew that Ben Contini's father had told his son where the rest of the paintings were hidden before he died last year – we got that out of Bergen at least.' He gazed at me. 'So the trouble is, like I said, this Ben Contini – he knows where the paintings are hidden as well. He's going after them now, over here, which is why we have to keep tabs on him.' The man was sweating. He looked over the canal basin, the line of boats on either side shimmering in the heat. He tapped the wheel. 'So don't think you can disappear again. I have to be off. You get back with Contini. He's with his American friend Broughton now. And keep your mouth shut about us. We're everywhere, all around you, and remember what I told you about Contini. Tell him about us, and we'll get you. Get on the wrong side of him, and he'll kill you.'

He left. I called Harry's number from a nearby phone box, as I'd arranged with Ben. I got through to Harry, then to Ben. Ben said he'd pick me up at the boat in half an hour. He was enthusiastic. 'We'll have lunch. Lunch in summer, in Paris! What better?' I liked him again. Ben a killer? Surely not. The little bastard was just trying to frighten me. I was still going to tell Ben everything, so I decided I might as well take the whole journal with me, not just the drawing.

Ben picked me up at the boat half an hour later and we walked down towards the river. He had the Modigliani in its bubble-wrapped parcel under his arm. He was impatient, on a high, as if he'd been drinking, his eyes bright and daring, as I'd remembered them at the funeral party in Dublin.

'Let's go straight to the Louvre,' he said, 'see if we can get any information on the picture. Then there's a small restaurant I always go to here, La Tourelle, just off the Boul Mich.'

We arrived at the Louvre and waited in the basement entrance under the glass pyramid in the courtyard. Finally we got to see an archivist of French twentieth-century paintings. A languid young man, tall, rather foppish, in a smart linen summer suit. He had a dismissive air that went with his tailoring until he saw the painting and examined it closely. Then he became animated, spoke as if it belonged to the Louvre and we'd stolen it. 'Where did you get this?'

'A legacy,' Ben told him shortly. 'It's genuine, isn't it?'

'Oh yes, it's a Modigliani. That winter of 1916 and 17, when he painted so many wonderful nudes.'

'Any idea who she might be, or where the painting comes from?'

'No. I've never seen this painting before, or heard of it.' He looked at Ben doubtfully again.

'Modi gave away many of his paintings,' Ben said, 'to girls, to café and restaurant proprietors, for drink and food. Could be one of those.'

'It could, and most he gave away like that were lost or destroyed afterwards. This one's survived – that's what makes it interesting. Astonishing.' Again the doubtful look.

'You have my name and address in Dublin – it belongs to me.' Ben was almost aggressive now. 'I wouldn't be here otherwise if it didn't.'

'Monsieur, I don't doubt you. It's just a surprise. Because you are the second person today to make such enquiries about the provenance of a lost Modigliani masterpiece.'

'I don't follow?'

'A man came to see me this morning asked if I knew anything about an unknown Modigliani nude, which he said might have ended up in Dublin after the war. I knew nothing of this, but I told him he might consult Monsieur Broughton here, the American expert on Modigliani's work.'

'What did this man look like?'

'Small, rather fat, English: and here you are a few hours later with the very picture he might have been referring to. You must forgive me if I seem surprised.' He looked at Ben gravely.

'Well, there's no connection. This is my painting and I can prove it.'

'Of course. Just coincidence.' A graver look.

'I've seen Monsieur Broughton already, a friend of mine. He knows nothing about it. It there anyone else in Paris who might be able to identify it? Maybe someone still living, from the old days?'

'Yes, the other man asked me the same question. I told him – Monsieur Martin-Beaumont. He was a young assistant to Madame Weill and worked in her gallery during the Great War. Modigliani had his first and only exhibition there, in 1917.'

'Is this man still alive?'

'Yes, he's an old man.'

'Can you give me his address?' The archivist was doubtful again.

'Look, I've given you my name and address. We're on my boat here, at the Port de Plaisance, the *Sorrento*. You can check it all out. So you needn't worry. I'm kosher.'

The archivist seemed reassured. He gave Ben Martin-Beaumont's address. When we got out Ben whispered urgently. 'Come on, let's go round and see Martin-Beaumont straightaway. He's only just over the river from here.'

Martin-Beaumont lived on the left bank, the Rue-des-Saint-Pères, an eighteenth-century *hôtel privé*, now converted into flats. We went through an arched gateway, across a courtyard, towards another arched doorway. A closed-circuit TV camera gazed down at us, with a coded entry system. We rang the concierge's bell. A young Algerian let us into the hallway. He called Martin-Beaumont on an intercom. No reply.

'Did he go out?'

'No, he's in. He had two people come to see him an hour ago. He's fairly deaf. May not have heard the buzzer.'

'Do you mind if we go upstairs? It's rather important. I have this picture for him to look at.'

'Go ahead. First floor, apartment two, end of the corridor.'

We walked upstairs. The corridor was silent. The apartment door was at the end, and the door ajar. Ben rang the bell. No answer. He pushed the door open slowly. 'Monsieur Martin-Beaumont?' No reply. Pushed it further. A dark hallway. Ben went ahead, towards an open door at the end. I followed. The place was airless, with a faint, tart smell, like lime juice. Ben was in the sitting room now. I was right behind. A big room, comfortable, good furniture, Persian carpets, pictures all round the walls. 'Monsieur Martin-Beaumont?'

There was no sign of the old man. Then we came on him, lying behind the sofa. I thought he was asleep, he looked so comfortable, stretched out on the carpet. He was dead, his tie round his neck, but not in the right place. Tight round his throat. He'd been strangled.

'Christ!' Ben was bending over him, holding his pulse, then touching his brow. 'Still warm. Not long ago.'

'Who? Who could have …?'

'We could have. In fact it was those two men here an hour ago who must have killed him. One of them was a man called O'Higgins, I bet. You smell the lime in the air?' I nodded. 'Well, O'Higgins is an antiques dealer in Dublin I sold some furniture to last week, and he was doused in some lime aftershave lotion when he came to see me. Upstairs, in a cabinet of my father's, he saw a list my father had made of pictures that included the Modi nude. So he came over to Paris to find out more about the painting, first from that archivist in the Louvre who told him about Martin-Beaumont, and then on here. But two of them came up here, the concierge said. The other guy was a hit man. O'Higgins must have become involved with some mob in the stolen art business, to help him find the Modi and all those other masterpieces in my father's inventory. Just like us, he found out that Martin-Beaumont might give them some information on the painting, and put them on the right trail, but the old man failed to cooperate. In any case it'll mean the police – a lot of questions. Have to get out of here. Take it slowly, we'll be on that closed-circuit TV on the way out.'

Downstairs Ben thanked the concierge. 'Yes, we saw the old man. A bit deaf. He didn't hear the bell when you called him.'

The concierge nodded. 'I have a parcel for him, just arrived. Looks like another painting. I'll take it up to him.'

We let ourselves out and walked casually through the court-yard, and once out on the street, we walked fast.

'Once the concierge gets upstairs and finds the body the police will be right over.' We turned onto the quay. 'Come on, we best go see Harry. A safe house.'

SEVEN

We were running now, with the painting. Crossing the Pont Neuf, I noticed a youth skating along on roller blades behind us. He seemed to be following us. And he was, still behind us as we came into the Marais quarter. When we reached Harry's square, Ben stopped. A police car was parked in front of Harry's house.

'Christ, that archivist must have told the cops about my being a friend of Harry's. No future there. Let's go. The boat.' We left the square, taking a new direction, through narrow streets we hadn't been in before, turning left, then right, then stopping. We were lost. 'It must be that way.'

We turned, walked down an empty, dusty street, the sun casting harsh shadows across old, boarded-up apartment buildings to either side. Then footsteps behind us, two men, the younger one who had been on the boat with me an hour before in baggy track-suit bottoms, the other in slacks and dark glasses. We started to run, but there was nowhere to run to. A cul-de-sac. The side wall of another apartment building blocked the end of the street, the doors of all the other buildings on both sides firmly boarded up.

But there was another smaller door, further on. No boards across it. Ben threw himself against it. It gave way with a crash, and I was right after him, running fast, along a dark corridor, up some stone steps, through a swing door and into a big open space, a marble-tiled hall, lit by high windows, sunlight streaming down on two empty bathing pools. To either side a score of cubicles, partitioned and fronted by white curtains. We'd made a full circle round the pools. We were in the old Turkish baths, only recently closed, for there were still dirty towels strewn about the floor.

Running round the end of the pools we ran into a cubicle halfway along on the far side, drawing the curtain behind us. Inside was a slatted wooden massage table.

'Up! Up on the table.' Ben clambered up and I followed him, crouching on all fours. I saw why now. All the curtains fell an inch or two short of the tiled floor, so that anyone taking a worm's-eye view along the row of cubicles would see our feet.

We waited. Running footsteps, up the stone stairway. The men were in the building. Silence. Footsteps starting again, softly now, but going in different directions, on the far side of the pool, to both ends of the other row of cubicles. The violent swish of curtains then, every few seconds, the men moving down the row in a pincer movement, hoping to trap us in the middle.

We had to get down the far end of the line, while we had the chance, towards the back door and make a run for it.

Easing ourselves off the table, we ran through the partition curtain into the next cubicle, hitting the massage table, and then into the cubicle beyond. By then they'd heard the racket and were running over towards us, one to either end of the line, blocking off our escape.

We got up on a massage table again. Trapped, waiting for them, helpless. There was a broom against the wall of the cubicle. Ben picked it up, then gestured to me. We both stood up on the table, but right against the wall this time, Ben holding the broom.

The footsteps starting again, softly in the silence, coming towards us from either side. Ben held the broom out, against the partition curtain to our left. The repeated swish of curtains as both men converged on us. Three cubicles away, two, one. Ben stabbed at the curtain viciously with his broom.

The shots rang out, bullets tearing through the curtain on our left, through the other to our right. We heard the second man fall heavily in the cubicle to our right. We ran fast, over the body, in a flurry of curtains, through all the other cubicles, towards the back door, ending up in the last cubicle. This was a larger one, without a massage table. There were cupboards, lockers, old towels, sponges littered about, and a fire hydrant against the end wall. A big canvas hose, flattened and coiled on a drum with a wheel tap above it.

Ben spun the tap. A vague hiss of water. Then, with another turn there was full pressure. He pulled the hose out, hand over hand, the drum spinning furiously, the canvas swelling, writhing about in his hands now, before a great jet of water emerged from the metal nozzle. He let it rip into the curtains ahead of us, tearing some of them clean off their rails.

The other man was still out of sight somewhere behind us along the row of cubicles, hidden by the sheets. Ben moved forward, hosing one sheet after another in a fierce torrent of water. Suddenly the man was in front of Ben, but only his shape, the drenched white curtain pressed against his body like a mould. He started to shoot again, wildly, through the material.

The curtain flew off its rails, enveloping him like a shroud. He stumbled out into the hall, struggling to free himself. It was easy for Ben: he directed the full force of water at the man's chest. He fell back like a ten-pin into one of the empty pools, six feet to the tiled bottom, a motionless heap, wrapped up in a sheet like a load of old laundry.

Ben climbed down, took the shroud off him and turned him over. I saw the soaking baggy tracksuit bottoms, the matchstick legs. He was unconscious. Ben went through his pockets. Nothing, no labels on his clothes. Nothing to identify him.

Then the other older man, lying in the cubicle. He looked dead. Ben went through his pockets – nothing to identify him. He picked up his gun, pocketed it, went back for the Modi nude where he'd left it on the locker, then looked at the fire hydrant. The hose was still spurting full tilt into the pool. 'Let it run. It'll either drown him or wake him.'

'No, we're not killers. Turn it off.' He didn't. 'We don't have time,' he said. Then we were out the back door and running. 'The boat!' he shouted. 'The boat!'

We got to the Port de Plaisance, crossing the footbridge over the basin, moving towards the *Sorrento* moored halfway along on the other side. We could see it now, a hundred yards away. Ben stopped. 'Wait a moment.' There was a man up by a pay phone beyond the bridge, seemingly waiting to use it, but there was no one using it. 'A look-out,' Ben murmured. 'I bet there's someone waiting to nab us on the boat. The police. That archivist must have told them about the *Sorrento*.' We were still walking towards the boat. 'Just turn round and walk back over the bridge – easily, slowly.' We did. Then we heard the footsteps behind us again. We ran.

We crossed the bridge and ran down onto the other quay, losing ourselves among the crowd of tourists and afternoon strollers. Further down there were two big steel refuse skips set above the moored boats. We hid behind them, waiting, breathless. The running footsteps came towards us, paused, then passed us on the other side.

Just behind us, low down in the water, wedged between two smart yachts, we saw an old converted barge, *L'Etoile*, with a line of washing and two bicycles on the deck, and a sign above the wheelhouse: *Bateau à Louer*.

Ben went straight down the gangway. I had to follow. He looked into the wheelhouse. No one there. He hammered on the door.

'Christ! Hold your horses, whoever you are.' A man shouted in English, rising up from the hold as if from a stage trap door. A big man, seemingly more wide than tall, rings of fat, middle-aged, white-haired, a stormy beard, deeply lined face, like a crumpled boarding house bed. A Falstaff in grimy shorts and a T-shirt. He'd hardly opened the door before Ben spoke, pushing into the wheelhouse.

'Hi! Saw your sign. We're interested in renting your boat.'

'Come on, come on in then.'

We were in the wheelhouse, hidden from the quay. The place was a mess. Books, papers, dirty mugs and bottles all over the place. I could smell the man's aniseed breath. The bottle was nearby, a litre of Ricard. Two drunks now, I thought. Just dandy.

'A drink?' He picked up the bottle. He might have been expecting us.

'Thanks, but it's a bit early for me. Sun's not yet over the yard arm.'

'Oh – a sailing man yourself?'

'Yes, out of Poole harbour. We have a racing five metre. Over in Paris on a break and saw the sign, thought we might hire the boat and take it up one of the canals here.'

'Yes, why not? You have RYA helmsman's papers? Need that over here.'

'Oh, yes, I have all the papers. What do you charge?'

'Hundred quid a day. I'll give you 20 per cent off, if you take it for a week. Sleeps eight, most mod cons, and you get the theatre thrown in.'

'The theatre? What sort of …'

'All sorts. Straight, farce, commedia dell'arte, cabaret, old-time music hall, conjuring, illusionist's tricks, and potted Shakespeare:

bilingual, French and English. On the deck in summer, below deck in the hold in winter. We cruise the canals, moor in towns and villages. "Les Saltimbanques de Bateau" we're called. We're having a break for a week or so, and I need to get back to London for a bit. But any income we can get meanwhile…'

'Of course.'

The man was enthusiastic now. 'Take a look below.' He turned back. 'I'm Geoff, by the way. Geoff Wakefield.' Ben took his hand. 'George Hayward,' he said at once. 'This is my friend Isobel.' I shook his hand. More than a hand. It was a huge paw, to go with the huge everything else.

We were coming down the steps to the hold, into a narrow central corridor. There was quite a decent-sized galley to the right, bottled gas cooker, fridge, dirty sink, plates and wine glasses. Further on he opened a cabin door. 'The master bedroom, bathroom en suite.' We looked inside. Chaos again. 'I'm sorry – haven't done it over yet.' No bunks, but a double divan filled nearly all the space, with a headboard, gilded plaster cupids playing at the top. Two portholes, hundreds of dead flies and a pot of brown geraniums on a shelf beneath.

'Great,' Ben said.

'I'm sorry – no chairs. No room.'

'Doesn't matter. We can just sit on the bed.'

'There's a shower here.' He pulled a curtain across on the far side. 'Have to be a bit careful with the water, but you'll always get a minute or so out of it – warm water, I mean.'

'We … I don't shower much.'

Geoff swayed as we left the cabin. We moved into a long, narrow space, the covered hold of the old barge, wooden benches piled up on each side, a small proscenium arch at the end, curtained and crowned by two more gilded cupids.

'A lot of cupids,' Ben said.

'Yes, from a movie studio clear out here, a job lot.'

'Glut on the market these days I expect, gilded cupids,' Ben murmured. Then he was enthusiastic. ' "The smell of the grease-paint, roar of the crowd"!'

'Interested in theatre?'

'Oh, yes, used to act a bit.' Ben had gone forward, peeking through the curtain. 'May I?' Geoff nodded. Ben got up on the small stage, disappeared and then returned. He was wearing a shiny top hat, holding a silver topped cane. He did a little dance, swinging the cane, doffing the hat. He laughed. I didn't.

'Great!' Geoff shouted up. 'That's part of my 'The Man who Broke the Bank at Monte Carlo' act.'

Ben immediately started on the song, in an off-key voice. ' "As I walk along the Bois Boolong, with an independent air, you can hear the girls declare, he must be a millionaire ... He's the man who broke the bank at Monte Carlo!" '

Geoff clapped vigorously. 'A bit of make-up and my dress suit and you'd be perfect.'

Ben jumped down from the stage and shook hands with Geoff. 'Great! We'll take it.'

'But Ben ... George ...'

Ben turned, looked at me fiercely. 'Yes, a bit of make-up and a dress suit. Wouldn't recognize me, would you, *Isobel*?'

'No. No, I wouldn't.' I saw what he had in mind. Disguises. He was mad.

'We'll take the boat, for a week.'

We went back up into the wheelhouse. 'I'll take that drink now.' George poured Ben a large Ricard, with just a splash of water, then offered me the bottle. I shook my head. He added a little water to his own glass. They toasted each other. Ben took out his wallet and counted out £550 in crisp £50 notes. They toasted each other again. Ben handed him the money.

They drank again and talked of the trip. 'Where would you like to go?' Geoff had some maps by the wheel, the canals of France. Ben turned to me. 'Where would you like to go, darling?'

'I don't know.'

'The Marne and Rhine canal might suit you,' Geoff put in quickly. He opened up a plan of it, in a tall, narrow book, with the route detailed on each page. 'Goes east through some fine country, and some good pike fishing if you wanted it. There's two rods in the stern locker. A week's trip – to Bar-le-Duc – here.' He pointed a finger. 'There's a little restaurant just off the square, Le Coq d'Or. Tell you what: would you leave the boat at Bar-le-Duc for me, and give the keys to the patron of Le Coq d'Or? Monsieur Jacques is an old friend. I said he could have the barge for a family holiday, until I get back.'

Ben took another gulp of Ricard and looked at the map. 'Fine. We don't want to come back the same way anyway. We'll leave the boat at Bar-le-Duc, and take a train back from there. Can we leave today? Now?'

'Sure. Just sign a few papers. What about your luggage?'

'Back at the hotel. We'll – I'll – go pick it up, and get some food.' Ben turned to me. 'Since you're feeling tired, why don't you stay here, darling, take a rest down in the cabin, while I do the chores. That okay, Geoff?'

'Sure. Come up and fix the papers, then I'll get my things and go with you.' Geoff was in a hurry now and Ben more or less pushed me downstairs. He joined me a few minutes later in the cabin and closed the door. 'What would you prefer?' he said at once. 'The men who got Martin-Beaumont? Or the guys in the Turkish baths? They'll have friends. Or the police who went to see Harry? They'll be looking for us now. Or those men back at the *Sorrento*, whoever the hell they are. We have to get out of Paris on this barge.'

'We might get out some easier way.'

'What way? The stations, airports, main roads out – they'll be checking them, they know what we look like, we're on video. This way, on the barge, no one will know.'

'Great.'

'We can get off at Bar-le-Duc, take a train, get straight back home from one of the channel ports.'

'And your boat?'

'Hell, that can wait. We can deal with all that when we get back safe on home ground. Just not get tied up here in France, with the police or with any of these other guys. That's all that matters now. You got a better idea?'

'No, I don't. Just – frying pan, and now the fire.'

'There's no fire here. Geoff's not going to make any trouble. He's pissed already, and not the sort anyway.'

'Ben –'

'Either that or you can take your chances on your own.'

'No, I was going to say – this is all really crazy. What are we doing?'

'I'm not sure. You might know better than me.' He looked at me pointedly. 'I'll leave with Geoff now, pretend I'm picking up our luggage and get some food and things.' He tapped the Modigliani, secure in its bubble-wrapped parcel. 'Keep an eye on this, Isobel.' He put it under the divan, turned and left.

I looked out the porthole. Part of the quay was visible above me. I saw a couple of cops, and then another two, walking up and down, looking around. Christ, Ben would surely be caught. He wasn't. I watched as they left the barge – Geoff with a big backpack and carrying another one. They walked along the quay, laughing, swaying, boisterous shipmates taking shore leave. The cops took no notice of them.

Ben was back an hour later, with tins of food, vegetables, wine, two T-shirts emblazoned with the legend 'J'aime Paris', two flimsy windcheaters, a toothbrush and some toothpaste, all stuffed into a Euro Disney rucksack with a picture of Mickey Mouse on the back.

'Sorry, they only had one toothbrush left in the pharmacy. We'll have to share it.'

'Thanks.'

'They're there – the river police, at the lock that leads out to the Seine at the end of the basin. Looking over all the boats leaving. Which means you're going to have to hide below deck while I take her out of here disguised. There's make-up back on a shelf behind the stage and loads of theatrical tat in a big skip there. So you'll have to lie low somewhere, while I play the drunken sailor topside.'

'Ideal casting.'

'Look, I've had more bright ideas drunk than sober. We're in a sheep or a lamb situation, and I don't intend getting hung for either. See?' He did his scowl-smile at me.

'Okay, but it'll be lambs to the slaughter.'

'No it won't. Come on.'

We went forward into the hold and up onto the little stage. The make-up, moustaches and things were there on a shelf. 'Darken my face, anything, make me look swarthy. And that moustache is made for me.' Then he opened the wicker skip. A terrible stale smell of old unwashed costumes emerged. He started to rootle round. 'Look, this is just the job – French matelot costume, striped T-shirt, blue sailor's cap.'

He got into the matelot costume. I brushed his face with some dark Leichner powder, stuck the moustache on. He added the cap, angled jauntily over his brow. He was certainly changed, and unsteady on his feet now. The drunken sailor, absolutely.

'And where am I going to hide?' I asked.

'Not in that big laundry skip. First place a cop would look.' He looked around the stage. In one corner was a tall wardrobe-like thing, colourfully decorated, with a sequin-bodiced woman in a tutu painted on the door, two fencing foils attached to the side. He went over and opened the door. Inside was a circular platform with two full-length mirrors angled at the back against a central pole. Ben moved the platform a bit. The mirrors moved, displaying a hidden triangular space behind. He moved the platform back again. 'Ideal. It's an illusionist's cabinet.'

'A what?'

'One of Geoff's tricks. You disappear in it.'

'No.'

'Go on, get into it! I'll turn the platform and you'll be perfectly hidden, that's the whole point of the trick.'

'And those two foils? What are they for?'

'I don't know. Just get in, hurry! We need to be off.'

I got in and stood on the platform. Ben closed the door, and suddenly, with a snap of some mechanism, I was swished right round and hidden in a dark space at the back. 'I can't see a thing!' I said. 'How do I get out?'

'Come to that later.' I heard his footsteps disappear.

'Christ,' I said. I heard the engine start, a gentle throb, and we edged out into the basin. Then into reverse, forward again, a more powerful throb, and we were moving down towards the lock leading into the Seine. Then we stopped.

I heard footsteps coming down into the hold and up onto the stage. Ben's voice, perfect French. 'Nothing up there, officer, just our theatre stuff. We have a date up at Joinville tonight, meeting the other guys there.'

Someone drew the curtains, climbed onto the stage. I heard the lid of the skip thrown back. 'Nothing there either, officer. Lot of old laundry.'

'Smells like a load of dead rats,' the cop said, then, walking towards the cabinet, 'What's in here then? This pretty girl on the door?'

'Illusionist's cabinet, but I'm afraid the pretty girl isn't inside right now.' The cabinet door opened. 'See, no one inside.' The door closed again.

'And these foils? What are they for?'

'Just to show the audience that the girl has really disappeared. You push them in, either side, those two holes.'

'You do?'

'Well, when I'm doing a show.'

'But if there's no one inside, why not?'

'Well …'

'Let me try.'

I pushed myself as hard as I could against the back of the cabinet. Was the cop going to impale me now? Kill me? I heard the foil swishing in behind my back. The second foil, from the other side, came through a moment later, faster, in front of me. I nearly shrieked.

'See? Nothing inside.' Ben's confident voice again. I heard them climb down from the stage, their footsteps disappearing.

Five minutes later the engine throbbed again. We were moving into the lock. Silence. The lock gates clanging behind us. The boat falling in the water. The other gates opening. The boat moving out onto the river.

I was stuck, and absolutely furious. Ten minutes later the engine died, and I heard him mooring the barge, and after that his footsteps, running down to the hold, and shouting, 'You okay?'

'I'm not okay, you bloody fool!' I shouted.

'Then you are okay.' He jumped up on the stage, pulled the foils out, fiddled with the door. Some mechanism cut in and I swirled round inside the cabinet. He opened the door. I got out, furious. He took no notice, just put his cap up at a jauntier angle. 'Well, what would you have done,' I said, 'if one of those foils had gone through me?'

'They wouldn't have gone through you. That's the whole point of the trick.'

'Thanks,' I said.

We went up to the wheelhouse. He'd pulled the barge into one of the quays a little way upriver. Now he cast off the bow rope, returned, started the engine and we moved out onto the water. Soon we were chugging upstream, going east out of Paris, the twin towers of Notre Dame behind us, cut through with the bright shafts of a midsummer sun, falling in the sky, a flame over the bridges, way downstream.

He started to sing quietly. ' "As I walk along the Bois Boolong, with an independent air, you can hear the girls declare, he must be a millionaire … He's the man who broke the bank at Monte Carlo!" ' He turned to me. 'See, it worked.'

'Yes, all very clever of you. I thought you were just a painter.'

'I thought you were just a cookbook writer.' He looked at me carefully. '*Isobel.*'

Con man? Killer? Or just a crazy innocent? I wasn't sure. Then he took the gun he'd had from the guy in the Turkish baths from beneath the dash board. I'd forgotten about it. A small gun. He looked at it, then at me. He hadn't been going to kill me with the foils. He was going to shoot me now.

EIGHT <<<<<<<<<<<<<<<<<<<<<<<<<<<<<<<<<<<<<<<<

'Don't shoot! Let me explain!'

He was puzzled. 'Shoot you? I was just moving the gun to a better hiding place. Explain what?'

'Everything.' I started to tell him what had happened to me and my father in Dublin a week before – the men who had visited us both, my father at home in bed, the morphine drip in his arm, which the nurse fixed up, morning, midday and evening, when she came to tend him.

'They killed him that way?'

'Yes, they tinkered with the drip – gradually pumped much more morphine into him than he needed – trying to get him to talk about where the art hoard was. He told them nothing, except that they were just making dying easier for him, but it was terrible for me. They made me watch.'

'God, I'm sorry.'

'So you can see why I was so nervous with you at the funeral reception and the next day. It wasn't my father who told me to go and see you – it was them, and they'd kill me if I didn't or went to the police. They said your father must have known where the art hoard was hidden as well, and must have told you before he died.'

'Well, he may have known, but he never told me.'

And then Ben told me everything. About the inventory in his father's cabinet, and how it had emerged, and all that had passed between him and Harry Broughton that morning. We came clean with each other, or almost clean. I didn't tell him about my finding the drawing of Katie in her journal on the boat that morning, that I knew she looked just like me. That could wait. The drawing and the journal were in my bag now. Meanwhile we talked and talked as the barge made its way slowly upriver into the coming darkness, and we emerged into something of the light together.

Later, when it was almost dark, and we hadn't got out of the dreary outer suburbs of Paris, we moored for the night in an old industrial backwater in the shadow of ruined warehouses, near Joinville, wedged between the bows of two great derelict barges, where we couldn't be seen from the shore or the river.

I was making a dish with what I'd found in the galley and Ben had bought in Paris, spaghetti puttanesca, with a hot Roman sauce of anchovies, olives, paprika and a tin of tomatoes. I was at the stove. He was at the galley door, still in his matelot costume, with a glass of wine.

'Those men who got onto you and your father in Dublin, and in the baths this morning must be neo-Nazis, or hit men working for old ones. As I said, it fits in with everything Harry told me. How most of this art was looted in Poland by Dr Frank and his pals, then hidden somewhere towards the end of the war, then some of it brought over to Dublin in those crates of marble my father imported from Italy, then secretly sold over the years in that back room of your father's Dublin shop. So my father and yours must have been well connected with the Nazis. Because there's the inventory of all Frank's looted art in my father's hand.' Ben had showed me the inventory earlier.

'Yes, but ...' But Ben rushed on.

'We can't get away from it, Elsa – my father and yours must have been involved in this business. Your father must have been a Nazi – in the SS or worse – and my father must have been involved with them all as well.'

'Come on, Ben. Maybe my father was a Nazi – there were millions of them. Why worse? He, and your father, could just have been dishonest, dealing in this stolen art. Middlemen, no connection with this monster Frank.'

'Yes, I'd thought just that.'

'My father was in the ordinary German army, not the SS. He could have come on this hoard, hidden somewhere, at the end of the war, thought he'd have it as a nest egg afterwards, and teamed up with your father in Dublin when he came back from Auschwitz.

'Okay, that's a reasonable argument, but there's a hole in it. How could just the two of them have fixed up all this on their own? Nearly everything in that inventory can be identified as Dr Frank's loot, taken from private art collections, churches, monasteries – and Jews – in Poland and elsewhere. So at some point they must have been involved with Dr Frank and his SS thugs. There were a whole crowd of them, Harry told me. Especially a man called Pfaffenroth, an SS major, Dr Frank's sidekick. I can't buy the idea that your father or mine just stumbled on this hoard. They must have been involved with the SS in Poland so that my father was able to hide the loot for them, maybe in one of his Carrara quarries, and had the means to get all the stuff out from Italy to Dublin after the war, by boat, hidden in his crates of fine cut marble. I don't know how he met your father, maybe in some DP camp in Europe after the war or in Dublin later on. But when they did meet, they had the means to sell it in your father's Dublin shop, to support them both after the war, having double-crossed the other Nazis in on the game, which is why they're after us now, fifty years later, to get their share.'

'That's a worst-case scenario.'

'Take the worst case first, and you can work back from that. Think of innocence first and you're bound to be disappointed.'

'That's really cynical.'

'Only because your father's involved. So you have to deny it.'

'No! You're just a cynic.'

'Facing a very likely truth isn't cynical, it's honest, and that's our business, isn't it? Being honest.'

'Yes, but not this time. My father – innocent until proved guilty.'

'You think I want to see my father as guilty?'

'Seems very like it.'

'A Jew in Auschwitz, who was involved in all this dirty business? I may have to face something worse than anything your father might have been up to.' He turned away, fretting.

'I'm sorry,' I said.

'Anyway.' He turned back. 'There's one sure thing. All these people are after us, and it seems they're not likely to let go.'

'Bastards.' The olive oil was heating in the pan. I threw in some diced onions, letting them brown. 'I didn't want that man drowned in the baths. Now I hope he was. Just as that little squirt on the boat who cornered me told me. He said his friends were everywhere.'

'Yes, and one of them is O'Higgins: he must be working with those two guys in the Turkish baths. All of them art crooks, and maybe working with neo-Nazis. In any case the police will be after us when they've seen that closed-circuit footage and talked to Harry.'

He put down his glass, rolled a cigarette. It was hot in the galley and he was sweating. The brown make-up had smudged and run down his face. He'd stopped acting. The show was over. He'd saved us, for the moment, and that was great. He'd been great. He was no killer or crook. A bit raffish, mildly lecherous, but a good man. I liked him. But now I wanted out. Of everything – him, them, France, Dublin, the lot, just to go home to New York and try to forget about the whole business. The onions had browned. I threw in half a tin of tomatoes with them.

'Right,' I said. 'So with all these people after us, now's the time to get out.' He didn't reply, no agreement with this obvious point. The sauce started to bubble in the pan. I tipped in the anchovies, olives, diced red peppers, stirred them about. A pinch of oregano, paprika. A dollop of the red wine, turned the heat up, sweating myself. There was a roll of kitchen paper. I mopped my brow.

'Have a glass of wine,' he said. 'I bought some white. It'll be chilled in the fridge by now.'

He got the bottle out, opened it, poured me a glass.

'Happiness!' He held his glass up. 'Like that first time, the reception in Dublin with that white Châteauneuf.'

I sipped it. 'This is better. That was a terrible party.'

'I told you I'm not good at parties, or deaths,' he added. 'My mother, well, that wasn't a surprise. Katie – that was different.'

'Yes, yes, I can see.' I hadn't told him yet about how I had his dead girlfriend's journal and the drawing of her in my bag; how I knew she looked just like me. I didn't want to talk about this. At some point I'd just give him back the journal, without telling him I'd seen the drawing.

'So it all fits.' He turned to me, intent now, serious.

'Does it?' I turned up the gas under another pan of water for the pasta, put in some salt, olive oil. 'I'd say we've come to the end of the story now,' I said.

He was fiddling with his roll-up. 'Have we?'

'It would be crazy to mess with any of these people. We've nothing to gain, and everything to lose. Get out of here now, any way we can. You have the Modi. Sell it. No cash problems for you anymore. So we can both forget about it all.'

'Yes, except I still want to know what my father was up to in the war. And, yes, okay maybe we can forget it all, but these other guys won't. They'll be looking for us – or me at least since they think I know where the stuff is hidden.'

'Go to the police, then, when you get back home. They don't know where you live in England.'

'Easy to find out.'

'Well, what's your alternative?'

'I don't want to sell that nude. I like her.'

'Okay, just go back home with her then, sleep with her under your pillow and keep your head under it too.'

'And you?'

'Me, the same. Go back to New York. Keep my head down. I can put the Killiney house on the market from there. I don't want the house. I don't want anything of that house again.'

'Wait a moment, Elsa!' He was roused now. 'You're saying drop everything. So you don't care a damn about what our families were up to in the war? Well, we should care. We're them.'

'No we're not!' I was furious now.

'Same flesh and blood.'

'Okay, but that doesn't make us anything to do with whatever they might have done in the war, and certainly not if it means getting killed for something they did and we were no part of.'

'Christ! How could you live the rest of your life not knowing if your father was a Nazi war criminal or not?'

'Very easily.'

'Well, I couldn't.' He screwed up his eyes and some more of the sweaty make-up ran down his chin. He rolled another cigarette. 'What about your olives and olive oil book?'

'I tell you – I can surely do that some other easier time.'

He poured us both another glass of wine, and sniffed the air. It was full of anchovies, olives, tomatoes, peppers. A whiff of oregano, paprika.

'Well, why don't we do the olive groves tour now? Like we said we would in Dublin. Drop the boat at Bar-le-Duc, hire a car and go down south. They'll maybe look for us back home, but they won't look for us in the olive groves.'

'No.'

'I haven't painted you yet, either.'

'You left all your stuff on the *Sorrento*.'

'Easy to buy some more paints, a canvas or two.' He smelled his wine. 'This isn't bad, you know. Yes, let's go south. "Where the vine and olive thrive and the Brussels sprout doesn't grow at all."'

'No. I just want to get back to New York and eat some cheese-cake from the deli round the corner.'

He drank the wine, came over to the pan, brushing past me, sniffed the mix. 'This is good,' he said.

I don't know what made me instantly want to do just what he'd said – go to ground, down south, do what we said we'd do in Dublin, as if all this terrible business had never happened. Then I thought I knew. It was his brushing past my body, in the small space, glancing against my backside as he went over to smell the sauce. Oh, it wasn't Martha brushing past me in our New York kitchen, on her way to sniff the supper I was making on the stove. It was a body. Of course I wasn't going to go south with his body or anyone else's, but the thought crossed my mind.

We nearly fell asleep over the tart's spaghetti before we went to our separate cabins. I had the master cabin with the double bed, tepid shower, the Sanilav, and the gilded cupids. Ben had a cabin somewhere down the corridor. I couldn't sleep. My life had turned so many strange circles in the last week, I barely knew where I was.

All I had was a past I knew about, where I'd been happy. I thought about it, looking for an anchor, lying beneath the gilded cupids, listening to odd sighs and murmurs of the water moving along the flanks of the barge outside the porthole.

I couldn't concentrate on any one aspect of my old life, and what I most couldn't focus on properly was my father. Even if what he'd been up to in the back room of his Dublin shop wasn't war-criminal stuff, it seemed he'd been doing something crooked. This didn't sit with my memories of my father at all. I'd loved him. He'd been a good man. If I believed Ben's theories I had to hate him now, but I couldn't.

If I hated my parents now I'd have to see my whole childhood and youth tainted. It was often idyllic, at home in Killiney, with the sea and the long crescent beach down the road, bathing and lolling about, gazing at the blue haze over Killiney Head in midsummer. All this should have seemed corrupted now, but it didn't: you couldn't corrupt the past if it had been happy for you.

My father – gentle, always courteous to everyone, and so Catholic, like my mother. Mass every Sunday and on holy days, fish on Fridays even when that ceased to be obligatory in Ireland. A quiet man, preoccupied with old books and manuscripts, playing the piano sometimes in the evenings, the easier pieces from Beethoven and Mozart. Dipping into Goethe and Schiller.

How could someone like this be involved in Nazi art looting? My mother, the worn, tired face, but always happy in the kitchen making apfelstrudel or Wiener schnitzel. What possible clue was there, in either of their lives, which might have led one to suspect this sort of evil past in them? I couldn't deal with these thoughts about my parents anymore. I had to switch to something else, to a much happier time: going to America when I was eighteen and staying near Charlottesville, Virginia, with wealthy German friends of my father's, the Kochs. They had a stud farm out in fields with white fences, big chestnut hunters, some arabs, palominos, a long row of stables.

They hunted in the Fall with the Albermarle County pack. I spent a whole year there and loved it. Riding out into wild country, up into the Blue Ridge Mountains, forested, with tumbling streams, old ruined homesteads and apple orchards from early settlers in the mountains, with deer and wild turkeys jumping up in front of you and having to stay clear of the bear tracks.

I could keep my mind on this for a bit, until I realized now that Mr Koch might well have been a war criminal. Since he was an old friend of my father's – they had been in the army together – he and his stud farm could well have been financed by the looted art. The Blue Ridge memories were at risk of being tainted as well.

I'd liked the Kochs and they helped me get into the University at Charlottesville, where I studied languages, French and German. I knew German anyway and had good matriculation French. I didn't have any problems until I met Curtis, one of the English professors, at a frat party in Rugby Road. He was young and brilliant, vividly engaging, from an old Southern tobacco family. A gentleman. He'd just had a novel published, which had apparently been well reviewed. He'd described it to me as a 'literary' novel that first evening. I didn't know then that there was any other kind.

Indeed there was, he said, and he talked to me about all the other sorts of novels in the following months. Except the sort of novels he also wrote, which I didn't find out about until after we were married a year later and were living outside town in an old clapboard house off the Military Road.

He wrote hardcore pornography, under another name, for a publisher in Paris. I found out by chance when I discovered some of the books. They'd been posted over from France, the parcel had partly broken open, and Curtis was away. One fell out. I glanced through it. Brutal sexual athletics, where the woman, who was clearly me, was doing things we'd never done. I saw how he'd lied and used me as a sort of sexual guinea pig in reality and then in his fiction, as the manipulated, degraded 'heroine' in the novel.

I hadn't slept with anyone before Curtis, but when I found out about his other literary efforts and how I figured in them, I exploded. I'd been used as his muse, but a soiled muse. I gave men up and decided never to be used again. That's when I met Martha. Martha seized my real heart.

I'd been down in New Orleans researching an article on French-Cajun cooking. There'd been a hurricane raging round the Gulf and no flights out of New Orleans that day, so I'd taken the train back, the Amtrak Crescent to New York, as she had too. She'd been giving a lecture at the Maritime Law School at Tulane.

We met in the dining car, first night out, both of us alone, so the steward put us at the same table for two. She had a delicate, rather plain face, with two swathes of straight hair either side of a central parting. Narrow-shouldered, unfashionable, in a beige wool skirt, a dun-coloured silk blouse, a cameo brooch. Though in her mid thirties she had an air of immaturity and innocence, a fragile, other-worldly appearance. I didn't know then what drew me to Martha, but I knew what this was several months later, after we'd met again in New York and she'd moved into my West Side apartment.

It was her adolescent restlessness, that first night on the train in the storm. The way she fidgeted with her cutlery, her napkin, looking out the window aghast, like Dorothy in *The Wonderful Wizard of Oz*, as if the hurricane was going to hurl itself upon us at any moment and overturn the huge train, and we'd all be sucked up into the raging skies. She was so earnest, naïve and frightened. And I thought I knew, five years later, how it was just these quali-ties, which at first had attracted me, that took her away from me. Her appealing fidgets, her seriousness, that quizzical gleam in the eye – these were the seemingly innocent seeds which were to grow into exotic hothouse blooms, an overweening ambition to take a leaf out of my creative writing books and write a virgin-attorney-working-death-row-in-Miami novel.

I asked her later what had attracted her to me. 'Almost the first words you said in the dining car, looking at the menu – "I'm going to have the New York Strip Steak." The daring way you said it. It was somehow sexy.' It must have been. We shared my small sleeping compartment that first night out in the train from New Orleans.

That meeting with Martha was more than a dozen years later, though. After I left Curtis I went back to Dublin and moped a while with my parents in Killiney. Then I went back to New York. I did a cookery course, at the Cercle de Cuisine, near the Lincoln Center. Then I worked as a guide on the Circle Line Manhattan boats, and then the same in the UN. I did other odd jobs, in restaurants mostly, waitressing at first, then the cooking, which I suppose was what I'd really wanted all along.

I was lucky. I was waitressing in a small West Side restaurant, the Brittany du Soir. Red check tablecloths, bistro style, damn good. Seafood a speciality. The chef burnt his arm badly early one Saturday evening, and the place was booked out, with only the French patron there. He knew I could cook a little, we'd talked about food. And of course I spoke French. '*Vas-y, Elsa!*' he said. 'Get in there and help me out. The scallops are one of the specials tonight – see what you can do.' Coquilles St Jacques. I did them okay, and Lobster Mornay, and oysters quick-fried in batter with a dash of white wine and parsley, a Brittany dish. I did the cooking for several weeks. The chef never came back, and I got his job.

I loved the work and the place and the people. Happy days. Then the restaurant and my cooking were reviewed in *The New York Times*, so that soon there were smart-ass types over from the East Side, showing off or making ignorant complaints, and I didn't find it so congenial. I wanted out. The patron didn't find it so congenial either, but he was coining money. So he said one day, 'Why don't we write a Brittany du Soir cookbook?'

We did. It was a success. I became a cookbook writer. Three other books followed, where I travelled in Europe, India, China, Russia. Part diary, part travel book, but the underpinning was always accounts and recipes of simple or unusual food and traditional cooking methods. Talking to the locals in remote places. Venison and sun-dried fig kebabs, and sweet champagne, high in the Georgian mountains. Honey and breadcrumbed Porca Alentejano and very fresh vinho verde in a riverside café I found halfway up the Tagus. And French-Cajun cooking in New Orleans, which is how I met Martha.

Martha. My mind stopped flashing about. I tried to think of something else quite unsullied. The time in Lisbon, the vast, fabulous seafood platter in what had looked like a McDonalds, right next to the hotel. It was after I'd finished my Portuguese article, the first evening of a holiday with Martha, when she'd flown over and we had a few days together doing nothing but walk the mosaic sidewalks, letting the wind swirl round our ankles, that ever-sweet wind off the Tagus. But the only world then had been us. I'd said to Martha on the plane back, looking at her, 'If I never wrote another cookbook again, I wouldn't mind.' Shaking my head, looking at her, in wonder.

Next morning I woke early, just after dawn, and went up on deck. The sky was pearl-grey, but brightening, the sun about to rise over the hulks of the great barges. There was no sign of Ben. A sudden panic. Then I saw him. He was behind the wheelhouse, sitting right on the stern with a fishing rod, gazing intently out on the grey water. I moved round the wheelhouse. He was looking at a float, motionless in the water.

'Ben?'

'Shh …' He turned, eyes alight, and spoke softly. 'Perch, roach, who knows what? I'm trying anchovy as bait. So I might even tempt a great pike. They like smelly bait and murky backwaters like this. I'd like to get a big pike. You know how to cook them?'

'Bake them slowly for hours in tinfoil, stuffed with as much herbs and white wine as you can get into them, and even then they're filthy, oily and full of bones. I didn't know you fished.'

'Oh, yes. On lakes up in the north of Ireland. Big pike there, monsters. I used to go with my father. He loved it. Early morning, or twilight.'

'Okay, but it hardly seems the moment.'

'It's the ideal moment – told you, dawn.'

'No, fathead! I meant generally. We're on the run, Goddamnit! Supposed to be trying to get out of here, not taking a fishing holiday.'

'Get out of here later. Maybe you could make some coffee?'

'Okay.' I turned back. 'Look,' I said, 'there's something I didn't tell you last night. On the *Sorrento*, when that guy went through your bag looking for your father's art inventory – well, he thought he'd found it, but it turned out to be some sort of scrapbook or journal. He threw it on the floor. I rescued it. Thought it might be important for you. I have it in my bag.'

He was gazing intently at the float, and then he spoke, still with his back to me. 'Oh, yes, that journal's important all right. Katie left it behind in her bag, in my barn, that afternoon before she set off to kill herself. I drove after her to give it back, but I was too late.'

'I see.' I wondered if he was going to tell me now how I looked just like her.

He didn't. He continued quickly: 'I've only read bits of it. So I don't know what she's really said there. A diary, yes, partly about us. Which is why I didn't go on with it.'

I wanted him to tell me the truth, about how I looked just like Katie – but just then the float dipped violently in the water and the reel spun out viciously with a great whine. He had some big fish hooked.

'God! This could be it.' He stood up, playing the fish back and forth back for the next five minutes, the rod bent – reeling the line in to breaking point, it seemed – before he released some mechanism and the line spun away. Then reeled it in slowly again. To and fro, arms braced, muscles bulging. A great battle. 'Christ!' He was shouting now. 'It must be a big one!' He was beside himself. 'That net behind me,' he shouted. 'Get the net, be ready with it, over the stern here. I need both hands.'

It took another five minutes. Then we saw the fish, the shadow of it first, then the mottled green and yellow skin, twisting viciously about just beneath the water, when it ran deep again, and was pulled back. Finally he had it, bringing it towards the net, which I held over the stern, as he pulled the fish over the wire lip.

It was a pike. It must have been nearly three feet long, its great flat head and wide gaping jaws staring up malevolently at me, chomping at the wire lead, with a disgusting, sagging white belly. It was nasty, ferocious, its huge mouth snapping. I could see its sharp run of teeth – as if famished, biting on nothing except your fingers. I was thankful when Ben took the net from me and lifted it up onto the stern boards, where it flashed and flew about, struggling in the net, its body arched in a semi-circle.

'God, it must be nearly twenty pounds. Just look at the brute!'

He hit it on the back of the neck with an iron mooring stake. 'Hook's too deep to get it out, swallowed it right down. I'll have to kill it.' It lay inert, just the odd twitch now.

'It's far too big to cook with what there is in the galley,' I said.

'Fillet it. Or cut it into steaks.'

Then something distracted him. He looked up. I turned round.

The sun was rising, and there, illuminated on the high deck of the derelict barge to our left, were two men, in caps and uniforms.

'If only you hadn't gone bloody fishing and shouting!' I said, shouting myself, 'we could have been out of here long ago!'

'Yes, but we wouldn't have had the fish – and what a fish!' We ran to the wheelhouse.

NINE

They were only private security guards. Alerted by our ridiculous shouting and splashing they'd come running from somewhere behind the old warehouses. They shouted at us in French, from the prow of the big barge above us. 'Can't you read? "Private Property – Keep Out – No Mooring".'

Ben placated them, and we headed upriver. 'Trouble is,' he said, as we chugged east into the morning sun, 'they may remember us if they get to hear the police are looking for a man and a woman out on the river. They'll know the direction we're taking as well.'

'What direction are we taking?' We were in the wheelhouse drinking coffee. A vast commercial barge, the deck loaded with cars, was bearing down on us, producing a great wave to either side of its prow. I was worried. We seemed to be headed straight for it.' 'What side of the road do we drive on here?'

'The right, and every big commercial barge has the right of way.' He slewed the wheel round and we made for the shoreline, just in time, I thought. The great barge hooted at us. 'That's only to thank us,' he said. 'The *"camaraderie des chaloniers"*, comradeship of the bargees.'

'Thanks. I do speak French. And it's "mariners". You can't turn the barge, "la chalande", into the "bargees".'

'Yes. Well, where are we?' He got the map and showed me. 'We turn off the Seine about four kilometres ahead, left onto the Marne. Then along for about fifteen kilometres to Vitry-le-François, where we turn left again onto the Canaux de la Marne au Rhin, and that leads us to Bar-le-Duc, about another forty kilometres. Okay?'

'What's that? About a day's run?'

'We're not driving a car, you know. We're on the water. Four miles an hour, and there are locks, about fifteen or so of them. Bar-le-Duc? Three or four days.'

'Wait a moment! We're supposed to be on the run, not swanning along at four miles an hour on a holiday. We should get off this boat as soon as possible. Dump it and make for one of the channel ports, like you said.'

'*You* wait a moment – swanning along slowly is the best game we can play. Let the trail go cold, before we make for one of the channel ports. And furthermore, I'm not going to dump Geoff's boat, his livelihood, until we get to Bar-le-Duc, where we said we'd leave it. And I'm captain of this boat – so there!' Taking his hands off the wheel, he started to roll a cigarette. Another great barge was bearing down on us.

'For God's sake … watch out!' I shouted.

'Calm down.'

'Look, you can have yourself run over, but not me!'

'Christ, I wouldn't like to drive a car with you in it.'

'You won't ever have to, I can assure you. Just let me out!'

'Let you out? We're not in a car you know – I keep telling you. That's water out there. You'd drown.'

'I can swim.'

'Wouldn't if I were you. That big barge, or the next would certainly get you then. First it'd suck you under, then you'd be mincemeat when you got to the propeller.' I could hear the throb of big engines now. Ben finally turned out of its way.

I was panting with annoyance. 'You're playing your bloody games again. First in Paris with Geoff, then with that damn great fish, getting us into trouble, now dicing with death with these huge barges. What is it with you? You really think this is the way to go on? Risking our lives with every damn great barge that comes along. You got a death wish or something?'

'No.' He turned. 'Just the opposite, and it's always been my reading of things to do what the crooks and the cops won't expect. And they won't be expecting us to swan along at four miles an hour in this barge enjoying ourselves.'

'Okay, well I'm not enjoying myself, so you can let me off at the next stop and I'll make my own way home.'

'Right.' He didn't look at me. 'Let you off at Vitry-le-François. Should get there this afternoon. You can get a train there back to Paris in half an hour, then fly straight out, back to New York. You could be eating that damn cheesecake in your local deli this time tomorrow.' He turned and looked at me, downcast, so that for several seconds I was tempted to stay on board with him. But no, that'd be crazy. He was crazy.

'Okay, let me off at Vitry-le-François.'

'Right, another four or five hours. Maybe you could cut a few steaks off that pike and cook it for lunch?'

'That fish has caused us trouble enough.'

'Well, you could cut it up for the cats.'

'Cats?'

'Yes, there are two cats that Geoff forgot to tell us about, in his cabin. I heard them this morning, mewing, went in and gave them some anchovies. They didn't like them.'

'Cats – well that's just great.'

'We'll need to get cat food at Vitry.'

'You didn't find anything else in there – a couple of mad dogs?'

'Yes, almost. Cabin's stuffed full of bits and pieces, like an antiques shop, props for his theatricals, I suppose. All sorts of strange things.'

'I knew that guy was nuts.'

'So why don't you give the cats some of the pike? They're starving – and take a look at the things in there.'

'Okay, I'll feed the cats, but I'm getting off at Vitry.'

I left the wheelhouse, cut some flesh off the disgusting pike, diced it up on a plate, went below, opened the cabin door and saw the two tabbies, mewing, tails in air now. They started to eat hungrily. I looked round the cabin. It was extraordinary, packed out with things on shelves and on the floor. An old horn gramophone, a Red Indian headdress and a tomahawk, other things I couldn't identify. Over his bunk a full frontal photograph of a naked African girl. Another lecher.

Then I saw it and sprang back: hanging by a cord at the end of a shelf was a pitch-black, shrunken human head, bulbous nose with a ring in it, elongated lobes with strings of beads hanging down, long shanks of matted dark hair trailing round the back, the eyelids and lips roughly sewn together. A nightmare. My God, I wanted off this boat.

I told Ben about the shrunken head when I got up to the wheelhouse again.

'Yes, I saw it.'

'He's really nuts. That's a human head.'

'Sure it's a human head. It probably comes from some South American Indian tribe. Spoils of victory over another tribe.'

'Maybe, but it was a real person.'

'What did you think it was, something from EuroDisney?'

'How would you like your head smoked and shrunk and hung from a shelf?'

'I wouldn't know much about it, would I, but I do see their point: it's a way of keeping power over your enemies, and much less harm than cruise missiles or cyanide showers.'

I got off near Vitry-le-François. We'd moored half a mile out of town, to avoid anyone on the lookout for us at the quay in the town. It was nearly three in the afternoon, and very hot.

'Look,' I said. 'Don't think badly of me.'

'No, I don't think badly of you. That's your privilege, running away from things. I'm just sorry I didn't get to paint you.'

'Maybe some other time. I'll come back to Dublin, or your place in England. Paint me when all this has blown over.'

'Yes, but the trouble is we're involved in something that can't ever really blow over.'

'We're not involved in all this looting. They were – if they were, which I very much doubt.'

I left him.

I walked along the riverbank into the town. The main square was surrounded by heavily ornate, turn-of-the-century buildings: the town hall, library, a museum; a sign pointing to the Gare SNCF. I was near the station. The light was blinding. I badly needed a pair of sunglasses. I'd lost mine sometime yesterday. There was a touristy shop next to the museum entrance and a circular rack of sunglasses outside. There was a selection of mirrored sunglasses and in the mirror of one of these I saw a man and a woman crossing the square behind me, coming towards me. The woman with a headscarf, dark glasses, rather dowdy, in a flower-print dress. The older man, over-weight in a linen suit and a Panama hat. An owlish face. Just a couple.

But somehow I was on alert. They were such an incongruous pair. I had no reason to think they were interested in me but I felt there was something wrong about them and I wasn't taking any chances.

Without turning around I walked up the steps into the museum, paid three francs, and was pointed to another flight of wide stairs up to the first floor. The high-ceilinged rooms were cool and quite full of visitors: exhausted tourists sitting on benches, a few old men escaping the hot weather, a group of noisy schoolchildren with a teacher. An interesting provincial museum full of Celtic, Roman and Frankish things and display cases, filled with old coins, porcelain, silver goblets, swords and gilded daggers. Portraits of grandees in suits of medieval armour.

I moved round, keeping an eye on the door I'd come in by. The couple I'd seen were almost certainly nothing. Just nerves. Nobody could know we'd be stopping in Vitry-le-François, or that I'd be leaving the boat alone. The couple didn't appear at the doorway, but I'd give them time, just in case. I wandered round.

There was a marble bust of François Premier, the founder of the town, with a garland of laurel on a plinth, looking very military and proud and satisfied. Just behind him was a doorway. '*Dames.*' I wanted a pee. The place was clean and modern and no old woman waiting to take pennies off me inside. It was empty.

When I came out of my cubicle the woman in the headscarf and dark glasses was staring straight at me, a gun in her hand. She must have been in her forties, a thin, rather raddled face. I finally said, 'What do you want?' I was shaking.

'Out of here,' she said in English in a coarse, north-country accent. 'And when we're out of here, and you meet my friend, you will walk between us, carefully, and tell us where you and your friend have put the stuff you were supposed to deliver to us in Paris. Which we paid for, half the agreed price. And if you shout or do any other stupid business when we get out of here I'll shoot. The gun is silenced.'

She gestured with the gun, then covered it with another silk scarf she had in her hand. We moved out into the museum. The middle-aged man in the Panama hat met us. His face was round, the skin very white and smooth and frozen, like marble. Only the eyes moved, but he was affable. He raised his hat a fraction to me. 'How good to meet you.' A real gent. He gestured towards the doorway. 'Let us go and have coffee, shall we?' His English was perfect, but the very slight accent was German, I thought.

We moved down the first of the two flights of the wide marble staircase. I saw the big mahogany door on the half-landing marked '*Privé*'. It was ajar.

I was on the inside by the wall as we went down. We were alone on the staircase. As we passed the door I threw myself at it. It flew open, and I ran. It was dark inside after the glare. A storeroom, a big room full of broken statuary, pillars, bits of old masonry on the floor, suits of armour, swords and halberds.

I turned and ducked left into one of the dark corners. Then right, behind a group of statues. I could hear footsteps and peered out. It was the woman in the headscarf. I'd no idea what to do. I'd assumed there'd be someone, one of the museum staff, in the room, which was why the door was ajar, but there wasn't.

Then, in the gloom beside me, I saw the exhibit. It was a mock-up of a room in a Roman villa, wooden-framed, with figures: a *tableau vivant*. Figures in togas, men, women, children, in lifelike poses: two women going about various domestic tasks, one combing her hair, a second baking bread, two children beside her; two men in togas in the darkened background, conversing, with wine goblets in hand; a third man, behind them, sharpening a short sword on a grindstone, and sheets littered about.

I stepped into the *tableau vivant*, picked up a sheet and draped it around me, and went back to the shadows, beside the guy sharpening his sword. To hide my face I bent down by his shoulder, as if I was helping him, and stood stock-still.

I heard nothing for a minute. Then I saw the woman, gun in

hand. She came towards the exhibit, stopped, looked at it, seemed to stare straight at me for a moment, then moved on. I thought I had escaped, but she reappeared, and now she stopped for longer, looking at the motionless figures. Then she stepped into the room. But no, she hadn't seen me. She stopped at the woman baking bread, gazed at the one combing her hair. Then she came towards the two frozen men holding their wine goblets. She looked at them carefully, and then turned past them, towards me.

I knew if she came close, she'd know I was real. I gripped the wooden broad sword. I saw her out of the corner of my eye coming up to the grindstone, behind the stooped soldier. She stopped, looking at him, then up at me. And in the second she saw I was real I let her have it with the sword, catching her on the cheek, then again on the shoulder, and again somewhere else as she fell. I felt like decapitating her, but there wasn't time.

I ran for the door and then I was out on the stairway with the schoolchildren, and an attendant in a tight blue skirt was shouting at them not to run. I mixed in with them all, down in the lobby now, then out into the blinding sun and across the square. I was halfway across before I realized I was making for the river, not the train station. I kept going in the same direction, back to the boat. Better the devil you know.

When I reached the spot where we'd moored the barge, it was gone.

I sat down on the bank and nearly cried – but at least I knew that at Vitry Ben was going to turn left, up the Marne and Rhine canal and towards Bar-le-Duc. At four miles an hour and with all the locks I could surely catch him up. But I was on the Marne now. Where did the canal start? I would have to find out back in the town, and risk another meeting with the tarty woman and the man in the Panama hat. There was nothing else for it.

When I reached the main square I saw the sign. 'Canaux de la

Marne au Rhin. Port de Plaisance'. The arrow pointed right across the square to the town hall. And across the square, outside the town hall and museum I saw the police and a police van, and a crowd of people. I had to risk crossing the square, passing through the crowd, and possibly being seen by the police, or wait. But I couldn't afford to wait. I'd miss Ben and the barge.

I crossed the square, head down, and stepped onto the other sidewalk, near the town hall, pushing through the crowd. I hadn't gone five yards before I heard the voice, loud, excited. 'Yes, there she is! That woman, she's the one in the storeroom.'

I turned. It was the museum attendant. She was standing on the steps on the museum with a cop. Pointing at me. I ran.

Round the corner, and another corner. There was a big super-market and a parking lot ahead of me busy with crowds of people, children eating ice creams in the forecourt and playing with red balloons. I rushed through the doors, took a basket, moved away, right to the back, moving among the high shelves. The cheeses. Then the wines.

Then I saw Ben. He was holding a basket full of cat food and cheeses and inspecting the wines. He had a bottle in his hand, looking at it carefully.

I came up behind him. He didn't even jump. 'Thought you might come back,' he said. He held up the bottle. 'What do you think of this? A Barton et Guestier claret, a good '89. The Bartons are an Irish family from Kildare. They still run the firm now in Bordeaux. Go well with the Pont-L'Evêque I've got, and I've bought some quite good-looking steak as well, for two...'

'Christ, will you stop babbling and listen!' I said, infuriated by his blather. But I don't think I was ever so pleased to see anybody.

'Well,' he said, when I'd told him what had happened and about the couple. 'The barge is up in the basin leading into the canal. The police won't look for you there. Just walk out of here.

I'll tell you what, all those balloons they're giving away out in the front here … get some. Hold them down about your face. There are tourist families from the boats buying provisions here, all going back to the basin. We'll get in among a group and walk back with them.'

Which we did: I held three balloons just over my head, and we walked to the basin with two English families, chatting with them, children trailing behind, all of us weighted down with bags of food and drink. Ben turned and said to a little girl, 'If you like, I'll carry that bag for you.'

'No thank you,' she said primly. 'Mummy told me never to talk to strange men.'

Her mother scolded her. 'Don't be rude, Sophie! He's not a strange man – not when you're with us.'

Sophie started to cry. It was very hot; I didn't blame her. Ben took her bag and gave me his, and picked Sophie up, put her on his shoulders with her balloons, and bounced along towards the basin, singing 'The Man Who Broke the Bank at Monte Carlo'. She stopped crying.

We left the basin at once, into the first lock, then along the canal. Ben was relaxed at wheel. The canal was straight and narrower than the river and the barges coming towards us, when they did, were much smaller. Safer travelling, but now there was another worry, if not a real danger.

'Look … don't you think … who were those two people?'

'Your guess is as good as mine.'

'Come on, Ben! You're supposed to be the bright one in all this. The woman told me we had to deliver something to them, which we didn't do. Something important, since she had a gun.'

'Must be the Modi nude. What else could it be?'

'No, she said the "stuff". And that we'd been paid half the agreed price for it.'

'Maybe they paid your father for some items in the past and now they're after the rest of the art loot.'

'So they must be with the guys in the Turkish baths, but there's no chance that any of them could have known we – that I was going to be walking about the middle of Vitry this afternoon.'

'No. Pure chance, but then that's exactly how you met me in the supermarket. So much is just pure chance.'

'How did they come to be in Vitry in the first place? No one knew we were headed in this direction, or that we were going to stop in Vitry.'

'I don't know, but they must be looking for the paintings in my father's inventory, maybe somehow involved with O'Higgins and the Modi. They were following us in Paris, they saw us leave in the barge, and followed us in another boat. And followed you off our boat into Vitry to get you alone.'

'So, if you're right that means they know the boat we're on and they'll still be following us.' I looked behind. There was a smaller cruiser a hundred yards away, but it was one of the English families.

'Not at once they won't. Seems you gave that woman a real bash with that sword. She may be in hospital now. And her gun! The cops may have found that, and if they have, she'll be held on a charge. In any case we have a good head start on them.' As if to underline what he said, he moved the throttle forward a bit. I was encouraged. We must have been doing all of five miles an hour.

We were soon out in the country, a small breeze in through the open windscreen, the evening sun slanting behind us, a long row of poplar trees on the bank casting their shadows away into cornfields dotted with poppies.

'What made you think I'd come back?' I said. 'I certainly wasn't going to.'

'I thought you'd be a fool to give all this up – the poplars and poppies, high summer on a French canal, Pont-L'Evêque and a fine claret – for a slice of cheesecake in sweaty New York.' He rolled a cigarette. 'Oh, and the steak,' he added. 'You might consider showing your paces with it tonight? I threw away the pike.'

'How insouciant you are.'

'Thanks. I speak French, too, and I'm not unconcerned. You are. That's why you want to do a runner back to New York.'

'Touché. Though all the same, if you thought I'd come back why didn't you wait for me where we'd moored on the river back there? You couldn't have thought we'd bump into each other in the supermarket.'

'All right – I hoped you'd come back, let's put it that way.'

'I know you did.'

'Oh? How on earth did you ever guess that?'

Here was my opportunity, and I might as well take it. 'Because I look just like Katie, your dead girlfriend – that's why.' He didn't bat an eyelid. Hand on the wheel, gazing into the middle distance, frozen. 'I'm sorry, I didn't tell you before. When I found the journal on the *Sorrento* in Paris I glanced inside and saw it was Katie's, saw the drawing you'd made of her, how it was just like me.'

He turned to me. 'The drawing?'

'Yes, the drawing. So that I knew then why you'd been so star-tled to see me at the funeral party in Dublin.'

'Well now you know, there's another reason for you to run, isn't it? Who wants to be liked – loved – just because they look like someone else?'

'Why not? It must be quite a thrill, except I can only look like her surely? I can't actually be like her. Must be different in every other way.'

'No, you're like her in other ways, too. All her better ways.'

Silence again, until I finally said, 'Well, there's nothing to be mournful about. I'm not like her in one way. I'm alive – that's the big difference.'

'That's exactly what I thought.'

'It's lucky you don't look like Martha. I think I'd have run a mile from you if you had, or done something stupid.'

'Was it that bad?'

'Wasn't it for you? Must have been worse: Katie killed herself, Martha just went off to write smart-ass novels.'

'I think it was so bad with Katie because it never had to happen.'

'That's usually why the worst things happen. They have to happen.'

He perked up at this. 'You mean – fate?'

'No, some people just attract trouble. Like we said that day on the boat out from Killiney. They set themselves a lousy script – then they have to produce it, won't be denied. Even kill themselves, rather than see they're wrong and chuck the script.'

'Seems that's just what Katie did. You can see it happening in her script. Here.' He leant forward, took the journal from the shelf beneath the wheel, thumbed through it, stopped near the end, offered it to me. 'I've been reading it – but only bits of it.'

'No, it's private.'

'Please, I'd like you to.'

I took it from him and read the passage, several pages from the end of the journal.

Now that I'm going to lose him – why not go back to the beginning? That first time, before we even met. One of my riders, Monika – Monika, who does watercolours – she said one Sunday, five years ago, did I know the painter Ben Contini? That he lived not far away. I said no, and that I'd never heard of him. Then she came out with it. They wanted a portrait of me, to mark my twenty years of running the riding school. I said no, it was nonsense. Then, for no good reason, I repeated his name. Ben Contini, and I had a fluttery feeling. Can one fall in love with just a name? I must have done. Two or three weeks before I met you, and it was this that made me agree to the portrait, as an introduction.

I was already making a date with you before I met you, but I was losing myself, making a commitment I sensed I couldn't fulfil. And so, when it came to it, as it has – it has to be either me or you. One of us has to go. And it won't be you, I know. Fidelity is your strongest card. How hard you tried not to lose me, and the more you tried, the more you loved me – the more I couldn't face your love.

So, a portrait of me? You painted so many. Of the woman you wanted me to be – but never the woman I was, someone who couldn't live with you.

But when you came to the riding school that first time, out of your old Bentley with your paints and canvas in the back seat, and said brightly 'Have I come to the right place?' – both of us full of conventional smiles – I knew I was suddenly living again, after years of nothing that way, that I wanted you already. Just looking at you, that windy March day, your head to one side, ruffling your hair. You made me, that instant, know what a very forward person I could be – how I wanted to be painted by you, wanted to seduce you, and wanted to spend the rest of my life with you, too. But I couldn't.

I'll go and see you this afternoon, and make love with you in the flax field, or your old barn, the doves warbling above us, on the great tatty divan. Warm against the huge fire in winter, or bright with the 'Larks in the spring air' as you once said. But even then I was already going away from you. Leaving such happiness.

I looked up at Ben. 'It's painful. I don't understand her. It's all about her being no good, not you, and she gives no reason for wanting to leave you. Was she in love with someone else?'

'Her father, I think, when he came back home after years of womanizing.' And I told Elsa all that I knew of Katie and her relationship with her father.

'Well – they both sound kind of mad.'

'That's what I've thought. But was she really … disturbed?'

'I don't know. But whatever, she doesn't like herself. And it seems she's trying to justify this by chucking you, and that's pretty twisted.'

'Maybe you could say she blamed herself because her father left home when she was a child, and she left me because when he returned she felt he had forgiven her.'

'Sounds even more twisted. Who's to know the truth about her?'

He looked at me, as if he was trying to corner me now, instead of his dead mistress. 'Ben, I have to – we have to – get off this boat and get back to our own lives. We could take a slow boat to China and I'd still not love you.'

'Okay. Except for one thing. If you really wanted out so badly why didn't you run straight for the train station in Vitry when you left the boat instead of coming back to the boat?'

'I …' I hesitated.

'You were running back into the fire when you could have been in Paris by now.'

I remembered why. 'Better the devil you know …'

'Thanks.'

'I was frightened.'

'So we must count for something together.'

'I suppose so. Yes, we must.'

I wasn't certain exactly what. So I let the issue drop, went away and made us mugs of tea. Later I went down to the galley and started to prepare supper. I got the pots and pans organized and rummaged through the two shopping bags. The steaks looked reasonable. Thickish centre cut. There was fruit, salad and bread, and lemons, as well as a sealed pack of Alaskan smoked salmon. And more olives: big, green, herby Provençal ones. I opened the jar, ate one, then two, and took a hunk off the baguette. I was hungry. And that key opened a door, fiddling about with food again, the smells and the tinkering, and fingers getting moist with juices. Living again.

The best foil against evil and folly was to get involved with food. Preparing, cooking, eating it. I'd known this for years, of course, which was why I was in the business, but I'd forgotten how you could cock a snook at evil in a kitchen. I got out the steaks. Not the best. They'd need a bit of whacking and marinading. I cut a lemon, squeezed half of it onto a plate with a thin film of olive oil, then ground black pepper into the mix, and some grain mustard. There was a string of garlic, and butter. I opened the pack of sliced smoked salmon. An oaky smell of the sea. Nibbled a bit. And another bit. Ate another olive, unwrapped the Pont-L'Evêque, to air, and opened one of his friend's bottles of claret to air as well, and tasted it. The wine was good, a big nose. Then I looked for something to soften the steaks with. I opened the cupboard beneath the sink. There was nothing, just some cloths and, surprisingly, since there was no washing machine on the boat, six jumbo packs of Persil washing powder. I finally used a tin of tomatoes to beat the steaks, put them in the marinade and ate another olive.

Returning to the wheelhouse I was back in a less happy reality, before it struck me. I said to Ben, 'We can hardly stop and eat supper if we're supposedly on the run from all these people?'

'We'll have to stop. All the lock-keepers on this canal go off duty at seven.' We'll be in time for the next two locks, here at Adecourt and Brusson, but not the one after that at Ponthion.'

'But those two monsters back at Vitry – they'll know about the locks closing as well. Don't even have to follow us by boat. They can come along the old towpath there.'

'Possibly.'

'In which case?'

He got out the map again. 'Look, there's a small basin, here, just before the lock at Ponthion. There'll be other boats moored there for the night, because they won't get beyond the Ponthion lock tonight either. We'll moor right alongside one of them, away from the bank. They're not going to start gunning for us in the middle of a flotilla of tourist boats.'

'Gunning for us?'

'You said she had a gun.'

'Yes.'

'Well, I have one, too.'

'Come on – these people are professionals, Ben. Killers. You're not going to …'

' "This dog is dangerous. He defends himself when attacked".'

'I see.'

We got to the Ponthion basin just after seven. The lock was closed, and there were five or six boats moored there, as Ben had forecast. No space by the bank. We asked one of the English families if we could tie up alongside them. That was no problem.

I started to cook the steaks beneath the gas grill.

'We can eat up in the wheelhouse. Keep an eye out.'

And so we ate in the gathering twilight, lights in the village coming on ahead of us, dappling the water with streaks of yellow, midges annoying us. 'Rub some lemon juice round your face and your ankles. They always seem to fancy your ankles most.'

'Yes, I know.' I was on edge. 'Doesn't look like you're going to get any painting done. These villages aren't likely to have any art shops.'

'No, but I could get some paper and sketch you for a later masterwork.'

'Like that sketch in the scrapbook?'

'Yes.' He looked at me, like he'd looked at me at the funeral reception in Dublin. Appraising me, without clothes. It was hot in the wheelhouse. I was wearing all I had to wear: shorts and a billowy, thin cotton blouse.

'Well, you said I could paint you any way I wanted that day out on the boat.'

'But it's not quite the same now, knowing you'd really be painting Katie.'

'Not now, I wouldn't.' He turned away, sipped his wine.

'Listen, even if I didn't look like Katie, you'd have no future that way with me.'

I told him about Curtis and the hardcore porn novel he'd secretly written about us back in Virginia.

'I'm sorry – that's tough.' Then he added in a brighter tone, 'Though at least it shows you weren't always into women.'

'Right, but I'm not likely to revert to men.'

'And not likely to find another woman just like Martha. I was lucky in finding you.'

'You're right. You found a nice symmetry: with me, though not quite the same.'

'That's what attracted me. The same, but not the same.'

'But that's your real problem: you're still looking for that dead woman, and as long as you're doing that you're sort of dead, too. You said I was avoiding the issue in all this art-looting business, but you're avoiding something more serious: your life. And you're not going to find your life in me, no more than you did with Katie. So forget her and get back home.'

'Just what Harry said. You Americans, so keen on swapping love for work. The old puritan ethic, I suppose. But why should I swap love for work?' He was in his fierce mode again.

'Okay, I agree. I suppose it was the same with Martha.'

We'd finished dinner. He was eating a last wedge of Pont-L'Evêque, drained his wine glass. Preoccupied, he was silent at last. He looked over at me quickly, concentrating his gaze for a moment, then turned away, half-closing his eyes, as if what he saw in my face was a sun, too bright to look at.

What happened in that moment for me? I don't know. There was sympathy and liking for him already. Now there was something else. It wasn't hunger for him, or love, but it was something just as overwhelming. I felt irradiated, cut to the quick by warmth and joy, and the need to give this to him in some way.

I got up. His hand was on the table. Without looking at him, I took it and rubbed it, put it to my cheek, kissed it. Then rubbed it hard again, as if this way I could rub out all his pain.

'Thank you,' he said. 'And for supper. You're a damn good cook. Hey, I tell you what ...' He stood up, went over to the wheel, folded back a blank sheet of Geoff's log book, found a pencil, came back to the table, and sketched me very quickly. He handed me the drawing. It was good, and with something of the warmth and joy I'd just felt for him in my face.

'See. It's you,' he said. 'Not Katie.'

'Yes. It's very much me, for you.'

We took the dirty plates and cutlery down to the galley and I started the washing up. We'd run out of washing-up liquid. 'I know,' I said, 'There's loads of washing powder under here. That'll do.' I opened the cupboard and got out one of the jumbo Persil cartons. Opened it, sprinkled some over the dirty plates, then a flow of tepid water from the tap. No suds. The water didn't even go milky. The powder just dropped to the bottom of the sink.

'That's strange. Must be past its sell-by date.' I peered into the carton, put my nose to it. 'Sort of sweetish smell. Quite pleasant. What's wrong with it?'

Ben took the carton, smelt it, then dipped his finger in the powder, licked it, tasted it. 'Nothing wrong with it – as heroin. It's pure heroin. Very pleasant.'

TEN ‹‹

'Six jumbo cartons of raw heroin don't have a lot to do with theat-ricals – so we won't be spoiling Geoff's livelihood by dumping the barge before we get to Bar-le-Duc.'

Ben was thinking of something else. 'Geoff, a drug-runner? Didn't seem the type.'

'No? He was suspicious from the start about the boat. So keen to hire it, no deposit, cut rate and without even checking your yachtsman's papers in the end. And dead keen to get out of Paris as soon as he could – with those two backpacks stuffed with heroin, no doubt. And that explains the man in the Panama hat and his woman. Geoff was supposed to pay them, with cash or with that heroin, but he double-crossed them. So they went after him on his barge, but caught up with us instead.'

'Okay, but why did Geoff want us to get the barge – and the rest of the heroin presumably – to the patron of Le Coq d'Or in Bar-le-Duc when he could just have disappeared with his heroin, and without renting the barge to us or anyone else?'

'Maybe he had a firm deal to deliver half the stuff to the patron, feared him and didn't want to disappoint, and saw us as carriers.'

'Maybe.'

'Anyway, one thing is sure – we have to get away now, dump this barge before we're in worse trouble.'

'Yes.' At last he agreed with me about this. 'But we can't leave in the middle of the night.'

'First thing in the morning then.'

He was resigned. 'Okay, I'll feed the cats. I left them to run about in the hold.'

'I'll open a tin.' I was happy to show willing about the cats, at least.

We went down to the hold. Ben turned the light on.

'Puss, puss, puss?'

'Where are they?'

'They were here when I left this afternoon. Puss, puss?'

'Maybe up on the stage, behind the curtain.'

I walked forward, pulled the bottom of the curtain aside, and saw one of the cats. It was nestling at the foot of a man's shoe, some costume stuff left there, I supposed. 'Come on, puss, food.' I had the plate in my hand. It didn't seem hungry. It was purring, nuzzling the shoe, playing with the laces. I pulled the curtain some more, and saw a trouser leg attached to the shoe, then the hem of a linen jacket. Then I looked up and screamed.

The man in the Panama hat. A motionless Buddha now, his round, ivory-hued face looking down at me. I screamed again.

'No!' The statue sprang to life. 'Don't scream again.' He came down from the stage, surprisingly agile, confronting us with a gun in his hand. 'Come,' he said, 'at last we may talk of things.' We turned for the wheelhouse. 'No, here – we will talk down here. Privately.'

We sat opposite him on some benches in the gloom of the hold. And talked.

His speech, his choice of words, his English – all were refined, polished, well-nigh perfect, if archaic, and with that slight accent – German? Dutch? He might have been an Englishman of the old school – discreet, courteous, benign.

When we finished our explanations, that we were simply tourists who had hired the barge from Geoff Wakefield in Paris and were to leave it at Bar-le-Duc, the man said 'Come now, if all that's the case, why, when you were out shopping and I came on board, did I find nearly three thousand pounds in £50 notes in the bag in your cabin – and an automatic in the wheelhouse locker? Why did I find that you'd already opened some of the "stuff" beneath the kitchen sink? And especially,' he turned to me, 'why, when you saw us in Vitry this afternoon, did you run into the museum and hide from us? Why all this, if you are just tourists and have nothing to do with Geoff and know nothing of all this business? I am not a fool, you know.'

'I – we – can explain,' Ben said at last. But clearly he couldn't, unless we brought up the real business of why we were here.

The man stood up, paced the hold. 'Yes? I am waiting.' Ben said nothing. 'Why not tell the truth? It's clear that Geoff, having received part payment for the 'stuff' he was supposed to deliver us in Paris, decided to run away with the cash and most of the consignment. But that he paid you three thousand pounds, and shared out the heroin with you, so that you could disappear with both, on his boat. All of you – you have double-crossed us. Why … beat about the bush?' He used the expression with mild pride, a small smile, as if it were an English expression he'd learnt long ago, and had been waiting all these years for an appropriate occasion to use. Emboldened by his success he used another one. 'You are not coming clean I think, Mr…?'

'Hayward. George Hayward,' Ben replied at once.

The man smiled again. 'No, Sir, Mr Hayward. More Mr

Benjamin Contini, I think, or so your passport has it, in your bag. Though a false name perhaps. With "Painter" listed as occupation. A nice touch, that. An artist, I assume? Not of houses?'

Ben glowered. 'Of houses.'

'Come Mr Contini!' He sat down again. 'You do yourself an injustice – that fine nude you must have painted, which I found under the bed in your friend's cabin.' He turned to me. 'Of you, possibly, Miss Elsa Bergen, according to your passport at least. Yes, a very intimate painting. Lovers, no doubt. I'm sorry you seem to have had a falling out … keeping separate cabins. No honour among thieves, or just a lovers' tiff?' He returned to the bench. 'No matter.' It was hot and close in the hold. He wouldn't take his jacket off, or his hat, but he wiped his face with a big spotted handkerchief. 'Let us to business. I have a proposition – at least I hope you will see it as such, well met like this as we are. I need just such innocent transport as you pair of estranged lovebirds will provide on the barge here. Transport for myself, the cash and the remains of the heroin.'

'Back to Paris?'

'No. To Strasbourg, then across the border, on the Rhine, into Germany.' Ben looked put out. 'You were not aware that this canal leads straight onto the Rhine?'

'No. Well, yes, but that would take some time – a week, two weeks.'

'I – we – are not in any hurry.'

'You could take the boat yourself. It's easy to work, I can show you.'

'But without my partner, who crewed with me on the boat we followed you in, how could I manage alone? There are probably twenty or thirty locks between here and Strasbourg. A man of my advancing years … you could hardly expect me to work all those locks by myself, and drive the boat?'

'I suppose not.'

'Besides, after that little fracas at the museum today …' He turned to me, 'Where you so savagely assaulted my friend, Miss Bergen, attracting the attention of half the police in the area – I need to "lie doggo" with suitable cover, and what better cover than that which you two innocents and the good ship *L'Etoile* will provide?'

'And when we get to Germany, what then for us?'

'That depends on if we get to Germany, and on your navigation. And discretion.' He stood up. 'But come, we are all tired. We should retire. We need to make an early start.'

He gestured us forward with the gun, down the hold towards the cabins. Ben stopped at his. 'No,' the man said. 'I can't keep an eye on you both separately. I'm afraid I'm going to have to play Cupid. You are going to have to make things up with your girlfriend, Mr Contini – in the same cabin. The double bed. And what better way, they say, to make up a "lovers' tiff" than in a bed?'

'Now what?' I asked, when the door was locked behind us.

'At least he doesn't know the painting is by Modigliani. Obviously knows nothing about all that business.'

I was furious. 'That's a great plus!'

'Yes, isn't it?'

'This is ridiculous!' I stamped my foot. 'We've swapped one hole for another! And now we're cooped up together in this tiny stuffy space.'

'At least we're cooped up with a double bed, a tepid shower and a Sanilav. Could be worse.'

I could have throttled him. 'And you intend to drive this guy all the way to Germany?' I was almost shouting.

'No, he does. And we don't drive, we sail. He has a gun, Elsa. Two guns. And keep your voice down.'

I lowered my voice. 'Maybe we could drop him someway, or call the police at a lock?'

'You forget the police are looking for us too. We have to play along with him. Which side of the bed do you like?'

I was furious again. 'Damnit! You might have contrived all this yourself, just to get me into bed.'

'Yes, I contrived it all myself, just to get you into bed with me.' He gave me that look, half-glare, half-smile. 'But I'm sure as hell not going to sleep on the floor – or what there is of a floor.'

'Nor am I!'

'Right then, we can sleep head to tail.'

'Oh, for God's sake! Why don't you put a sock in it?'

He laughed. 'Real Angela Brazil, riot-in-the-girls'-dorm phrase that. You should use it with the guy in the Panama hat. He seems to collect them.'

We eventually slept, head to head under the gilded cupids, far apart, in our pants. What little sleeping we did, for it was hot. Though I did doze off properly towards dawn. When I woke I found myself right over his side of the bed, almost next to him. He was already awake. 'Better be careful,' he said seriously. 'When I woke you had your arm right over on me.'

'I'm sorry.'

'No. It was great.'

We left shortly after sunrise, Ben at the wheel, moving with the first of the other boats into the lock at the village of Ponthion. Then out again, in procession.

The English family, with Sophie on the prow of their cruiser, waved at us. Ben waved back. Everything was so normal, except for the man in the Panama hat sitting in a cane chair behind Ben, out of sight, gun in his lap.

I brought up some coffee. The canal was straight now, heavily wooded to our left. Ben gazed out at the trees, which came right down to the bank. The man stood up.

'Thinking of jumping ship, Mr Contini? Good cover in those woods,' he said.

'No.'

'Something like that?'

'No. I was thinking you're not the sort to be in the drug-running business.'

'Nor you two.'

'We're not in it, I told you.'

'No, of course not. Nor am I then. We're all just having a holiday, making for Strasbourg and the Rhine.'

'You're German, must be.'

'If you like to think that. So why not call me – Kurt? Good solid German name. Better have a name, hadn't I, if we are to spend a week or more together. Kurt, Ben and Elsa. That's better isn't it? Though none of those are our real names, of course, but one needs to name things. One can't live with the unnameable.'

'Can't live with a lot of damn lies either,' Ben said. 'You're not Kurt, you're the man in the Panama hat. And we're not drug-runners. That's the only sure thing. So I'll call you Panama.'

'Your privilege.' He bowed slightly.

'Your English is remarkably good.'

'Yes, I –' He was about to give something away, so he stopped.

'You must have lived in England.'

'I might have done. I might not.'

'Cagey.'

'You can't expect me to come clean with you, when you won't with me.'

'All right then, we're drug-runners. Working with Geoff. We double-crossed you. So now what about you?'

He pondered this, a slight smile.

'Funny, in your admitting that at last, I feel I don't believe you.'

'Well, like your living in England – maybe we are drug-runners. Maybe not.'

'Indeed. Truth is so ambiguous, isn't it.'

'I've never thought so. And I'm not ready to be persuaded.'

'You will be.'

We came into the open lock at Germaize-les-Bains early in the afternoon. A newspaper seller called out above us, catering to the English tourists.

The lock gate closed behind us. Panama shouted up to him as the boat rose and gave him some money when we were almost level with the top. Buying two English papers, he took them into wheelhouse while we made fast to the quay.

When we got back on board, Panama, in his cane chair, was engrossed in the papers. We set off again, through the open lock and out onto the canal. Five minutes later we heard a loud guffaw. We turned. Panama was flourishing the *Telegraph* at us.

'I did you both an injustice, thinking you were drug-runners: you're obviously into something far bigger.' He read from an inside page. ' "Modigliani Nude Murder on Paris Left Bank" – lovely headline, the sub-editor must have dreamed of writing a headline like that all his life – "The couple with the Modigliani nude visited the Louvre just after midday, where M. Blois, one of the archivists, confirming the painting to be genuine, then gave them the name and address of M. Martin-Beaumont, the well-known art historian and collector living on the rue des Saint-Pères … a CCTV recording shows … the concierge found M. Martin-Beaumont dead from strangulation shortly after they left … The couple didn't leave Paris in their own boat but have gone to ground … The man gave his name as a Mr Contini. The woman is American. French police are continuing their search throughout northern France … The painting, one of Modigliani's finest nudes, is thought to have been stolen and was valued at between fifteen and twenty million dollars."'

Panama put the paper down. '"Fifteen to twenty million dollars"! That puts my business in the shade. "One of Modigliani's finest nudes." I got it all wrong! Nothing so vulgar as drug-running. You're in the major-league art heist business. And strangulation …' He fingered his neck gingerly. 'My goodness, I better be careful.' Ben was speechless.

'And yet you see,' leaning forward, Panama helped him out enthusiastically, 'somehow I don't quite believe it all.'

'Why not? You don't look or behave like a drug-runner.'

'Ah, but unlike you artists, in my business I have to look as conventional as any bank manager or dentist.'

'I see.'

'Good, but I don't. Because if you'd stolen that picture the last thing you'd do would have been to go to the Louvre with it, giving the archivist your name and address. And then you didn't return to your own boat, this *Sorrento*. Instead you escaped on Geoff's barge, when my friend and I took another boat, following you to Vitry. So all right, you're not drug-running for Geoff, but clearly you must be guilty of something?'

'Our deal was just to take you into Germany.'

'Never mind. Meanwhile, since clearly we're both on the run we could help each other out. I could put my gun, and yours, away.'

'I'm surprised. If you go by the facts in the paper, guns aren't our style. One of us might strangle you.'

'Yes, and I should fear that. Except I don't. I know the strangler type. Neither of you remotely fills that bill. So I'll tell you what's much more likely. Somebody else strangled this Martin-Beaumont, before you got there.' He smiled. Ben said nothing. 'And they strangled him because they wanted information from him. They applied the pressure, literally. Some very important information, which only he possessed, but didn't give them. Now do you see where this is leading?'

'No. I don't.'

'No, perhaps not, because, like the others, you failed to get this vital information out of him. But what information? "Martin-Beaumont: well-known art historian who, in his youth, knew Modigliani". Yes, Ben, now it all fits. The information Martin-Beaumont had can only have been about establishing the background of the nude, for his killers and for you.'

'Yes, all right, that's it.' Ben could no longer keep silent. 'We were trying to establish the provenance of the painting with Martin-Beaumont.'

'Now we are getting somewhere, but we face another problem. If you didn't steal the painting then it must be yours. It's not a crime to try and identify the origins of one's own property, yet you are behaving very much as if it was. In a most guilty manner, if I may say so. So there are some vital pieces missing in the puzzle.'

'Why not cut the cackle? What do you want?'

' "Cut the cackle"! – I like that. I told you, we could help each other.'

'You mean you want the painting. And fifteen or twenty million dollars, or whatever you can get for it from some crooked buyer.'

'Yes, exactly, but I'd cut you in on it. And when we get to Germany I'd see you both safe out of Europe. Plenty of money, new names, passports. I have friends in high places. Think about it.' He stood up, still covering us with his gun. 'And while you're thinking about it, I think the painting would be safer under my cabin bed, rather than yours. Would you bring it up for me please, Elsa?'

I went down and brought it up to him. He gazed at it. 'Sensuous, erotic, but all so understated. Who is she?'

'I don't know. That's what we were trying to find out.'

'Well, it hardly matters. She won't be going on public view.'

'Wait a moment, I haven't agreed about giving you the painting, or your selling it on. I've only agreed to take you into Germany.'

He looked at Ben, a kindly gaze. 'You are hardly in a position to refuse any of my requests.' He looked down at his gun, surprised, as if only then was he aware that he had it in his hand. That seemed about it. We were stuck with the genial bastard, right through to Germany.

In the hot days that followed, dawns rising to pink and pale-blue skies, and then the burning orange of midday, to midge-filled twilights and late deep dark, we fell into a routine where it was difficult to avoid feeling that the three of us were colleagues, at least, on holiday, cruising the lovely canal, through little towns and poppy fields with the other tourist boats.

A routine of opening and closing locks, moored by the bank in the midday heat, a snack lunch, mugs of tea and biscuits at teatime in the wheelhouse, wine in the evening with whatever decent meals I could manage. Panama was always polite. He praised my cooking and Ben's navigation.

Stuck with him? No, we were his prisoners. He kept an eye and his gun on us all the time. Except when he let me off the boat at some canal-side town or village to buy provisions. 'Remember, I have your "partner" here,' he would say before I left. 'So don't do anything rash. Like contacting the police, for example. I'll shoot your friend if you do.'

We were free of him at night when he locked us both in the cabin, but then Ben and I had to confront each other at even closer quarters. It was hot in the cabin, even late into the night. Impossible not to move around or shower or sleep almost naked, and though that hadn't worried me with Ben before on the boat in Killiney, things had happened between us since that made it more difficult. In our enforced physical proximity we could only find privacy in our thoughts.

Ben dipped fretfully in and out of Katie's diary, sitting at the foot of the bed, trying to appear indifferent to what he was reading. I lay out on the bed reading some of the theatre books Geoff had left in the wheelhouse. Alec Guinness's memoirs. Tennessee Williams's plays. *Sweet Bird of Youth, Small Craft Warnings, Suddenly Last Summer.*

One night Ben looked up from his reading. 'Strange how Katie absolutely insists on remembering things in a particular way. She writes how "he contradicts me about obvious facts", when I know what I said to her that time was absolutely true.'

'Don't you see? She had to be right. The sanity clause: seems she couldn't face the truth with you, about whatever she was up to with her father, which was why she had to chuck you without giving you a reason. It was the same with Martha – I've no real notion of what took us apart.'

'No idea?'

'No. Except it was something she came to dislike in me. Something grated. Like your friend Katie she just left me swinging in the wind.'

'Silence, admission of guilt?'

'Yes, except I was somehow on trial, not her. She was the prosecutor, but wouldn't say what my crime was. I think she came to believe our sort of love would tell against her with her very proper bosses in the New York legal firm, but since she couldn't admit this nonsense, she had to find some other reason to leave me and go straight, and rise in the firm. Find some false evidence, phoney exhibits which would prove the case against me.'

'She must have produced something concrete against you?'

'Now and then, towards the end, yes, she let several mangy cats out of bags. She hinted she couldn't love me, because I was using her, in love only with her youth. Well, she was hardly that young, and I was certainly not that old. Or that I was unfaithful:

she once astonished me by asking if I had one-night stands with other women I'd met on my trips away.'

'Did you?'

'Of course not, and I told her so. Then she said I was unreliable, a maverick, too demanding, that I was beyond the pale of reasonable emotion. She actually said we were incompatible.'

'That's always a good one. I got that one, too. Then they can chuck you without a qualm. Anyway, everyone is more or less incompatible, and isn't that the attraction? We often love people because we're so much not like them.'

'The chalk-and-cheese clause. Except Martha couldn't read beyond the incompatibility clause.'

'The cook and the lawyer! Well, you were certainly very different. Maybe too different? Like Katie and me. I couldn't ride a horse to save my life, nor she paint. And Martha probably saw you as a bit raffish, like Katie saw me.'

'Yes. Frivolous. I'm sure she saw all my cooking and eating and writing about food as frivolous, and I had to be punished for that.'

'How did she go cold? What did she do?'

'Oh, I don't know … Well, yes, I was away on a job, a seafood article up in Maine. Just a few days. We'd arranged to have friends over for dinner that Sunday evening. She was doing the cooking. The flight back was delayed and I didn't get home till after nine to find they'd not waited. That was okay, but Martha hadn't kept any food or wine for me, except the remains of a meringue and apricot tart, just a few crackly mushy bits on a platter. A tart which I'd made myself, too.'

He laughed. 'I'm sorry.'

'So what's your example with Katie?'

'She said to me once, when I asked her why she'd only sleep with me, never do anything else – trips away and so on like we'd done so often before – "It's easier this way now that I've lost respect for you."'

'She sounds a bitch. Unless maybe you really did something terrible to her. Did you?'

'Of course not. I just put up with her saying terrible things to me. Maybe that was part of her charm.'

'No. You're plenty idiotic sometimes, but you're not a masochist.' I laughed again. 'Sorry,' I said, 'but one has to laugh. All the ridiculous shabby manoeuvrings one goes in for – "in love"! If we'd just been tougher and told them to bugger off, they might have come back with better sense.'

'Martha might have done. But Katie wasn't going to come back. If she had, she'd have to have written a whole new script, and she couldn't face the truth of that.'

We dropped these painful topics. Ben dozed off and slept, but I couldn't. Why am I making such a meal of losing Martha? As if I was the first to lose like this. But you always feel you are. And you're right – you are the only person who's lost in this particular way with that particular person.

It was my particular skin, after all, my body: it was your mouth, Martha, and mine – at that particular time, in that particular place – when we ate pastrami and rye one afternoon, sheltering from the rain, that particular Saturday afternoon, in that particular crummy Second Avenue bar, famished for each other. It was us, and no others, that Christmas when we watched the skaters on the ice at Rockefeller Plaza and you said, 'I'd love to skate, but I don't know how.' And then you turned and kissed me, as if to say, 'My not skating doesn't matter a damn, because I have you.'

Two mornings later we approached Bar-le-Duc, a little hillside town with medieval buildings already in view on our right. We were all in the wheelhouse, but as we came towards the open lock just before the town, Panama got up. 'I'll go below, just in case there's anybody unpleasant to greet us here.' He went below.

'I hope Geoff's drug-trafficking friend at Le Coq d'Or isn't the unpleasant person to greet us,' Ben said.

'What'll we do if he is?'

'Ask him on board. Tell him his consignment is downstairs, under the kitchen sink. Then he and Panama can sort it out, while we disappear.'

'Sort it out? How?'

'Shoot each other. That'd be ideal.'

The patron of Le Coq d'Or wasn't looking out for us when we moored at the quay beyond the lock. Instead I saw the tarty woman walking towards us, in her headscarf and dark glasses and a flower-print dress. She stopped in front of the barge and stepped on board. The headscarf covered half her cheek but it didn't quite hide the big bruise there. She had another scarf hiding something in her hands. Her gun.

I thought she was going to shoot us. I took Ben's arm, about to duck, run, retreat, anything. 'It's her,' I whispered, urgently, 'the woman I hit in the museum.'

'That's all right,' the woman said. 'It's him I want to see, not you. Where is he?'

'Downstairs,' Ben said, 'in the hold.'

She pushed us into the wheelhouse, locking the door, and, gun openly in her hand, I thought she was going to shoot us. But she walked straight past and went below. We waited. Almost immediately there was a short muffled noise from the hold, the 'phut' of a puncture, a sudden escape of air.

After a minute the top of the headscarf appeared on the wheelhouse stairs, then the dark glasses and finally the whole woman. She looked pleased, the gun with a silencer still in her hand. Now it was our turn, I thought, about to duck again. 'No,' she said. 'I need you two alive. You're going to help me. It's him I wanted dead. Abandoning me like that. I loved him, you see.'

She turned and slapped me viciously on the face, once, twice, so that I stumbled and fell, putting my hand to my stinging cheeks. Ben moved forward in a threatening way, before she covered him with the gun.

'No.' The coarse voice was quite calm. 'Nothing rash.' She glanced down at me. 'I just needed to be quits with her. Now I'll tell you how you're going to help me.'

ELEVEN <<<<<<<<<<<<<<<<<<<<<<<<<<<<<<<<<<<<<

'Help you?' Ben said, glaring at her, helping me up from the wheel-house floor. 'Can't say I feel inclined.'

'You will, you will.'

'That's just what your friend Panama used to say. Same English teacher?'

'Panama?'

'The hat. We came to call him that. He wouldn't give us his real name, of course.'

'His real name was Kurt.'

'Oh? So he was telling the truth there.'

'If he told you his real name he must have trusted you.'

'He had to, stuck together on the boat, since he couldn't work it alone.'

'I won't trust you so much – you can be sure of that.'

She waved the gun at us, but then, beyond the bridge, the lock gates opened. We were second in line. Ben said, 'I'd put that gun away if I were you – there'll be a lot of people about when we move into the lock.'

She sat down in the cane chair behind the wheel, which her late lover had occupied – at least I assumed he was late. She hid the gun, on her lap, underneath the second headscarf, the barrel pointing towards us. 'Go ahead,' she said to Ben. 'Do whatever you have to do.'

We went under a bridge, with the other boat ahead of us. Then into the lock. The gates closed behind us. The boat rose slowly. The gates ahead opened. I was outside, fending off. My cheek still stung. What a bitch. I came to think of Panama quite fondly. This woman was a very different kettle of fish. Poor old Panama – he'd have relished that expression.

We were soon in open country again, but now there was just a narrow strip of scrubby pasture by the canal, and beyond, to either side, the land rose – hilly country, scattered trees, then forests rising up the slopes beyond. We could jump ship, but there was at least a hundred yards or so of open ground before the tree cover. And Headscarf was clearly handy with her gun.

Ben was at the wheel. 'So, what sort of help had you in mind?'

'You'll take me to Strasbourg – then onto the Rhine and into Germany – with the money you and Geoff double-crossed us on. And the rest of the heroin. Where is it?'

'Downstairs, beneath the kitchen sink.'

'And the money?'

'In our rucksack – Panama took it. In his cabin on the right. Check it now if you want,' Ben said.

'I'm not such a fool. I'll check it all tonight, when you two are safely locked in your cabin.'

'What about us? When we've got you into Germany?'

'No more need of you. Do what you want. Where do we stop for the night?'

Ben looked at the route map by the wheel, then at his watch. 'Village of Trevernay, I think, three or four kilometres ahead. They have rubbish facilities there.'

'You have rubbish to dispose of?'

'No. You have. Your friend downstairs in the hold.' Ben turned from the wheel a moment. 'Or did you think to just leave him there?'

'Yes.'

'In this heat – in a few hours he'll stink to high heaven.'

'I see.' She paused. The nasty processes of the flesh after death were clearly unknown to her. Or it may have been that she didn't want to think of her ex-lover in that way. Who would?

She said, 'Dump him overboard then, at a suitable opportunity. Some backwater. You'll see to that. Not something I'm going to be involved in.'

Ben turned to her. 'Dump him overboard? He must weigh a ton. And there are no backwaters here. This is a canal.'

'You'll think of something.'

Ben returned to the wheel.

I said, 'Isn't it rather extreme? Just knocking him off like that without talking to him? After all, maybe he wasn't abandoning you and had some plan to meet you later.'

She turned a glassy eye on me. 'No. We did everything together. We were inseparable.'

'Perhaps that's why he ran out on you?' Ben remarked casually. 'Got to feel the relationship was getting too constricted?'

'You keep your fucking thoughts to yourself.' She flourished the gun at him, moving restlessly about in the cane chair, as if there were ants foraging at her rump.

I was nervous. 'Of course not, Ben. Why it – it must have been a perfect relationship … else she wouldn't have killed him when he left her, would she?'

Headscarf turned to me, pleased with this apparent logic, almost a smile. 'Exactly. It was perfect.' She turned to Ben sourly. 'A woman would understand that.'

'Yes, of course I do,' I said. 'And so all the worse when he sold you down the river.'

'Down the canal,' Ben murmured. 'I keep telling you both – this is a canal.'

'Listen carefully, you two jokers.' She was restless again. 'You'll dump him overboard after we've stopped, late tonight.'

'There's a problem,' Ben said. 'He'll just float on the water, all the gas in his stomach by then, and since there's no current, he'll stay there all night. Next morning he'll still be there, a big balloon, belly up in the water, and some other boat behind us will see him, or someone on the towpath, and call the police. We have to dump him while we're moving.'

'Sink him with weights then,' she said shortly.

Later, towards seven, a mile or so before Trevernay, the canal widened. There was a single mooring space beneath a grove of willow trees arching over the water. 'There,' she said. 'Pull in there. Just the spot for the night. And towards dawn you'll dump him.'

Ben pulled in. It was still hot. Flies and midges, disturbed from the willow leaves by our pushing in under the canopy of branches, started to devour us. We moored the boat, fore and aft, with iron stakes.

It was supper time, but I wasn't hungry. I was tired, and with what little energy I had left I was furious.

When we were moored Headscarf said, 'You better have an early night. Your cabin – get down to it.' She waved the gun at us.

We went down the steps into the corridor and stopped outside our cabin. She was a few paces behind us. 'This yours?' Ben nodded. She tried the door. It was locked. 'Where's the key?'

'Panama has it. He kept it on him.'

'Go and get it off him then.'

When Ben got back, holding the key, she stopped him at the doorway. 'Just a moment, take everything out of your pockets.' She stood back, pointing the gun at him. 'Throw it all out on the floor.' Ben emptied his pockets. Handkerchief, a wad of money, tobacco, cigarette papers, lighter – and a pair of handcuffs.

'Handcuffs?' she asked. 'What were you going to do with these? Open the cabin and get inside.' Ben unlocked the door and we entered the tiny space. She stood at the doorway, looking at the big divan, pointing at the headboard cupids. 'So what's this – cosy lovey-dovey in here, is it?' She laughed briefly. 'You two look a bit long in the tooth for that.' I swear, if she hadn't had the gun, I would have strangled her. 'Where are your bags?' she added. 'The money?'

'In Panama's cabin.'

'They better be.'

'What did Panama expect to use the handcuffs for?' Ben asked.

'You two. I told you – he was slack about things.' She slammed the door in Ben's face and locked it.

'It's all right,' Ben said, when we'd heard her move away down the corridor. 'I've got another pack of tobacco and papers under the bed, and some lighters, too.'

'That's your only worry is it?' God, I was angry. I could have strangled Ben as well.

'Calm down,' he said. 'The best way to keep control in a tricky situation is to think laterally, take a quite different approach. Get to grips with the real problem then.'

'Okay, you've thought laterally. Now think vertically. What are we going to do?'

'Well, hump that corpse overboard first.'

'Just you and me?'

'That's what she said – finer feelings, you know. Doesn't want to touch him. When you see him you'll understand.'

'Thanks. And when we've got rid of him?'

'Well, we're back where we started with Panama – take her to Strasbourg, then across the Rhine and into Germany.'

'And?'

He shrugged. 'You go back to New York and eat cheesecake and I go on looking for the provenance of the Modi nude.'

I turned away. The cheesecake seemed very remote now. I turned back. 'You didn't find Panama's gun when you went to frisk him?'

'No. Glad I didn't in a way. I might have shot her, and that's not really my metier.'

I exploded. 'Ben, none of this is our bloody metier! It's all a nightmare.'

'Worse – it's real.' He paused. Then he turned, brightly. 'But look on the good side, Elsa. She doesn't know about the Modi nude. When I went to get the keys off Panama, I went into his cabin and hid the picture under his bunk. So she knows nothing about what Panama found out – about us, the looted art, all that. See? She did us a real favour by bumping him off.'

He knelt down, got his pack of tobacco out, sat on the bed, started to roll a cigarette. The two portholes were open. I went over to one and looked out. We were right up against the falling branches of a willow tree. I reached out and picked a green leaf, crunching it in my hand, smelling the juices. There was still a real world out there.

'Yes,' I said, 'bumping him off like that, no questions, tears, recriminations. Just shot him. One sure way to end an affair.'

Ben drew on his cigarette. 'She has guts that way. We hadn't.'

At four next morning, an hour before sunrise, Headscarf opened the cabin door. Gun in hand, she gestured towards the hold. Ben had stripped one of the big sheets from our bed. 'The sheet,' he said. 'We'll need it to carry him up.'

'Do it how you want. You're the undertakers.' She turned and went up to the wheelhouse.

Panama was lying just beyond the galley, at the end of the corridor. Stretched out, his coat open, shirt stained red, torn, distended white stomach showing, belly up, like the filthy pike Ben had caught. The battery lights weren't very bright, and I was glad of that. I couldn't see much of him to begin with, as Ben laid the sheet out and started to turn his great body over on to it. But then, bending down to help him, I saw the pool of blood and a dark shitty mess seeping out on the floor, and the same on the sheet, as Ben turned him and covered him with it. And the stink. I held my breath, then gulped air in through my mouth.

We pulled him, slithering along the corridor, towards the steep steps that led up to the wheelhouse. Now the difficult part. Ben had tied the sheet firmly round the body, head and foot. Now on the first step, he started to lug it up. He didn't get very far. Panama was really heavy. Ben stopped, panting for breath. Wrapped in the bloodied winding sheet, Panama now had his great rump on the third step, his back against the next three, his legs propped up crookedly on the floor.

On the top step above the body, Ben took the twisted end of the sheet and started to pull. This time he managed to get it right up, leaning against the sharply angled stairway. Then, stepping up into the wheelhouse, he started to pull again. But it was no use.

'We'll have to rope him, and both of us pull from the top.' Ben left Panama balanced against the stairway and went up into the wheelhouse. I stood there, looking up at the grisly, bloodied mummy-fold.

And then the whole fat white cigar was falling forward, the body bursting out of the sheet, the heavy torso coming straight at me. I screamed. It almost fell on me, swollen and purple, brushing past my face and landing with a great squelchy thump, doing a belly flop on the floor beside me.

We got it up in the end, both pulling on a rope, into the wheel-house. Ben tied on some big ballast bricks he found under the floorboards in the hold. The sun was nearly up. We dragged the body through the wheelhouse door, back to the stern, and then, with a last great effort, pulled it over the stern board, and let go. It fell into the placid water like a stink bomb, a cloud of gassy bubbles rising to the surface.

I stood back, and turned. The sun was just up over the horizon to our left beyond the willow trees. There'd been no sign of Headscarf throughout all this, but now she emerged from the foredeck with her gun. Ben was already going back to the wheelhouse.

'Well done,' she said. The first comment she'd made in anything like a friendly tone. Then she added, a concerned voice now, 'You see – I was worried about him.'

Ben said nothing for a moment, then shook his head. 'Right, let's get out of here.' He went into the wheelhouse, started the engine, and I went ashore, casting off, then leapt on board, as the boat moved off. I went downstairs to the cabin, into the tiny shower cubicle to wash. I saw my hands clearly then in the rising sunlight. Smeared with blood and shit. I saw my face in the mirror over the basin. The same. I started to retch. I turned just in time, spewing everything out into the Sanilav.

Later that morning, in the wheelhouse, Headscarf gave out the rules for our voyage to Strasbourg. 'You'll stay on the boat all the time, except when one of you needs to attend to the locks. You asked what the handcuffs were for. They're for both of you, and that's why Kurt had them, and should have used them. But he was daft. So I'll be buying the food, and you'll both be locked together in your cabin when I'm out.'

'Wait a moment,' Ben turned on her. 'There's no need, we're not going to escape.'

'No?' She bared her teeth in a crooked smile. 'Pull the other leg. You know I can't drive this boat alone, so precautions are in order, for your own good. Because if you try to run I'll shoot you.'

And so it was. Every day or so, moored for an hour at some

village, she'd take her gun, direct us down to our cabin, throw Ben the handcuffs, and tell him to fix one cuff to his wrist and the other to mine. 'That's right, now click both cuffs shut.' When she returned from shopping, and always keeping her distance, she'd throw Ben the handcuff key and the process would be reversed. With one difference. Before she threw him the key she always made sure both portholes were shut. I asked Ben why she did this. 'So I won't throw the key out later, after I've opened the cuffs. If I did, she'd be able to lock the cuffs again, but not to release us, to crew the boat.'

The handcuff business was painful. It meant Ben and I had to sit or lie on the bed right next to each other, for an hour or more, sweating in the heat. Otherwise the next week passed much as it had with Panama. We moved due east now, through wooded, hilly country, rising up the lower slopes of the Vosges, lock by lock, village by village, into Alsace.

Except that Headscarf was a good deal more vigilant than Panama, and far less interesting. She kept silent unless she had to speak, ordering us about on the boat, or down to our cabin. She asked no personal questions, was quite uninterested in us. She just wanted to get to Strasbourg and into Germany.

That afternoon, mooring at Chesnais-les-Eaux, she went out shopping, having gone through the handcuff routine and locked us in the cabin. We sat chained together on the bed.

'She's a tough cookie,' Ben said.

'She's a fucking bitch.' I was sweating, exhausted. I wanted to lie down, but Ben wanted a roll-up, as he always did after lunch, and normally he made a few beforehand, kept in reserve, for when we were locked together. This time he'd forgotten. He fiddled about with the paper, the tobacco pack, pulling my hand over to his as he worked at the cigarette.

'Couldn't you roll it with one hand?'

'Christ – I'm not John Wayne!'

'No. Been out of all this long ago if you were.'

'All right – you play the heroine and make a run for it. I don't want a bullet in my back. Then you'd have to tip me over the side, floating belly up – think of that.'

'What I'm thinking is it was the worst moment of my life, meeting you.' I rattled our chain furiously then, in frustration, so that his tobacco and paper fell on the floor.

'For God's sake! Just let me have my fag – a few puffs, and then we can lie down.'

He finally got his cigarette together, had a few puffs, and then we started to lie down. Quite a performance. His left hand was handcuffed to my right, so he had to lie on the inside. It was a struggle – careful positioning, levering about and leg swinging – but we were getting used to it. We made it, heads under the gilded cupids, lying as far apart as we could, arms outstretched, semi-naked, chained together – a thrilling picture, I'm sure.

'You know something?' he said when we were vaguely settled. 'It's just struck me – we wouldn't have to go through all this manoeuvring, if we lay down the other way, heads at the end of the bed. Would we?'

'Of course we would. Just the same bloody manoeuvrings, except I'd be on the inside then.'

He thought a moment. 'You're right. You would.'

'Don't you start losing your marbles.'

He said nothing. We dozed fitfully.

We reached Strasbourg port two days later, then through the huge Rhine-Marne connecting lock, and out onto the broad river. Ben asked which way she wanted to go – up or downstream, and where she wanted to be dropped off.

'Upstream,' she said shortly. 'About ten miles, there's a small town near the river, Erstein, and just after that there's a marina and a riverside inn. We'll stop there.' Ben had got out another map in the locker, of the upper Rhine. 'I see the town, Erstein. About two hours away.'

I was relieved. We had a port in view, an end. The weather had changed. It was still hot, but also humid, with huge purple-bruised clouds on the horizon, slowly gathering from the south. The fine weather was changing.

'You'll leave us our bag and things,' I said. 'Our passports. We'll need them to get back home.'

'Yes, you can keep your bag and passports with you.'

'And some money. Maybe you could give us a little of that £3000 Panama took from my bag – just enough to get home with.'

'Okay, but economy class.' She spoke so reasonably I almost smiled in thanks at her.

Two hours later, passing Erstein, nestled beneath a tree-covered bluff of land, we saw a quay, some sailing boats, a line of buildings to our left, a red-tiled, conical-towered inn facing the river.

Closer up, we saw three jetties and a sailing marina, but Headscarf directed us to a smaller quay beyond the marina. We pulled in here. There was a chandler's shop, a fuel pump and rubbish disposal facilities for motor cruisers. We moored below two other untended boats there. A big Mercedes van was parked some way back from the quay with two men standing by it. After we'd moored, they came on board. Nothing special about them. By comparison with Panama and Headscarf they were very ordinary. In their thirties, smart-casual dress, one of them in an expensive blue designer windcheater.

We were all in the wheelhouse. The barge rocked easily in the swell from the river. In a moment or two they'd all leave.

The man in the windcheater looked at us both quickly, then spoke to Headscarf in German. 'The handcuffs?' he asked her. They were in her bag. She handed them over. The other man took a gun out. Headscarf turned to us.

'Now listen carefully – my friends don't have much English.

You'll walk off the boat with us, and no fuss, no shouting – to the car. You won't try and escape, because you'll be handcuffed. And –'

'But you said!' I burst out. 'That once we were in Germany, you'd leave us, we could go back!'

'Go ahead,' she said to the windcheater man, in German. 'Before she starts to make trouble.'

While the first man covered us with his gun, Windcheater stepped forward with the cuffs, took my wrist, then Ben's, and clipped them on to both our wrists in a flash.

'Ben!' I shouted. 'Can't you …'

'Can't I what? I told you, I'm not John Wayne.'

'Well, what about the cats?' I turned to Headscarf. 'You can't just leave them here to starve.'

'You must be joking.' She turned to Windcheater, in German again. 'The stuff's in the galley, underneath the sink, six Persil cartons, and get their rucksack, in my cabin. The cash, their passports and so on.' The man went below. Returned a minute later with the cartons, went down again for our Disney rucksack, emerged again. The other man took the rucksack.

Windcheater made a stack of the cartons on the table, then picked them up.

'Okay, let's go.' Headscarf looked around the wheelhouse, then turned to us. 'Right – remember, no fuss. You walk across to the van, holding hands. Right?' She smiled then, or as much of a smile as the bitch could manage. 'Yes, holding hands, just like lovers.'

They locked the wheelhouse door, paid a mooring fee, and we set off for the van – leaving the cats, the Modi nude and Katie's journal behind us, hidden under Panama's bunk.

TWELVE 〈〈〈〈〈〈〈〈〈〈〈〈〈〈〈〈〈〈〈〈〈〈〈〈〈〈〈〈〈〈〈〈〈〈〈

'Why take us?' Ben asked, as we walked towards the van. 'We're not going to squeal on anybody.' Silence. 'Where are we going?' Silence. The van had a sliding side door, facing away from the quay, against a wall. They bundled us in. It was dark. 'Lie down and shut up,' Headscarf said. We lay down. The van moved off. We were chained hand to hand anyway, but Ben gripped my hand now. He knew what I was thinking. He'd told me. Headscarf had killed her lover without a qualm. She could do the same to us.

I had the feeling we drove south first, for an hour or more, along the winding river road, before turning off, up a steep hill rising from the river valley. Then we were moving fast and straight, over a motorway at one point, for I heard the rush of heavy traffic beneath us. The three in front barely spoke, and I couldn't make out what they said anyway, except once, when one of them said to Headscarf – in German, of course, which they didn't know I spoke – 'They weren't pleased to hear about Kurt.' Headscarf raised her voice in reply – 'I don't care a damn what they think about Kurt,' she said. 'Kurt was my business. I loved him.'

After that I lost all sense of direction. We drove for about another hour, at speed, on a well-paved road, turned off onto a rougher road, in lower gears, continuing uphill. It started to rain, a hammering of rain drops on the roof of the van. Another turn and we stopped. A gate was opened. Then we bumped along a rough twisting track for about fifteen minutes, until we finally pulled up. They dragged us out of the van, and there, hidden in a clearing of thick forest, was a long ramshackle wooden lodge, raised off the ground on one side by a dozen pine trunks – since the lodge on that side straddled a roaring stream, rushing from a narrow defile in the rock behind. A long thatched roof, low sloping overhanging eaves, a witchy Hans and Gretel lodge, straight out of Grimm's fairy tales.

So I was pretty certain I knew where we were – in the middle of the Black Forest. We were on higher ground. There was a smell of pine. It was still raining. There was a roll of thunder from beyond the trees.

Immediately behind the house the forest rose sharply, and it had clearly been raining hard in the woods for the stream was in full spate, running under the lodge before disappearing into the forest again lower down the slope.

An older man was at the door as we pulled up. Burly, in Bavarian lederhosen, long woolly socks, boots, braces, an embroidered shirt and a hat with a feather in it. A sour-looking man. We were dragged out of the van, then marched up some rough wooden steps to one side of the house, through an arched oak door and led into the hall. A large dark panelled hall set right over the flooding stream, a log-beamed ceiling high above, a long Gothic-style table in the middle, vast fireplace to one side, a rack of sporting rifles, and hunting trophies all round the walls. Deer, wild boar, the lot. It was an old hunting lodge. The air was warm and oppressive. I shivered.

'Along here,' Headscarf said to us.

'What are we here for? What are you up to?' Ben still had a dash of his old cheeky self.

'You'll see. Come on.'

Windcheater went behind us, upstairs, along a corridor. He opened a room at the end. A bedroom. A window looking over the front. A large bed with huge bolsters and a duvet with a folksy canopy. Chairs, a table, wardrobe, all in the heavy Bavarian style. The man slammed the door and locked it.

Ben pulled me over to the window.

'For Christ's sake! Stop dragging me about the place. I'm not a horse.'

'Oh shut up. Want to see if there's any way out.'

There wasn't. The window had an iron grille outside. The rain was heavier now, so heavy that the water made a silvery curtain, almost blotting out the view. Beneath us the noise of the rushing stream increased. Ben pulled me over to the wardrobe, then the chest of drawers and the bedside table. He opened doors, drawers. There was nothing inside anything.

'People sometimes leave interesting things in old cupboards and drawers,' he said.

'Like what? Hacksaws? Loaded revolvers?'

'You never know till you try. You're always bloody giving up.' He bent down, pulling me with him, peering under the bed.

'A chamber pot?' I asked.

'No.' He pulled out a pair of old leather slippers. Flapped one in the air, glared at me. 'Like to give you a good whack on the backside.'

'Oh, so it's macho-man woman-bashing now, is it?' I started to struggle with him.

'If I wasn't chained to you I'd dump you, here and now, and you could go back to New York and stuff yourself with cheesecake 'till it comes out of your ears.'

'Thanks.'

'I'm only trying to save our lives, or aren't you bothered?'

'Yes, but I'm scared.'

'So am I!' He was shouting now.

We heard a car draw up outside. From the window we saw a Mercedes four-wheel-drive. Two well-dressed men in their forties got out, dark suits and ties. One carried a black briefcase. They went inside quickly.

Another minute, and we heard raised voices in the big hall immediately beneath us; Headscarf's voice the loudest.

'What's she saying?'

'Can't get it – something about "deserved it".'

'Who?'

'Must be about Kurt. In the car – the driver told her someone wouldn't be pleased about her bumping Kurt off.'

'I thought Kurt was Mr Big in this drug-running business?'

'No. That guy with the briefcase more likely.'

We said nothing more, until I turned to Ben and said what must have been on both our minds. We were quite possibly going to die. 'Look,' I said, 'I'm sorry for all these bad things we've both got each other into, and things I've said. I just wanted to say –'

'No. Don't say it.' He put his cheek on mine, and kept it there, warming the skin. 'God, you smell good.'

'What?'

'Like lemons. Lemony.'

'You smell good, too. Like vanilla.'

We lifted our arms, and chained together, we did our best to hug each other. We hugged hard.

He drew back, our chained arms dropped, and he smiled. 'Lemon and vanilla!' His tone was surprised. He was charmed by the idea. 'Well … they can't take that away from us.'

'No, they can't.' I felt better. If there was to be an end for us in a minute, it would matter plenty, but for those long moments, hugging and looking at each other, it didn't.

A few minutes later the door was unlocked. One of the minders came in with a gun, and prodded us downstairs to the big hall. Headscarf and the other thug weren't there. Still handcuffed, we sat down at the long table, opposite the older of the two smart-suited men. He had wispy reddish hair. His briefcase was open in front of him. He looked at us carefully, then down into his brief-case where he clearly had something relevant hidden.

'Yes,' he said to his companion in German. 'It's certainly them.' He closed the briefcase. He must have been looking at a photograph.

He looked up and started to speak in barely accented English. His tone was quite flat. 'So, a dangerous couple. You nearly kill one of our men and drown another in that Turkish bath in Paris. You avoided us again at your boat, then jumped on that barge and made a clean getaway. And but for the fact that two of our other friends followed you and caught up with you, we'd have lost you altogether.'

'I don't follow,' Ben said.

'The paintings, Mr Contini, all those Renaissance masterpieces, gold chalices, illuminated manuscripts. Your father knew where they were hidden.' He turned to me. 'As did your father, Miss Bergen, and you will remember what happened to him in Dublin.' He looked at Ben. 'You know where the paintings are hidden, too.'

We both knew what it was all about now. We were back to square one, with the art crooks, drug-runners, neo-Nazis – whoever they were, and however they were all in it together.

'We need to find those paintings.' The man scratched his wispy hair. He had a long thin face, the air of a pedant, a schoolmaster, perplexed for the moment with two difficult pupils, frustrated and just waiting for an excuse to get the cane at them.

'I don't know where the paintings are.' Ben was still cocky.

'No? I think you do. And we simply ask you to share that knowledge with us.'

'Do you think I could have a cigarette?' Ben asked. 'I left my tobacco on the barge.'

'Nobody smokes here. A filthy habit.' Ben sighed. 'Two ways we can go about this,' the man continued abruptly. 'You can tell us, willingly collaborate, or we can go the other way. Think about it. I have some business to see to here. We'll meet again this evening.'

'Food,' Ben said. 'Do you think we could have something to eat meanwhile?'

'This evening.'

'Well, these handcuffs – could you take them off? They're beginning to rub our wrists badly.' Ben jangled our chains in front of him.

'At six, Mr Contini, after you have helped us, they'll be taken off.'

The minder took us back to the bedroom. It was nearly five o'clock, and still raining hard.

Ben looked around the bedroom. 'Probably bugged,' he murmured. 'Don't talk. Whisper. And not by the bed. Bound to have something there, for the pillow talk.' He went over to the window, then turned. 'We're back with the same lot. The ones you said were everywhere. You're right. They are.'

'So it's a pretty simple choice, isn't it? We tell them what we know. We don't want those damn pictures, wherever they're hidden, we just want our lives.'

'I suppose so.'

'Come on, don't be a fool. We'll tell them, or I will.'

There was another roll of thunder from the south. The rain hadn't stopped. The clearing in front of the house was partly flooded now, the stream a raging torrent of noise beneath us: a whole sea of water falling all at once.

Suddenly there was an ear-splitting crack below us, then a crash of splintering timber rocked the room. A succession of splintering sounds, as the whole side of the building began to sway on its wooden stilts. The stream, bursting out of its narrow course, must have torn away some of the pine trunks that held the lodge up on that side. The bedroom door buckled, and the wall to either side folded like cardboard, leaving just the door and its frame standing. The vaulted ceiling cracked. We dived for cover by the bed. A shower of thatch, broken rafters and lathes fell all round us. Then the floorboards began to creak and tilt, and in a few seconds the whole lodge was lurching to one side, tilting on its collapsing stilts like a boat sinking, and we were sliding down the slope of disintegrating walls and floorboards, clinging desperately to the wreckage.

There was no chance of holding onto anything. We were falling fast, along with great roof timbers and walls and beds and furniture, as the lodge and its contents tipped right over. Then we were out in the pouring rain, still sliding, the handcuffs biting viciously at our wrists as we fell together.

I was lying on a pile of rubble. Ben was almost on top of me. I had the taste of blood in my mouth.

'Are you okay?' I could just hear Ben's voice.

I nodded. I could feel blood trickling around my neck. Ben wiped it away with his arm. 'Your chin,' he said. 'Just a small cut.'

'Thanks.' I tried to sit up. But I couldn't, with him almost lying on me. 'Are you okay?'

'Yes.'

'Well then, get the hell off and let me breathe!'

He struggled away from me. 'My foot's caught.' He struggled some more. I could see his leg caught beneath a plank. I tried to help him pull himself away, but chained as we were I couldn't get to him properly.

The rubble we were lying on suddenly tilted, and then we were sliding down the mess of timber and plaster again, until we hit the ground some way out from the front of the lodge.

Or what was left of the lodge. Only the far end of it, away from the hall and the roaring stream, was still standing. The middle, and the other end where the hall had been, was just a mound of rubble with the water frothing out from beneath it. Something moved from behind the rubble. A figure emerged. It was the burly guy in lederhosen: the hat was gone and his clothes were torn and covered in white powder, but he had one of the sporting rifles in his hand. He saw us, half-raised the gun, then stumbled and fell.

Ben pulled me to my feet. 'Come on. Run!'

We ran, as fast as two people handcuffed together can, charging through deep pools in the clearing, falling into torrents of muddy water, picking ourselves up, making for the forest fifty yards away to the side of the lodge.

A shot rang out behind us, but we made it to the cover of the fir trees. And kept on running, uphill now, the going more difficult, the undergrowth thicker. Twisting and turning, the handcuffs really cutting into our wrists, pulling one way and another, falling into rushing drains of water that flowed down between the rows of trees.

It was dark in the forest, dank, dripping dark. The thunder rolled above us but it growing more distant, and after ten minutes we had to stop for breath.

Our wrists were bleeding. We had no handkerchiefs to staunch the blood. We had nothing. No money, passports, no rollup tobacco and no Modi nude. It was nearly seven o'clock. It would be getting dark and cold in an hour or so and I was shivering again.

We kept on up the hill. Safer away from roads. Half an hour later, with no sound of any pursuer, we emerged from the thick pine belt and into a glade of beech trees.

The storm had passed. The sun burst out, a bright evening sun that almost warmed us. We slackened pace, walked under the cathedral-like canopy of trees, their tall smooth white trunks like pillars, separating great shafts of light, shining through the leaves and branches, as if from a series of high windows, making mottled patterns on the floor of leaf mould beneath our feet, dappling Ben's face and drying his T-shirt as I turned to him.

He raised my arm, looking at our wrists. Bruised, still bleeding slightly. He licked the rivulet of blood away from my wrist and took my hand. We walked on into the dazzle of low sunlight.

The beech glade ended a little further ahead, the land began to dip, and we were in another belt of dark fir, going downhill. In chilly shadow now, the light fading.

We stopped. 'What do we do? These trees could go on forever.'

'Have to just sleep beneath them. Cover ourselves in leaves. Babes in the Wood.'

'This isn't a fairy tale.'

'Isn't it? This is surely the forest of the Brothers Grimm.'

'Oh for God's sake!'

'Okay, you tell me what we should do.'

I looked about in desperation. 'Find somewhere, someone, give ourselves up.'

'In this forest – who to? The old witch who lives in a house made of human bones or the big bad wolf?'

Then we heard an engine starting up, somewhere down the slope ahead of us. In another five minutes we came to the edge of the forest. Looking out from the trees, below us lay a gravelled clearing, an empty car park, picnic tables, a log hut, with a sign above the door: 'Café and Black Forest Souvenirs'.

We waited. No sound, nothing, nobody. It was getting dark and starting to rain again.

'Come on.' He pulled me forward. 'We'll find some shelter here.'

Skirting round the clearing, we came at the log building from behind. A back door, with a porch, firewood stacked in big piles, some rubbish bins. The door was locked, of course.

'What did you expect?' I said. 'A sign saying "Welcome! Come on in"?'

'It's a Yale-type lock. If we had a credit card we could push it in between the jamb and the lock.'

'We haven't got a credit card.'

'No. So I'll just kick it in.'

He stood back and started to kick the door repeatedly, so that at last half of it gave in with a splintering crash, and we were inside.

A storeroom, shelves everywhere, down the centre of the room, against the walls, stacked with tacky souvenirs of all sorts. Alpenstocks, phoney spiked Prussian helmets, embroidered aprons, and wooden cuckoo clocks of every size. We could see them in the half-light: long-eaved, wooden-tiled roofs, ornately decorated and painted, small clock faces, each with its cuckoo beneath, hidden behind a little doorway, mute, but waiting its moment.

The rain started to drum on the roof. It was dark now. We were famished. We moved to the front of the shop. I looked for a telephone. There wasn't one, but above the café counter there were soft drinks and bags of crisps, biscuits, cakes and a freezer filled with ice creams. 'Might as well hang for a sheep as a lamb,' Ben said, so that very soon we were gorging on a supper of crisps and dry fruit cake washed down with big dollops of peach ice cream and soda pop. Afterwards, lying on a mattress of crushed cardboard boxes and wrapped in embroidered Bavarian aprons we found in the back room, we lay down under the cuckoo clocks, dozed, then slept.

One of the cuckoo clocks woke us. Some vibration, something that released the impertinent bird from its house and set it going, cuckooing out the hours. It was pitch-black. Ben pulled me up, drugged with sleep. We stumbled about, feeling along a central shelf, found the clock, stopped it. Silence.

'Wait! Listen. Something else.'

We listened. The faint whimpering of a hound. In the distance. Coming closer, and then at the back door, barking furiously. Torchlight coming through the splintered wood. Then the rest of the door was kicked open and there were heavy footsteps coming towards us.

In the dark we ran back towards the main shop and straight into a shelf of cuckoo clocks, pushing the whole lot over, spilling them all on the floor, where they set up an outraged cacophony of cuckooing. A man was in the storeroom now, the torch searching us out. We'd fallen on the floor, among a debris of clocks and splintered wood.

The beam came towards us, spotlighting us; the voice in German: 'Now I have you!'

For a moment, as he adjusted the beam, I saw the man's face. It was the burly Fritz, in his tattered Bavarian outfit, rifle slung over his shoulder, torch in one hand, a snarling Alsatian on a lead in the other.

We were on our feet, Ben pulling me round behind another shelf of clocks and curios. A great cracking sound, Fritz smashing through the shelves in front us, the wood splintering, throwing out another load of souvenirs and clocks, releasing a further flock of outraged cuckoos. The room was loud with sound from the wretched birds and the barking dog.

Fritz blundered forward through the splintered remains of the shelves, big boots crunching over the souvenirs, the cuckoo clocks and the Prussian helmets with their sharp plastic spikes lying all over the floor. He was moving towards us. But then he stumbled, falling heavily, the torch flying from his hand. The dog snarled and the cuckoos continued their uproar, but there was no movement, no sound from Fritz. Ben pulled me to the torch, picked it up, turned with the beam.

Fritz was lying motionless among the souvenirs, the Alsatian still leashed to his hand, snarling. And then he saw the Prussian helmet and its sharp spike driven in somewhere below his neck. Blood was starting to seep over the floor – and Ben was pulling me then, over Fritz's body and out the back door. And now, torch in hand, he was dragging me across the dark picnic area and into the woods again. The torch barely showed our way and we stumbled and fell into drains of storm water, brambles and the spiky branches of fir trees. After twenty minutes I was bruised and breathless. I dragged Ben to a halt.

'Ben, this is crazy! If Fritz is dead, it'll be perfectly clear that we didn't kill him, that he fell on that spike. We should go back to the shop and wait for someone …'

'No. They'll find out who Fritz is – he's certainly mixed up with these drug-running, art thieving neo-Nazis – and the police will arrest us as their accomplices.'

'But they handcuffed us. Why do that if we were with them?'

'Because we double-crossed them!'

'But we didn't! And we can prove that – take the police back to the barge, tell them the whole story.'

'They won't believe it, and we'll be held here for months.'

He dragged me on, and then we fell over the edge of something, and tumbled down a steep slope, where I felt a bad jag of pain in my ankle when I reached the bottom. I couldn't move, my ankle twisted, with Ben almost on top of me.

'Christ!' I shouted. 'My ankle – you bloody fool, if only we'd stayed in that shop. For God's sake! Get off me!'

He moved. I managed to bend down, trying to reach my foot. Then, the blood going to my head, I was suddenly dizzy. I fainted.

I came to – ten minutes later I suppose. It was almost light, sunbeams glinting faintly through the trees, a dozen feet above us, both of us lying at the bottom of a leafy pit in the forest.

'I'm sorry,' Ben said, looking down at me with real concern.

In frustration he jangled the chain that held us and we sat there, our backs against the steep slope, saying nothing, as the sun rose above us. Then after a few minutes, he suddenly started shouting. 'Help! Help!'

'You're not in England,' I told him. 'You better shout in German.'

'They'll get the message.' And he carried on shouting, every few minutes, in English.

They didn't get the message. Nobody came. I would have cried if I hadn't been so exhausted. Ben, too. He gave up shouting. We both lay back, dozed, slept.

When we woke the sun was above us, illuminating a man standing at the lip of the slope, looking down, holding a rifle. Young, a short beard, green forester's cap and green serge jacket, jodhpurs, hunting boots. My ankle jabbed with pain. I shouted up at him, in German.

'Please help us. My ankle – help us.'

'Yes, of course,' he said easily, as if finding two handcuffed people in the middle of the forest was a regular occurrence. He took out a walkie-talkie and spoke into it; I couldn't catch his words. When he'd finished, he just stood there, looking down on us.

'Did you call the police?' I asked the man, speaking quickly in German, before Ben could make any more nonsense about our not contacting the authorities. 'You see, we fell into this hole last night and –'

Ben interrupted. 'You said "police" just now. We don't want them.'

'Oh yes we do. That's where I'm going, and you too, since we're chained together.'

Ben said nothing, resigned to common sense at last.

The man spoke again. 'Yes, you will need to go to the police. I've called my friend. He has transport, not far, just at the end of the track.'

'Are you hunting here?' I asked.

'No. We are park wardens, here to see that others are not hunting. This part of the forest is a nature reserve. Hunting is forbidden.'

Silence. It was getting hot. Birds twittered in the thick foliage far above us. I lay back on the mossy bank and closed my eyes. '*Danke schön*,' I said. I was happy to speak German again.

Five minutes later, the sound of an engine, stopping somewhere below us, beyond the dell. Another green-clad man arrived. They came down into the dell and pulled us up carefully. Then, one of the men carrying me, they took us down the slope to a forest track and levered us gently into the back seats of a four-wheel drive.

We set off along the track, beneath the trees, sunlight dappling through the leaves, a smell of fresh pine after the night's rain, warm summer air blowing in my face from the open window. God, I was happy to be doing something safe and sensible at last.

'Where's the nearest police station?' I asked.

The first man turned. 'You will need to see the chief at police headquarters in the town of Ulm, not far, less than an hour's drive.'

'Good,' I said. 'Thank you.' My ankle was feeling better already. Ben said nothing. I turned to him. 'It's the only thing to do,' I said.

He nodded. 'I suppose so.'

THIRTEEN <<<<<<<<<<<<<<<<<<<<<<<<<<<<<<<<<<

Ben's Story

'So …' The chief superintendent had been speaking English easily, but now he shifted uneasily in his chair after hearing our story. He was wary, with the air of someone who wanted to keep out of this particular trouble. One of his men had released us from our handcuffs and now we sat in his office, in a meticulously recon-structed medieval building, high up on the ramparts overlooking the Danube at Ulm, a town to the east of the Black Forest.

'This talk of looted art, Herr Contini, of Nazis and neo-Nazis and drug traffickers – and of your being handcuffed and held by these people in the Black Forest, in a hunting lodge on stilts which collapsed in a flood from the river – it sounds like a fairy story, no?'

'Superintendent, do you think we handcuffed ourselves?'

'You told me you were handcuffed on a canal in France. That's outside our control.'

'Yes, by that woman in the headscarf. She was one of the group who took us from the barge to the hunting lodge. It's all true, Superintendent, and if you get out to the remains of that lodge, wherever it is, and the souvenir shop where that guy Fritz tried to get us, you'll see.'

'Yes, we had a report – a man was found wounded in a Black Forest souvenir shop this morning. We are investigating, but he was not called "Fritz". He was called Bruckner. Hans Bruckner. He was simply a robber who broke in and got himself injured somehow in the back of the shop. Not an art thief or a neo-Nazi.'

'No? He was the caretaker in that hunting lodge for the other men. The man with the thin red hair and his thuggish friends, and the woman in the headscarf: the place must have been a hideout for these neo-Nazis.'

'Herr Contini …'

'The fact is they are all crooks, Superintendent. Drug traffickers, neo-Nazis, art looters, whatever. On that barge we took across France, in that hunting lodge, all in it together. Drug trafficking and looking for this hoard of looted art to pay for their new Nazi schemes.'

'Indeed.' He smiled. 'And where is this hoard of looted art?'

'I don't know. Are we being charged with something?'

'No, Herr Contini. We are simply making our enquiries.'

'Are you? If you were, you should get out to that ruined hunting lodge straight away and look among the debris. The man with the red hair and the briefcase, he was the boss of this group. You'll find plenty of neo-Nazi evidence in the ruins of that lodge.'

'We have had no reports of any hunting lodge collapsing in the Black Forest, but we will look into it.' He closed a notebook, in which he had written nothing. He wanted no formal record of our meeting. 'So, you have made your statements, both of you. You must return home now.'

'Yes, except that we've nothing to get home with. No clothes, passports, money, nothing. All in the ruins of that hunting lodge. Maybe we could all go back there?'

'That will not be necessary, Herr Contini. You will go to your consuls in Munich for new passports. I will arrange money for you both, to get to Munich and then on home. Now, in fact. There is a train in an hour.'

He wanted to get rid of us. Old Nazis? Neo-Nazis? Looted art? All far too hot to handle, in front of us, at least. He picked up a phone, spoke for some minutes, then turned. 'You will have an advance of fifteen hundred marks. That will cover your hotel in Munich, food, new clothes and enough to get home with. You will repay us when you get home. One of my officers will accompany you on the train and see that you get to a hotel and your consuls, that you get temporary passports and that you leave Germany. Safely,' he added politely.

Every service, I thought, in the cause of putting all this unpleasantness under the carpet. A can of worms he wanted to reseal. But I wasn't going to let him, if I could help it. 'Look,' I said. 'We're not making this up. It's all true.'

'Herr Contini, stop creating trouble for yourself.' His tone was suddenly hard. 'Go home. Forget it all. All your fantasies, all this Nazi nonsense. It never happened.'

'That's what they all like to say, don't they? It never happened.' The superintendent said nothing.

A clerk arrived with an envelope. The superintendent opened it and handed me a wad of cash. Fifteen hundred marks, which I signed for. A plain-clothes policeman arrived later to take us to the station. We stopped on the way to buy some new clothes, then onto a fast train to Munich. The cop, a youngish, lively man, sat on the seat opposite. I knew he was listening to us. I'd managed to talk to Elsa briefly alone before we got on the train, telling her to say nothing to me of any of our previous troubles or plans. The man would report back anything we said, I was sure.

On the train we spoke of easier things – cooking, dishes we liked. I told her how, on the trip to Italy I'd made with Katie two years before, to the marble town of Carrara up in the Apuan Alps, where I'd taught painting and sculpture at the local Academia delle Arte for a week – how I'd cooked us both Irish stew one evening. With barley, onions, carrots, and diced hunks of lamb, cooked it slowly for hours, so that it was nearly solid and you could cut it almost like a cake.

'Sounds dire.'

'No. It's the old way in Ireland – how you're supposed to do it.'

'I see.'

'All right, cook us something better when we get home.'

'I'll try.'

The cop took us to a small hotel off the Königsplatz. He met another plain-clothes cop here – young, polite and eager – who took over from him, escorting us to our room. A double, but with twin beds.

'It's okay,' I said to Elsa when he'd gone. 'Don't worry – twin beds and no handcuffs.' Then I went over to her and whispered. 'Don't speak of anything in here.' I pointed up to the ceiling, the lamps over the beds. 'Could well be bugged.'

Elsa's ankle wasn't badly twisted, just bruised and blue. I said we'd get some ointment for it and she had a bath, and I took a beer from the minibar, and sat looking out the window, which gave onto a restaurant terrace, coloured lights and an empty barbecue pit. No customers. I wouldn't have wanted to eat there anyway. I wanted to be out and about in the ordinary world again. I was hungry and we had money in our pockets.

When we reached the lobby half an hour later, the cop was still there, chatting up the blonde girl at reception. Clearly the place had connections with the Munich police.

'Look,' I said to him, 'we're going out to eat. But don't worry about us, we're not going to run away – no passports.'

He feigned surprise. 'Worry? Of course not, Herr Contini. I am only here to see that all goes well for you and that you both get home safely.'

'Good. We'll be back in an hour or so.'

'Try the Bierkeller in the next street along. Excellent Bavarian food, Herr Contini.'

He saw us out the door.

'I bet we're being followed,' I said, taking her arm.

'Christ, you're being paranoid again.'

We didn't go to the Bavarian Bierkeller – last sort of place or food I wanted, and probably another cop haunt as well.

We walked on and found an Italian trattoria off the Amalien-strasse, the Luna Caprese. We went through the restaurant to an open terrace behind and were given a table by a wall at the far end, where drifts of potted red geraniums cascaded down beside us.

At once I remembered – the same tumble of red geraniums falling down from the balcony of our apartment overlooking the Piazza Gramsci in Carrara with Katie, two years before. And now a woman sitting in front of me who looked just like Katie, so that the real Katie, and that view over the piazza with its lion-mouthed fountains and heroic statuary, flashed before my eyes.

The Luna Caprese was an old-fashioned trattoria – check tablecloths, candles in Chianti bottles, an Italian crooner, with a guitar, on a small stage to one side. Very Italian, and the past begun to run in my veins, that week with Katie in Carrara, the wine, and the water of those fountains.

We ordered a bottle of chilled Frascati. A warm August night, rumours of pomodoro and garlic, the romantic chatter and the sentimental singer. I raised my glass.

'To the real world at last!'

She was slow in raising hers. She was fretful. 'Yes, the real New York for me. And you?'

'There's the Modi still on the barge on the Rhine, and Katie's journal with it. And the cats. I'll have to get the picture back at least.'

'I can't help you there, Ben.' She was terse. 'You'll have to do that on your own.'

'Not certain I can even help myself. You see, besides Briefcase and his pals at the hunting lodge – and some of them may have survived – there must be others in that gang of crooks. They'll have known how we were taken from the barge to the hunting lodge and escaped. So if I go back to the barge they could be waiting for me to turn up, so they can put the screws on me about where the rest of the looted art is hidden.'

'Okay, Ben, so it's perfectly clear – don't go back to the barge. You've lost the picture, and that damn journal. Leave it at that, for God's sake. We've had enough. You've got us out of everything, and you've been great, but I'm not taking any more risks.'

'You're right. Except …'

'Except what?'

'Carrara – I'd like to go there and see if the stuff is really hidden somewhere up in those hills.'

'Crazy.'

'Maybe.'

'Why don't you stop "maybeing" and "excepting" and just stop this art hunt, which is really only an excuse for not going back to your real work?'

'You've said that before. Just like Harry. That's what everyone says, when there's something unpleasant lurking up the other path in their life.'

'Right, you play the hero – go on looking for something nasty up the other path. The truth hunter.'

'You were that once, on the boat out of Killiney. Saying how you had to be truthful.'

'Yes, I was so bloody conscientious about my principles. That's probably why I lost Martha: I tyrannized her with them.'

'Really?'

'Yes. I don't have any principles now. They kill you, or what you have with someone you love. I just want to go home.' She wouldn't look at me as she spoke. Then at last she turned to me, vehement. 'I'd prefer to be happy now, not truthful.'

Maybe she was right. I wondered if my heart was really in it anymore. What did it matter? Maybe all this high-principled crusading of mine was just a way of avoiding my painting again, back in the empty Cotswold barn, without Katie. In the balmy scented evening, the chilled Frascati on my lips, I wanted Katie then, and it was easy to forget principles.

I said, looking at her over my glass, 'I'd throw away my principles, too, if I had the flesh-and-blood thing with someone again.'

She said nothing, a vague nod, but it was clear enough – I wasn't going to have these things with her. We ordered the food: a big plate of antipasti, then kidneys and parsley cooked in white wine. The crooner sang an old Italian song I remembered, 'Volare', and I ordered another bottle of Frascati.

Italy was really moving in my veins now, whether I wanted it or not. And suddenly I wanted it. Wanted to fly there – to Carrara, to that apartment on the Via Plebiscito looking over the Piazza Gramsci, the chestnut trees, bandstand and heroic statuary where I stayed that week with Katie, with the white-marble quarries scarred into the mountains high above us, like snow. The summer art school, leaning over the shoulders of a dozen happy amateurs, lavish with their colours, or working away at small blocks of Carrara Cremo, dreaming of Bernini and Michelangelo.

I could stop playing the hero and let that looted art rot up in the marble hills, if that's where it was – along with whatever secrets I might find there about my father, or Elsa's. I could lose the Modi nude and Katie's journal. I'd loved the woman in the painting, and I'd loved Katie, but I wasn't going to die for either of them by returning to the barge. All I had left was that last time with Katie in Carrara.

A whole unencumbered week, eating in the evenings on the apartment terrace beneath the geraniums, high over the piazza gardens. The town band playing *La Traviata*, our lemony fingers tickling the *frittura mista*, little fish and clams doused in batter, flamed in oil, with the local white wine. Later, in the pool of light from the white-globed lamp above us, the blue flames from our coffee-beaned sambuca, smoke from my rolled tobacco keeping the midges from our golden halo.

I looked again at Elsa, but the face I was pursuing now was the original picture – Katie's face, vivid in the soft light from the lantern above our balcony in Carrara. And her face next morning, still as marble, in the gauzy Tuscan dawn from the bedroom window, when I turned and saw her, deep in peace, asleep on the crumpled pillow.

Just remember this, I thought – Katie in the flesh, our bed, her lies, whatever. The lies didn't matter, and nor did the marble quarries at Carrara or the sins of my father. All that mattered was the memory of Katie.

All right, maybe it was crazy, thinking to resuscitate the love of a dead woman among the fountains and heroic statuary of those baroque gardens. But why not? I raised my glass to Elsa. 'To us,' I said, remembering Katie.

FOURTEEN ‹‹‹‹‹‹‹‹‹‹‹‹‹‹‹‹‹‹‹‹‹‹‹‹‹‹‹‹‹‹‹

Elsa's Story

We had to spend several days in Munich while our consuls checked us out before giving us temporary passports. I had time to go to the American Express office and get a new credit card. So, with the marks we had already, money was no problem for either of us now. Having my own money again, and the freedom of summer in the city – the nightmare was over.

On the second balmy evening, tempted by the open terrace and accordion music coming from a cheerful-looking restaurant beyond the Königsplatz, we were eating and chatting when Ben, glancing over at a table with only a lone and incongruous-looking occupant – an elderly, very sombre German – remarked casually, 'I wonder what he was doing sixty years ago, in the war?'

'What does it matter now?'

'No.' Then he added, following his thought, 'All the same, I'd not realized, Dachau, that camp – it's just outside the city here. I've never seen one of those camps.'

'Well, you go ahead then.'

'Something to do while we wait here.'

'Plenty of other far better things to do while we wait here.'

'Why don't we go?' Then he rushed on, almost enthusiastic. 'We can make a real end to all the things I've been worrying you about – the looted art, the war, the whole caboodle. Finish with it all. Here and now.'

'You go on your own.'

'Maybe I will.'

But overnight, thinking of it, his suggestion seemed reasonable. We were free at last. We had survived the very worst and so we could face anything now, and besides, we were good friends, and so, above all, I owed Ben the duty of friendship. Next morning I went with him.

Following him around the camp I hardly looked at the exhibits. Until one stopped me in my tracks. It was a glass case filled with old domestic and kitchen equipment. Broken tea cups, saucers and little wine glasses, rusted wire egg beaters, tin openers, tarnished knives and forks and spoons. These were the remnants of somehow precious things that the doomed travellers had taken with them to Dachau in their single suitcases, which the camp authorities had thrown out as rubbish and found years later buried in the poisoned soil.

Almost hidden at the back of a glass case I noticed a small knife, a soiled kitchen devil. Once it must have gleamed, sharp as a razor, and had some special importance for the cook – why else take it in a cattle wagon halfway across Europe?

Because it must have been very personal to the woman who had owned and used it, just as my own sharp kitchen devil was precious to me, and which I worked with every day in my New York kitchen. As I gazed at the little knife I thought of its use in good times before the war, used by some happy Jewish mama, all the family coming to dinner, cutting up a chicken for the barley soup.

It wasn't the mounds of hair, old shoes, the dissection tables and tins of Zyklon B that struck me in the other buildings. It was the little rusted kitchen devil that cut me to the heart, but when we left the huts and went out into the autumn sunlight all I said to Ben was 'Grim.'

'Yes,' was all he said in return, and there was nothing more to be said. And I knew then, that if my father had been any part of what had happened here at Dachau, I couldn't face life after what I'd seen today. We didn't speak of Dachau again, but it lay there, like a vague ache all over my body, for days afterwards.

The next afternoon, after getting our new passports, we were walking towards the Englischer Garten in the late-afternoon sun, moving through glades of chestnut trees, leaves beginning to droop, autumn creeping up on the calendar, a hint of an end to the summer.

We heard a murmur, like swarming bees, ahead of us, and the faint sound of brass music. Taking an empty path through some bushes, we came out into the open. And there was a marvellous theatre – hundreds of people, strolling, and sitting in the formal gardens, on little chairs, on picnic benches, eating sausages and grilled fish cooked on small barbecues, drinking beer in chilled litre-steins from kiosks dotted here and there along the pathways. At the far side a Japanese pagoda and at the centre a bandstand, where brass bandsmen, in comic-opera uniforms, having finished their last tune and mopping their brows, picked up trumpets and horns again and embarked on a lively polka.

Ben smiled over the whole proceedings. 'Rather my style,' he said. 'And this'll likely be even better beer than the real ale they have at my local in the Cotswolds.'

'All that grilled fish and spicy sausage. Probably better even than my local deli.'

'They do some things best of all in Germany.'

We made for the entertainment, bought food and beer, and found an empty picnic bench at the far end of the garden, beyond the pagoda. A frothy stein of Löwenbräu for both of us. He raised his glass and drank long. I did too.

'My God that's good,' he said. He shook his head. 'Best beer I've ever had.'

We nibbled at the food, saying nothing, letting the summer air and the music caress us.

'So,' he said. 'You're for New York and I'm for Carrara.'

'But Carrara? Your father? The rest of those damn paintings?'

'No, no, I told you, that's why we went to the camp. I've given up on all that now. The painting, Katie's journal, what my father did in the war, your father, Katie's father – the lot. Just Carrara.' He stopped, uncertain a moment. 'That last time I was with Katie abroad, that summer – it was good. I'd like to go back.'

'God, don't. You'd be opening the wound again. That strange stuff you showed me in her journal – she must have been nuts.'

'Was she, though? Maybe there was nothing going on between her and her father. I just use him as a stick to beat her with.'

'You don't kill yourself without a damn good reason, like you're really ill, depressed or someone really important has died. So there's very likely some connection between her father and her suicide.'

'Maybe. Hardly matters now, anyway.' He turned away, then turned back, abruptly. 'But why should you believe what I say about Katie? She chucked me. I'm biased.'

'I'll tell you why!' I sat forward, full of his old certainty and attack, which he'd lost. 'I believe you, and what you say about her, the madness or whatever, because I've got to know you as well as anyone could this last month. Stuck on that barge for weeks, chained together, practically sitting on that damn lavatory together, and all your nonsense talk and the rows. All the good things of you – the evening at the lock with the midges when you did that sketch of me, and when we hugged in the hunting lodge, thinking it might be the last hug of our lives, and we said how we smelt of lemon and vanilla, and a lot more. Apart from making love no two people could have been closer. And I've been just as difficult with you. We've seen absolutely the best and worst of each other. So I'm in a damn good position to tell you that – there's much more of the best than the worst in you. And she didn't want to see that.'

'But …'

'So why can't you just accept the fact that she treated you like dirt?'

'Because I loved her.'

I leant back from him. 'And threw that away. For no good reason, as far as you were concerned. Seems she was determined to chuck love out of her life, in any case. You were just the excuse.'

'Maybe.' He started to fiddle with his glass, downcast. 'Well, all right, but I have to get rid of this heavy-handed remembering of everything I did with her.' He looked up at me. 'It's a kind of torture. I must have lived so intensely with her, so that once I start thinking about her now, every detail, every place we did things, comes back to me … pubs where we drank and inns we stayed in, places in the Cotsworlds I can't drive by now without a bad jolt of memory. Particularly there's Carrara.'

'So don't go back there again.' I was sad for him. I wanted to help him wipe out those painful memories. 'I know exactly what you mean. I have just the same feelings about Martha. Bad jolts of memory, seeing places where we'd done things together in New York. It stops you in your tracks, knowing you're never going to do anything with her again.'

I wished I could go to Carrara with him, now. All the more since he'd given up on all those hopeless emotional ideas about me. He'd dropped the Modi nude, and we'd escaped all our pursuers.

We had money, we were free. I could go with him to Carrara.

He raised his glass, took another quaff, smiled at me, and looked away over the bandstand, froth all over his lips. The polka was done. Now 'The Gold and Silver Waltz'. Joy in this miraculous summer afternoon overwhelmed me. The elegance of the gardens, the chilled beer, the food, the music. Free, where all the rightness of life was ours again. In profile now, the low sun glinting on his hair, looking away into the distance, alone with his jolts of memory, he wiped away the froth from his lips. And in that gesture, that instant, I knew I had to go to Carrara with him. I had to help him get through the desert of love, just as I had to help myself get through it. Why not do it together?

So I said, 'Yes, those memory jolts, Ben, I know them too well. I'll come with you. We'll go to Carrara together and lay those two ghosts of Katie and Martha together.'

He'd turned, and now he raised his glass. 'Thank you,' was all he said, but his smile said a lot more. He was no longer alone with his desperate memories, and I wasn't either, and the waltz played on, and the world seemed even better than it had a few minutes before.

We booked a flight to Pisa for the following day.

FIFTEEN <<<<<<<<<<<<<<<<<<<<<<<<<<<<<<<<<<<<<<<<<

We walked about Carrara, and late in the afternoon sat outside a café in one corner of the Piazza Alberica, gazing up at the sharp green peaks towering above the far end of the square. The air was cool after the heat on the coast, the crush of tourists, the stifling rail journey from Pisa.

Ten miles above the sea, in the foothills of the Apuan Alps, the town was as fine as the air. The cobbled baroque square, the Malaspina palazzo to one side, a colonnade on the other, narrow medieval alleys running off it, one to the last of the old town gates, which gave onto a bridge over a frothy river, white from its bed of old marble fillings and chippings, flowing down from the quarries somewhere high above us. A town where just about every building was made of the pure-white, the creamy, or the greyish-veined hues of the local marble.

'It's really something,' I said to Ben, leaning back in my chair, revived now by the beauty of the piazza and a double espresso. 'Not a tourist in sight.'

'They stay down in the hotels at the marina, the beaches, the discos. You only get the serious marble types here in Carrara town – like the ones we saw back at the hotel, those rich Saudis; that American architect. They're fussy, and won't buy down at the marble yards at the port. They have to see it up at the quarries, choose their own blocks, like Michelangelo when he stayed here.'

'You've seen the quarries?'

'Just the ones you can see from the road, by the village of Colonnata, six miles up, where the road ends. Katie and I went one day. Most of the quarries are even higher, off the road: you have to make an appointment.'

'And your father's quarry?'

'Don't know exactly where it is, but it was one of the oldest, not far from Colonnata. Of course it's owned by another company now, but we're not worrying about that any more.'

'No.'

'We could just sit here for a few days, a bit more of the Baroque, coffee and Campari sodas, then hire a car and go over the mountains into the Tuscan olive groves.'

'So why not right now? And before that you can show me where you lived with Katie that week.'

'It's just around the corner, past the cathedral, sharp left and into the Via Plebiscito.'

At that moment we heard the sound of an orchestra strike up from somewhere away to the right of the square. Ben looked at his watch. 'Six o'clock, Saturday evening. The town band. They play most weekends in summer.'

We left the café and walked around the corner, into Ben's past on the Via Plebiscito.

'There' he said, 'That's the flat we had, second floor, with all the red geraniums pouring down over the balcony.'

And there it was, a beautiful three-storied baroque house, in a terrace that lay along the narrow sunken street below the gardens. We stopped beneath the chestnut branches, the trees leaning over a high wall from the gardens of the piazza above us, which we couldn't see, but where the bandstand was, with the town band blowing and fiddling away.

'It's the overture, *La Traviata*,' he said. 'Just like last time.'

He turned to me beneath the shadowy leaves, excited, but not in his usual way. There was a harshness in his face. 'You see,' he said, 'Just about now, around six, when I'd finished my classes – back there at the Academia delle Arte – I walked back this way, and she'd usually be up on the balcony, reading or writing or dozing, and I'd call up – you see that half-basement to the house, the sign cut in the marble above the door? Vini – it's a little bar. So I'd call up and say "What about a half litre?" And she'd come down –' He stopped, suddenly.

'Well, what about it?' I said. He turned and looked at me, puzzled.

'What about what?'

'A half litre.'

It was strange watching someone relive the very instants of their past. The man in front of me was living two lives at the same moment. A little flea-bitten terrier, with a lame back leg, was sitting in front of the doorway of the Vini. It barked as we approached.

'The bar dog, Toto,' Ben said. We went through a bead curtain, down some stairs, and into the bar. It was small, and very cool, a real workers' bar. Some old men at the back, arguing loudly, with tiny thimble glasses of vino in front of them.

'It's all right,' Ben said, listening a moment. 'They're not really fighting. It's just about the local football team.' I sat down at an empty table by the door and he went to get us the half-litre. A fat and rather sour-looking woman presided behind the long marble counter, with huge bottles of unlabelled red and white wine behind her, but she was jolly when she saw Ben.

'Ah, Signor Contini!' They shook hands. I couldn't follow the rest of her effusive greetings. My Italian was ropey and she spoke with a heavy accent. Ben returned with a cloudy yellowish wine and two thimble glasses.

He raised his glass, we drank. It was the roughest wine I'd ever tasted.

'You get used to it,' he said. 'Especially when she brings the titbits.' He smiled.

I said, 'Yes, I remember all that titbits stuff in Killiney. This is so much better.'

The big woman who'd gone to the kitchen returned with our snacks: two doorsteps of white bread, saucers of raw anchovy, chunks of *parmigiano crudo*, shrivelled black olives, half a lemon and a corked carafe of fresh, bright-green olive oil.

'See – the titbits!' Ben, leaning back, just looked at the food, the wine, the oil, making no move. 'But no funerals here.'

The band had stopped, but now it started up again. 'Overture, *Il Trovatore*,' Ben said. We could hear the music quite clearly and I noticed how some of the old football fiends, while arguing, had started to tap the beat out, unconsciously, on the marble tabletop. As familiar with Verdi as they were with football.

Toto came to sit by us, ears pricked, head to one side, quizzical. Ben gave him a crust. Then he laid out some anchovies on a hunk of white bread for me, squeezed some lemon on the fish, cut up some of the cheese on it, then put his finger on the snout of the olive oil carafe and flourished a sprinkle over the whole concoction. He passed it over to me, a real doorstep. Then he did all the arranging on the bread for himself, looked at his creation, quizzically, then took the plunge. Opening his mouth as wide as he could, he forced the bread between his jaws. There was no other way to do it. It was a grotesque sight.

Can you fall in love with a grotesque sight? I did, as he munched and I watched the last of the slippery, oily fish disappear between his lips. I looked down at my own doorstep, and couldn't touch it. I'd fallen in love with a raw anchovy slipping down someone's throat. It felt absolutely right, the sudden fluttery thing in my stomach. The only strange thing, I realized a moment after, was that the someone's mouth was Ben's, a man. I was so surprised I couldn't look at him.

Seeing my downcast expression, he asked, 'What's wrong?'

'Nothing.' I looked up at him. 'Those anchovies – just not hungry any more.'

'Well, don't worry, I'll eat them,' he said, 'and you can have something proper later on. There's a really good fish restaurant round the corner.' He looked worried. 'You're okay, aren't you?'

'Just lost my appetite. I'm fine.'

He ate half my doorstep, and we left and walked up to the tired public gardens, with their dusty paths and heroic statuary and fountains. The white-globed lamps had come on in the twilight. I put my arm in his as we walked towards the bandstand. They were belting through *Aida* now, 'March of the Slaves'. We stopped to listen and look – a tiny sweating conductor in tails, punching them through the loud march. It was exciting. I squeezed his arm. He didn't return the pressure, just kept nodding his head slightly to the music. A week before, or at any time during the last month indeed, had I squeezed his arm that way he would not have been so indifferent. At least, when we walked on to the restaurant, he didn't look back at the balcony flooded with red geraniums, where Katie had sat and waited for him.

We had separate rooms in the Hotel Michelangelo, but next door to each other, so that wasn't going to be a problem: and nor was the fact that I hadn't made love with a man for fifteen years. Lovemaking is not something you forget.

There was nothing for it but to take the bull by the horns, as it were, so that towards the end of the meal in the fish restaurant, out on a terrace, and after grilled swordfish with a creamy caper-and-lemon sauce, and a good bottle of some Tuscan estate white, I wiped my lips, looked across the table and said lightly, 'Ben, let's go to bed together.'

He was still prodding about among the debris of his swordfish, moping up the sauce with a bit of bread. The peasant. He looked up. There was no surprise in his face, just humour.

'My God, I know seafood is supposed to be an aphrodisiac, but this is ridiculous. You mean … you really want to?'

'Yes.'

Silence. He looked puzzled.

'You don't seem too certain.'

'No, I was just wondering if we might have a sambuca? I can light the coffee beans on top and keep the midges and mosquitoes off.'

'Of course,' I said. 'They're getting at my ankles.'

'Have to rub a bit of lemon on them, that's the best. Here, I'll do it for you.' He got up quickly, with half a lemon, bent down, squeezed the juice over my ankles, massaged the pulp in with his fingers. The juice pricked my skin, and his fingers were warm and firm, and my toes started to tingle.

You can't talk about lovemaking afterwards. Not if it really is that. The words get stuck in your throat, in the moments of it, and afterwards. What to say but that we made love, as famished people. And in our hunger we had banished the ghosts of Katie and Martha.

Next morning I thought we were about to embark on a spell of pure happiness, the olive groves over the mountains, God knows what other good things, for to have made love as we did that night was to forget the past, be careless of the present and sure of the future.

Sex is salvation, I thought – the sheer well-being, that happi-ness – salvation until, waiting in the lobby to speak to the manager about hiring a car, a small, almost bald man in an old-fashioned linen summer suit and red hanky in his breast pocket came into the lobby. He was carrying a bubble-wrapped parcel under his arm. Two younger, tough-looking men followed.

'My God. O'Higgins,' Ben said, walking up to him. I thought he was going to hit him. He might have done, but for the men with him. Instead he said, 'What the hell are you doing here?'

The man gestured to the parcel. 'Your property I think, Mr Contini. We found it on the barge, along with a scrapbook and a diary of some sort. I was sure you'd want them back.'

'The barge on the Rhine? How did you come to find out about that?'

'Ah, that would be telling. It's you who'll do the telling now.' We sat at the far end of the lobby. O'Higgins sipped a coffee, still holding the Modi, guarding it carefully on his lap, the two men sitting nearby.

'But how did you trace us here?'

'A hunch,' O'Higgins said easily.

'A hunch? Out of all the places in Europe, why Carrara?'

'Your friend's diary,' he said beaming. 'We found it on the barge.' He turned to me. 'With a drawing of you in it, and I read some of the diary.' Of course, he thought I was Katie. He turned to Ben. 'I thought there might be a clue in the diary as to where you'd gone.' He looked back at me again, sipped his cappuccino. 'And there was.'

'What was there?' Ben was fuming.

'An account of a time you both spent here in Carrara some years ago, happy times it seems, while you were teaching at the art school. So I played the hunch. I thought – well, lovers, you know – and knowing how much of the romantic there is in you, Mr Contini – I thought you might both have come back here. Renewing happy memories.' He beamed.

'You're a shit, O'Higgins.'

'That's harsh, Mr Contini. When I'm here to give you your property back. The Modi nude. Worth millions, I'm sure.'

'I'm not interested in that now. Given it all up.'

'Well, that's all right for you painters, you can go on and do new work. I've not given it all up, and can't afford to in my business. Have to rely on past artistic work. Especially great works of art – paintings by Raphael, drawings by Dürer and so on.'

'What do you want?'

'Those paintings.' The little shit narrowed his eyes. 'They must be hidden somewhere round here, maybe in one of your father's old marble quarries, and you didn't come here to renew happy memories – you came here to find them. It was suddenly all clear to me when I saw the mention of Carrara in your friend's diary. Because of course your father was in the marble business in Dublin. So he must have known about quarries out here, and that's where he must have hidden the rest of the paintings, and he told you exactly where before he died. So it all added up – you must have gone to Carrara to get them. I want those paintings now.'

'You've got it all wrong, O'Higgins. I didn't come here to find those paintings, because my father didn't tell me where they were, and I did just come here to renew happy memories. So why don't you just bugger off and leave us to enjoy them?'

'Ah, Mr Contini.' He was sympathetic. 'Of course I'll let the two of you go your own way with your happy memories.' Then his eyes narrowed. 'But not until you tell me where those pictures are.

'I see.'

'I hope you do. I hope you're going to be sensible this time. Where are the rest of those pictures?'

'I've no idea.'

'Come, it's a big area, forty square miles of marble mountains, they tell me. Clearly I can't take a needle-in-a-haystack approach.

You'll have to help me. Otherwise my friends here,' he gestured to the men behind him, 'will take a very unwelcome interest in you, particularly in your girlfriend.'

I looked at Ben. We were surely and finally cornered now. He saw this, too.

'All right,' he said, 'I don't know where they are, but I'll help you, tell you all I know.'

'Good. Meanwhile you'll stay in your rooms, with my friends here keeping an eye on you. I have things to see to at the marina. We'll meet at lunch – just you and me. And please don't make a fuss, or you'll ruin everything. Including yourselves.'

I looked across at Ben. He looked at me. I said to him with my eyes, 'Get us out of this one, Ben, and forgive me for ever questioning your crazy idiot schemes. Dear Ben, just get us out of this one.'

>>>>>>>>>>>>>>>>>>>>>>>>>>>>>>>>>>>>> SIXTEEN

Ben's Story

This was a scrape we really had to get out of. I sat on my bed and rolled a cigarette. The phone was dead. One of the toughs, putting us both in our separate bedrooms, had disconnected it and taken the flex away, and locked me in. I could hear him, and the other fellow, walking up and down outside in the corridor. They'd taken rooms on the same fourth floor.

Well, there was only one way out and that was to tell O'Higgins all that I suspected about where the paintings might be, but I knew no more than him about this. Would he believe me? I didn't know.

And then suddenly I thought maybe I do know. The Modi nude. Why had my father kept the painting hidden in the attic all those years, a painting in which he had no artistic interest? Why hadn't he sold it, legally or illegally? Because the painting must have had some very special importance to him. All I'd thought about it was the secret behind the woman, Emelia. The woman behind the inscription 'Emelia-Amedeo-Amore' written on the canvas turn-over, hidden by the edge of the hessian backing. But what if the real secret, something much more important to my father, was also hidden behind the backing, on the back of the actual canvas itself?

I went with O'Higgins for lunch at the Roma, a little restaurant next to the marble theatre just up the road from the hotel. One of the minders took another table close by, and I told O'Higgins all I suspected about where the hoard was hidden – somewhere in a cave in the marble-quarry mountains above us. And then I told him how I thought the directions might be hidden on the back of the Modi nude.

He had a slice of melon and a wafer of Parma ham almost into his mouth. He lowered the fork, and a glint of greed showed again in his eyes. 'Of course! To think I never thought of that. Come on, Ben,' he said, making me a friend and accomplice by using my Christian name, and finishing his melon and Parma ham in two mouthfuls. 'We must move quickly.'

Back at the hotel we went up to his room. He unwrapped the painting and asked me to tear the hessian up along both edges of the frame.

And there it was. Several lines of writing in dark ink, my father's hand, in Italian – and below it a drawing. O'Higgins was on tenterhooks. 'So? What does it say?'

I translated the Italian. ' "Colonnata Village. On a theodolite line taken from the top of the middle pinnacle on the church tower." And then there are some figures: looks like "Thirty-something degrees south-west and at an elevation of forty-nine degrees", I think it is, "In the valley of the twin peaks, between the Cave di Gioia and the Cave Cancelli di Gioia".'

'And the drawing?' It showed what seemed a sheer rock face, high up, since it was between and not far below the two mountain peaks which my father had referred to. Marked high on the rock face, quite simply, was an X, like something from a child's adventure book. X marks the spot.

O'Higgins beamed. 'So, that cross must mark the opening to a cave!'

'Yes. Those two quarries must have been my father's. He must have hidden all the paintings there after the war, in a cave in some old workings, which he knew wouldn't be disturbed later.'

'And this Colonnata – where is it?'

'It's the marble village, end of the road, about six miles up the mountains from here.'

'These twin peaks … they must be visible from the church tower.'

'Probably, but that X on the drawing looks high up on the mountain. Could be difficult to get at.'

'I have the men to get at it, trained in quarry and mountain work down at the marina, and a boat to get the stuff away.'

Elsa and I were guarded overnight by our minders, locked into our separate bedrooms. I couldn't talk to her. Next morning one of the minders stayed behind in the hotel guarding Elsa, while O'Higgins and I – with the other minder, and two new men up from the marina – left for Colonnata in a big Toyota Land Cruiser. The new men, Italians, had the air of professionals. One of them versed in mining engineering, I thought, since he had a theodolite, tripods and other electronic equipment with him in the back of the truck. The second man a mountaineer, for the back of the truck was full of big coils of nylon rope, pitons, picks, pulleys, hammers and iron stakes.

We drove up the twisting mountain road, lush green trees to either side, another of those hot blue Tuscan mornings, a whole arc of sky opening above us as we approached the great white scarred peaks. We stopped in the tiny square at Colonnata. A dozen old red-tiled houses, a village hall with a church and a church tower, with three small stone pinnacles, above the piazza.

'Well, that's one confirmation,' O'Higgins said. 'The middle pinnacle, looking south-west.'

It took some time, asking at the café-grocery in the square, to get the key of the church tower. We waited outside the café while the minder went to look for the verger. The square was empty.

'The locals all work down in Carrara, or in the quarries,' I said.

We could hear the faint roar of machine saws and dump trucks above us, down the valley, but not on the twin-peaked mountain to the south-west, which we could see in the distance now, old white scars on it, the rest unworked. One of the Italians gazed at the mountain through powerful binoculars. He turned to O'Higgins.

'No sign of any current workings,' he said in English. 'All old workings, and you can see a hairpin track, cut into the mountain, leading up to the most recent of them: but the track stops far below the summit, and way beneath that rock face where the oldest workings are, where the cross on that map is likely to be.' He handed O'Higgins the binoculars, and consulted a large-scale map. 'And if I'm right, the only way to get at that high rock face would be from above.'

The minder came back with the verger who opened the church and we climbed the steps inside the tower with the theodolite, tripod and camera, because they'd said they wanted to take photographs from the tower for an Italian travel magazine.

At the top there was a marvellous view, and a clearer sight of the twin peaks. They set up the theodolite just above the middle pinnacle of the tower, moved the lens first into the horizontal degree which my father had given in his directions, and then raised it into the vertical angle. The second Italian gazed through the lens, moving it slightly from side to side, then up and down, until finally he was satisfied.

'Yes, the cross-hairs focus exactly on that rock face, the old workings, thirty or forty metres down from the plateau between the two peaks.' He moved to gaze through the binoculars, which had been set on another tripod. After a minute he said, 'There's a line of old workings there. Partly cut blocks of marble, on narrow terraces down the rock face, dropping for about fifty metres, and then there's a sheer drop, no way up to the old terraces. Those high workings must have given out, so they started again, to the side or lower down the mountain. There's no way to get at those old workings except from above.'

'Do you have the exact part of the rock face – identifiable by one of those marble blocks – where that cross is on the map?'

'Almost exactly. It's the second terrace down, about thirty metres down and fifty metres along from the western end of the terrace, with quite a bit of partly cut marble blocks at that point. Somewhere there, behind those loose blocks – there must be an entrance.'

'Good. Good.'

O'Higgins was sweating, fidgeting with anticipation.

We drove out of the village, up one rough track and then along another, followed by a succession of rising hairpin bends, down through a small valley to the left of the twin peaks, then turning up behind them, to the west, along another twisting track that ended at an old disused quarry working. We had to go on foot at this stage, carrying the ropes and other equipment, up a slippery scree of old marble chippings, moving between the two peaks towards the level ridge, among alpine lichens now on bare craggy rock. At the top of the ridge, at three or four thousand feet, there was a sensational view. Carrara in the distance, the hazy pale-blue sea beyond.

We moved down towards the edge of the ridge, gingerly, because we were on a slope now and the stones were loose. The ridge ended in a sheer precipice. We stopped. One of the Italians crawled forward on his belly, looked over the edge, then crawled back, stood up, dusted his hands.

'Yes, it's there, the rock face we want and the terrace of old marble blocks – about thirty metres beneath us.' He hacked the rock beneath the loose stones with the heel of his boot.

'Absolutely solid. A couple of stakes, abseil down.'

The two Italians inspected the terrain thoroughly, and hacked the loose rock away with small picks, finding a secure place to hammer their stakes in. They uncoiled two lengths of nylon rope, attached them to pulleys at the top of each stake, now deeply embedded in the rock, and put on body harnesses and belts carrying pitons, small picks and torches. Then, feet first, they eased themselves towards the precipice, played out their ropes and disappeared over the edge.

O'Higgins, myself and the minder waited above in the fierce sun. After about fifteen minutes we saw the pulleys moving on the stakes. The two men returned, sweating, but pleased. The first man, who had the best English, spoke to O'Higgins. 'There's an opening between two half-cut marble blocks, the second terrace down, about fifty metres in from the southern end. There are no other possible openings anywhere along the terrace, all solid blocks, partly cut into the rock face. So that must be it.'

'How wide is the opening?' O'Higgins was excited.

'Several metres.'

'And how high?'

'About two metres.'

'That must be it. Tall and wide enough to get big canvases in. Did you go inside?'

'Yes.'

'How far?'

'Only a few metres. The entrance was closed then by a block of solid marble, but there is a narrow entrance beside the block, just wide enough to get through.'

'Well, that's the way in. So go down again, squeeze in and see what's inside.'

The two men crawled back, feet first, and disappeared over the edge again.

O'Higgins fidgeted, impatient. A gust of wind took his straw hat and it sailed away over the cliff, swirling about like a kite, before drifting down into the huge valley below. O'Higgins put a hand to his bald pate quickly, trying to cover it, as if his private parts had been exposed. The minder, mopping his brow, sat down on the rock near me. I rolled a cigarette. The three of us waited in the hot sun. Five, ten minutes, fifteen.

Then the explosion. Deafening. Just below our feet, it seemed. A cracking series of explosions, or it may have been the echoes reverberating round the valley, for half a minute. Finally silence.

'My God!' O'Higgins yelped. And then, to the minder, 'See if you can see anything below.'

The man crawled forward, and leant over the edge.

'Can you see anything?' O'Higgins called out.

The man half-turned. 'No, I can't see –'

And that was all he said before the entire edge of the precipice, loosened by the explosion just beneath, gave way and disappeared. We heard his screams on the way down.

That just left me and O'Higgins. I looked at him, appraisingly. I was bigger than him. He was frightened. Thinking of help from below he started to tug at one of the two ropes, but there was no weight on it. He did the same with the other rope, pulling it all the way up. Just blackened fibre strands at the end. He pulled the first rope up. It was in the same state.

I turned to O'Higgins, shaking one of the scorched ends at him. 'The entrance was booby-trapped.' I said.

I wondered if O'Higgins had a gun on him. I waited a moment. Clearly he hadn't. He would have got it out by now. Guns had been the minder's job. And, yes, I was bigger and younger and tougher than O'Higgins. I moved towards him, with menace.

'Don't!' he shouted. 'Don't throw me over there! For the love of God!'

'I think you'd do well,' I said, 'to follow your hat.'

SEVENTEEN

I wasn't sure what else to do with him. Truss him up with all the rope about? Leave him on the mountaintop? No, I had to take him back with me to Carrara and hand him over to the police. While I was thinking, he'd been thinking, too. And now he was talking fast.

'The police will be up here any minute, Ben. They'll have heard the explosion all over the valley. If we leave now in the truck we'll both get clear away, no questions asked.'

'You've got it wrong again, O'Higgins. I'm not one of you. Come on back to the car to Carrara and the police.'

'You're not one of us?' He laughed. 'Oh yes you are. You came back here to Carrara to get the stuff in that cave and you knew it was booby-trapped, so we'd go down first and you'd get us out of the way. You're in this up to your neck, like your father, both of you crooks – and the Italian police certainly won't believe otherwise. So you come on with me – now, while we have the chance.'

O'Higgins was right about my father. It was clear now that he was a criminal, and worse. The explosion had finally proved that he had hidden the rest of the art in the cave. Finally I had confirmation of all my worst fears about my father, the father I had loved. But I wasn't going to argue with O'Higgins. I said, 'I'll take my chances with the police. And so will you.'

He changed tack now, became petulant. 'All right, be like that. I'll take my chances alone.' He turned and ran, down the other side of the mountain, as fast as his fat little legs would carry him, which wasn't far. Unable to slow down, he slipped on the loose scree and started to roll down the hill, on and on, like a child playing a roly-poly game down a meadow slope, until he was lost to sight over a ridge.

I moved down carefully to the edge. It wasn't a steep fall, and he lay amidst some rocks, about twenty yards beneath me, spread-eagled, motionless. I got down to him. He was semi-conscious, bleeding from a head wound. I took the red hanky from the breast pocket of his torn and soiled linen suit, and staunched the wound on his bald pate. Embarrassed again, he tried to cover his head with a hand, but couldn't move his arm, wincing in pain. It was probably broken. He looked up, seeming to appeal to me with his watery eyes, and I pitied him a moment, and said, 'My God, O'Higgins, why didn't you stick to conning old ladies out of their heirlooms in Foxrock?'

There was a faint, rictus smile. He didn't speak. I covered his head with the hanky, making a sort of tight turban with it over his head, so that the blood was staunched. He fainted. I loosened his tie, opened his collar, propped him up against a rock, letting the blood run to his feet, and waited.

I'd already heard a siren down in the valley, and now I heard an engine groaning up the mountain track. Another few minutes and the carabinieri jeep appeared, stopping at the end of the track where they'd parked the Toyota. Two carabinieri got out and came up towards us. Of course there remained one vital problem – the other minder was still holding Elsa prisoner back in her hotel bedroom.

As O'Higgins had said, the carabinieri, like the superintendent at Ulm, were not inclined to believe what I told them on the way back down the mountain. They took O'Higgins straight to the new hospital in the upper town, then returned with me to the carabinieri headquarters in Carrara, a fine classical building opposite the Academia delle Arte. I spoke to the carabinieri chief, a tall, dark-haired man with a luxuriant moustache. A nameplate above his breast pocket read 'Chief Superintendent Giorgio Marello'.

'You have to believe me.' I spoke in Italian, in his airless office looking over the Academia. 'What do you think they were doing abseiling down that mountain? Did it look like a climbing holiday? They're all crooks. And the proof of that is back at the Hotel Michelangelo right now, where one of them is holding my friend in her bedroom. Elsa Bergen – we have to get her out without his harming her.'

The chief turned to a colleague, a younger man. 'Get a plain-clothes man down to the hotel and talk to Carlo, the manager – see if what he says is true.'

'Why would I bother to lie?' I was annoyed, exhausted, alarmed about Elsa.

'We have to check, Signor Contini. It's a difficult story to believe.' He brushed his moustache. 'Your father, Luchino Contini, hiding a vast store of paintings, Italian masterpieces, looted by the Nazis, up in that quarry.'

'Well, get up there and see for yourself. The explosion may have burst open the cave behind.'

He nodded. 'We'll do that.'

'Good. It's your affair now, Chief Superintendent.'

He stood up, moved about the room, went to the window. Turning, he said, 'Your father Signor Luchino Contini, he and his family owned those two quarries up there beneath the twin peaks. They were a very well-known family round these parts.'

'Yes, but they were Jews, all murdered except my father.'

'That's true. You see, my father worked for the Contini Marble Enterprise here. Not in the quarries, but down at the main office at the marina. He was an accountant, chief clerk to the quarry manager who lived up here in Carrara.'

'The manager?'

'Yes. A Signor Roberto Battaglia. He ran everything here, your father lived abroad, only came here once or twice a year.'

I became alert now because, as I had thought, my father surely had an accomplice: this manager must have collaborated with him all along, until the late sixties when my father, with his friend Joseph Bergen in Dublin – with their fill of the loot, and not wanting to take any more risks in getting the stuff out – had sold the quarries.

'This Signor Battaglia … is he still alive?'

'No. He died about ten years ago.'

'And your father?'

'Also dead.' I said, 'You see the implications? The cave was booby-trapped. And Battaglia must have had a hand in helping my father get the paintings out. My father couldn't have done all that on his own. The two of them were in it together, the manager getting a fat cut of the proceeds.'

'Yes, that makes sense.' The chief went to the window again, turned. 'My father always thought there was something suspicious about Battaglia. He knew exactly what his salary was from the Contini enterprise. And I remember in the sixties, when I was a teenager, Battaglia bought an old palazzo here, did it up expensively, and got a big cruiser down at the marina. Took us all out on it. I remember that. He'd clearly come into a large amount of money.'

'Pity he's dead. Could have picked him up. Was he married, had a family?'

'Married, but no children. His wife is still alive, very old. Lives in an old people's home, run by the nuns, just outside Carrara.'

'Maybe I could talk to her. She might tell me something.'

The phone rang. He came back from the window, spoke for a minute, then said. 'Yes, there is a woman up in her room at the hotel, a Signorina Bergen.'

'That's her.'

'Unwell apparently, being looked after by a man who comes down and brings her food up.'

'That's him. The minder. But how can you get her out? He'll be armed.'

'Have to see.' He looked at his watch. 'Lunchtime. Maybe take him when he comes downstairs to get her food.'

'Thanks, Chief Superintendent. You believe me now.'

'Yes. Apart from anything else, what you told me fits exactly with Battaglia's sudden wealth. Right, let's see about your friend at the hotel.' We moved to the door. He stopped. 'You might go and see Battaglia's wife. She must have known your father, may have something to add to it all, which she wouldn't tell me. Signora Emelia Battaglia – she lives just outside town, top of the hill.'

We were halfway out of the door before I stopped abruptly.

'Signora Emelia Battaglia?'

'Yes. Why?'

'Nothing.'

'Emelia-Amedeo-Amore'. The inscription hidden on the turn-over of the Modigliani painting.

The chief, out of his uniform, was casually dressed. There were four or five other carabinieri in plain clothes in the hotel lobby – by the reception desk, at the small bar having coffee, in the breakfast room or interesting themselves in magazines at a table beside the lift and the stairs, where we expected the minder to emerge to pick up food for the two of them upstairs. The minder would have recognized me, so I was hidden in the manager's office, to the side of the reception desk, where, with a mirror on a pillar opposite the lift door, I had a view over part of the lobby. Carlo, the manager, was at the reception desk, fiddling with accounts, chewing his wet cheroot, head down as if nothing interesting was afoot. He was a good actor.

Waiting. It was after one o'clock, a quarter past, twenty past. The reception phone went. Carlo spoke for a half a minute, put the phone down, spoke to the chief.

'Ordered two pizzas and a beer. Said he'd pick the food up in ten minutes.'

'What floor is he on?'

'Fourth floor, number 42.'

'He'll come down in the lift then?'

'Yes. Almost certainly.'

'We'll take him getting out of the lift as the door opens.' The chief moved away, directing two of his men flat against the wall to either side of the lift door. Ten minutes later we heard the rumble of the lift coming down. The two men braced themselves, ready to pounce. The door slid open and in the hall mirror I saw Elsa and the minder behind her – with a gun in her back.

They stood where they were, the lift door open. 'Move!' he said, in harsh Italian. 'The two of you hiding either outside the lift. Move, or this'll be the end of the woman.' He put the gun to Elsa's head. The chief, over the far side of the lobby, gestured to the two men, and they moved away from the lift.

'And the rest of you,' the minder continued, 'get over there, by the bar. All of you.' He pushed Elsa out of the lift, holding her with her wrist twisted behind her back, gesturing with his gun to the others as they moved to the bar. I'd ducked down behind the reception desk, so that the minder wouldn't see me. I heard him speak to Carlo. 'And you as well. Out of there and over to the bar.' Carlo left the reception office. I was on my own. And then, beneath the reception desk, I saw the hotel fire alarm panel, a lot of bedroom numbers, switches – and a big red button, with the word TEST above it.

I stabbed it. Immediately a high-pitched siren, an ear-piercing wail, like the torments of the damned, flooded the lobby.

I put my head up over the reception desk. The minder, on his way out of the hotel but stunned now by the noise, had stopped with Elsa in the middle of the lobby, looking wildly around him, his back towards me. I was up and out of the reception office and running for him. He heard me, turning with his gun before I crashed into him with one of my old rugby tackles. At the same moment there was a sharp crack, and I felt a painless thud on the fleshy part of my bicep, and then a stinging pain as I landed on top of him on the floor.

The chief and the other carabinieri by the bar were on us in a flash, pinning the minder down. I reached a hand up to my shoulder, and saw the blood seeping through my fingers. And I saw Elsa above me in her T-shirt and shorts, silhouetted against the bright sunlight from the lobby window, the light illuminating the fine hair on her legs.

I said, 'Great legs. I really want to paint you.' I looked at my left arm, dripping with blood. 'Right arm's okay. I can paint you.' My eyes clouded, closed and my head lolled back into darkness.

I lay on the hospital bed. The bullet had gone through the inside edge of my bicep. Blood loss; shock. Shoulder and upper arm bandaged, the forearm held in a sling. Elsa sat on a chair beside the bed.

'What else was I to do?' I asked.

'Where that bullet went, you were just a few inches from dying, you idiot.'

'We've been a few inches from that quite often this last month or so.'

'Why did you do it?'

'Had to. A bit of lateral thinking, to get us out of that mess. It wasn't just for your great legs.'

That evening we were back in the Michelangelo. Carlo had moved us to one of the suites reserved for visiting Saudis, and had sent a vase of flowers, a bottle of Asti Gancia in an ice bucket, grapes, chocolates and some antipasti titbits. Most of the traditional bedside trimmings for the ill. Propped up, lying out on the big double bed, I realized I actually was a bit poorly and needed attention. How nice.

And there was the Modi nude on a chair by the window, with Katie's journal beneath it. I looked at the nude, the peachy flesh colours, the yellows, shadows of lemon on her thighs, the darker ochre of the curtain behind her, the attempted privacy, a hand crossed over her breasts, the lowered face of a woman who had loved and lost.

But she was mine again now and I loved her once more. And the hell with Katie's journal. I didn't need it. I had Emelia. And better still, I had Elsa. My arm stung sharply and I groaned. The painkiller was wearing off.

'Oh dear me,' I gasped, holding my arm.

Elsa came and sat by the bed, took my good arm and held my hand. 'Don't worry,' she said. 'I know what you're thinking. But I'm not going to run away.'

'No.'

'And when you're better you can paint me. I'll come back with you to your Cotswold barn before I go on to New York.'

'And the meal?' I said eagerly. 'Let me cook us the meal I asked you to cook. Let me do it. There's a Tesco beyond Stow, on the Fosseway: they've got everything. Even good meat, not the wrapped stuff, but cut for you off the carcass at the butchery. Fillet steak. Or I could even do that Irish stew.'

'Dear Ben, stop wittering!' She drew back, looking at me, still holding my hand. 'Just get us a hunk of warm bread, with olives and anchovies. And a half-litre of white.'

'Right – we'll do that.'

She looked at me intently. 'You know, don't you?' Still holding my hand. 'What I feel for you. I can't quite say it, but I do.'

'Don't have to say it. I do too.'

She got up and poured us both a glass of the Italian fizz. I raised my glass. 'Thank you.' And then I raised my glass to the Modi nude. 'And to you, too, Emelia. "Emelia-Amedeo-Amore".' And then I told Elsa what the chief had said to me that morning, about an elderly lady who lived in an old people's home on top of the hill just outside town. Signora Emelia Battaglia.

She tried to hide her sudden unease. 'You really think she's …'

'I don't know, but the bone structure of a face doesn't change much, and the eyes never do. I think I could tell if I saw her.'

'Well, you go ahead. No point in my coming.'

Elsa was retreating once more. She feared something in this unknown woman. I was tempted by her.

They dressed my wound again next morning, and the day after, and said it was beginning to heal. I sent innocent picture postcards home, to my family and the Phillips' at the end of my lane, and Elsa and I found quiet things to do in our room, reading, or talking of things that didn't matter, and eating one-handed at the Roma. I was fitter and thought it better not to talk of the future with Elsa, and not to warn Emelia. I'd take my chances. Next morning I took a taxi up the hill. The Modi nude was the other passenger.

Past the covered market, over the frothy river, across a piazza and through an arched gateway – *'Domus Deo Fecit'* inscribed in heavy black letters on the arch. A winding drive up the steep hill, thickly wooded with ilex, cypress and laurel. Clearly a large private estate years before, with the expected ox-blood baroque palazzo on top of the hill. But there wasn't. It was a rambling, run-down late-nineteenth-century villa, white-stuccoed, red-tiled, paint peeling.

The taxi left and I turned on the steps of a porch, shading my eyes with my one good hand – a huge view south and west over the old town and the sea in the distance, but veiled in the morning heat haze. The glass hall doors were open. A thin tabby cat appeared at the doorway, tail aloft when it saw me, coming down the steps, rubbing itself against my legs, purring.

The long hall was empty. Cool white marble tiles, terracotta pots of rubber plants, a large urn filled with sticks and umbrellas, old prints of popes and other divines along the walls, a plaster statue of a dolorous virgin at the far end. A smell of pomodoro cooking somewhere, wafting through the still hallway. I went to the end, two corridors leading away to either side. An elderly nun in a white habit walked towards me along one of them.

'Good morning, Sister.' I gave my name and asked if it might see Signora Battaglia.

'Are you family?' A low voice, meek, hands clasped together.

'No. My father, Signor Luchino Contini knew Signora Battaglia years ago here. I'm just visiting Carrara.'

'She will be pleased to see you. She has few visitors.'

'She must be old.'

'Yes, she is ninety-five – so she says.'

'You don't believe her?'

'Sometimes we wonder.'

'Not right in her mind, you mean?'

'Oh, no. Just … we think she likes to tell stories.'

'Imaginative?'

'Yes, imaginative.'

The cat had followed us in, rubbing its flank against my legs again. She looked down at it. 'Hungry,' she said. 'And she knows we eat early, at midday. There are so few of us here now, and the cook has to get away early. Soon we will all have to leave. Even you, little White Paws.' She bent down and stroked the cat. 'We don't own the villa or the land, you see. They are going to sell it, develop it. Apartment blocks.' She looked at my bandaged arm. 'You have been hurt, I see.'

'No, it was nothing. I was careless. I slipped up in the mountains.' She looked at the parcel under my other arm, and curiosity getting the better of her, she said 'You have brought something for the Signora?'

'Yes, a painting.'

'She will like that, I'm sure. I will take you to her. She is out on the terrace.'

I followed her back along the corridor. We passed an open doorway to a large gloomy room. Elderly people were slumped in old leather chairs, asleep, or vacant-eyed, one tapping her stick repeatedly on the floor.

'Signora Battaglia prefers to be outdoors.'

We went out onto a wide marble terrace with a balustrade, vines growing wild, looking over the steep hill and the cypress trees to the distant sea. Some cracked marble tables, chairs, but only one person, a small white-haired woman, in dark glasses, sitting in a wheelchair beneath a parasol.

The nun introduced me. 'A Signor Contini has come to see you, Signora.'

The nun left. I introduced myself. 'I'm Benjamin Contini. Just visiting Carrara, so I thought I'd come and see you, since I believe you knew my father, Signor Luchino Contini?'

The old woman looked up. At once an impression of sharpness, the tracings of a bohemian girl. Wearing a shift of layered cheese-cloth, slippers, delicate feet propped up on the leg rest. A thin, wasted figure, but still perfect in its proportions. The face deeply lined, angular, the high brow running down past high cheekbones to a pointed chin. White sparse hair pulled back tightly over her head and held with a tortoiseshell comb at the back. Decay was making its final advances in the tightly stretched skin, the dappled brown age marks, the drooping ear lobes, the thin bloodless lips.

'Benjamin Contini?' She took off her dark glasses as if to confirm this. 'Indeed you are.' Now I saw her eyes, which were astonishing – large, oval, young and blue. And the look of alarm in them now was that of youth, the fear of a young woman confronted by a lover who had long abandoned her but had suddenly returned. And I knew at once that this was the Emelia of the painting. The same woman, seventy-five years older.

'Why have you come here? To tell the police about Luchino?' she went on. Her voice was dry, but firm.

'No, why …?'

She cleared her throat, turned and took a sip of something from a glass beside her. Then she said, in precisely enunciated Italian, 'It doesn't matter now.' Silence.

'What doesn't matter?'

'My son Luchino is dead. He wrote to me, last year, just before he died, from Ireland.'

'My son? You mean my father.'

'Both. My son and your father. You are indeed Benjamin Contini. If I didn't know about you, I could see it clearly in your face. You are my grandson.'

Standing over her, outside the shade of her tattered parasol, I blinked in the bright light, beads of sweat trickling down my brow. 'I see,' I said casually. This must be one of her fictions the nun had spoken about. 'The only problem is that my grandmother died in Auschwitz, along with my grandfather, uncles, aunts and cousins. All my family in Italy are dead.'

'I'm not exactly your family though – but you are my grandson, I assure you.'

'Yes,' I said, to humour her. Then I thought – well, there's one certain thing – the woman in the Modi nude and this old woman, they were the same person. I was sure of that. I could establish something firm about her with the portrait. I unwrapped it, propped it up on a chair in front of her. She looked at it, surprise and alarm in her face. With the same certainty as she had told me I was her grandson, I said, 'This is you.'

Silence. She gazed at it, frowning. 'Yes, your father always kept that with him in Ireland. Never with all the other paintings.'

'The other paintings?'

'All the other paintings …' She stopped. 'But that was special to him. Of me, his mother.'

'A wonderful painting. Modigliani. You must have known him.' I showed her the inscription behind the canvas. "Emelia-Amedeo-Amore",' I said. 'You must have known him well.'

'Yes, I did.' Her face was quite still as she looked at the inscription.

I said, 'Well, if you're my grandmother, one of my Contini family, my grandfather I suppose, must have … you and he must have produced my father, but without being married?'

'Oh, no, nothing like that. Amedeo and I produced your father.'

This surely was a fiction. I said, 'But that would make me Modigliani's grandson.'

'Exactly.'

'I was seventeen when I met him,' she told me later, 'when he came back to Livorno, briefly during the war, summer of 1915. My family in Livorno, the Montecchios, a big shipping family were as bourgeois as his, except his were Jewish. I was an innocent and he wasn't. He was sketching at the Café Metropole early one evening, I was there with my brother at the next table. He started sketching me, came over with the drawing, and that was how it began. We met secretly in Livorno that summer. I fell in love with him. First love, mad love, all that – so I followed him to Paris that autumn, lived with him at the Bateau Lavoir, a tumbledown atelier he and Soutine and some other crazy painters shared up in Montmartre. And he painted me and we loved each other, and he painted me again, and nothing mattered for several months, until winter came and it was cold, no heat and no money and little food in the war, and the rows started – other girls, models, when he was out every night with them, or sketching for his supper, and always drinking with his friends, and coming back drunk next morning. It became impossible. I went back to Livorno carrying that picture – and your father.'

'Born in Livorno?'

'No. In Pisa. My parents were horrified – a good bourgeois family with a pregnant unmarried daughter. My God! – a fate worse than death. They disowned me and farmed me out with the Contini family in Pisa. My father knew the boss, Mario Contini, very well. He shipped his marble out from the Contini quarries in Pisa and Carrara. And Mario had a younger son, Marcello Contini – late thirties, but still unmarried. A marriage was arranged with him, with a handsome financial settlement from my father. Or rather it was forced on me. It was marrying Marcello or being out on the street. So I became a Contini, and your father was born in Pisa, Marcello pretending he was our child.'

'All that must have been very difficult for you.'

'Could have been worse. Marcello was a dull but kind man who wanted a quiet life. We had our own house in Pisa, down by the river. We didn't have any children ourselves. Couldn't face him that way after the first few times. Marcello didn't mind, went to the local brothels quite happily.'

'I knew Marcello was my grandfather, and that my grandmother was a local girl, another Jewish family in Pisa – my father told me, and how he and his parents and all the other Continis had been rounded up by the fascist militia in 1943 and taken to Auschwitz. But why didn't they take you as well?'

'I wasn't Jewish, and the chief of the fascist militia in Pisa knew that I was a daughter of the Montecchios in Livorno, a rich fascist shipping family, with whom the chief needed to keep on good terms. So he wouldn't take me. I was left behind.'

'My father told me nothing of all that, and nothing about you being a Montecchio.'

'He had good reasons for not telling you the truth.'

'What was the truth?'

'When he finally got back from Auschwitz, some years after the war – he knew I was the only person in his family left alive – he came back to our house in Pisa. But I wasn't living there any more. Thinking Luchino and all the other Continis, including Marcello, were dead, I'd married Roberto Battaglia, the manager of the Contini quarries in Carrara, and was living here. Luchino soon found out where I was and came to live with us. Later he told me what he'd done in that camp.'

'What did he do there?'

'He'd collaborated with the SS.'

'As I thought.'

'How did you come to think that?'

'A list in his handwriting, an inventory I found in our Dublin house, of paintings: one by Raphael, and other Renaissance master-pieces. I found that they had been looted in Poland and elsewhere during the war.'

'Exactly. But that's not how he survived.'

'How?'

'Luchino was a civil engineer, remember. So at the selection when they arrived at Auschwitz, he wasn't sent to the gas chambers, like the rest of the Continis. He was put to work on construction projects

outside the camp. Factories being built where they needed quali-
fied men as slave labour. Well, there was a young German architect
in charge of his work group. Luchino got to know him. This man,
with another senior architect in Berlin, had been commissioned to
build a house, not in Germany, but in Poland, outside Krakow, for
one of the big SS men there, a major called Helmuth Pfaffenroth,
deputy to Dr Hans Frank, the Nazi governor of Poland.'

'Yes, I know about them.'

'Well, Luchino told this architect he could get him the finest
white Carrara Cremo marble for Pfaffenroth's house, from his family
quarries in Carrara. A glittering white marble palazzo. Pfaffenroth
was thrilled with the idea. The architect got Luchino out of the camp
and took him up to Krakow, to work on the plans with Pfaffenroth. Luchino – that charm of his – he played on Pfaffenroth. They
became friends. Luchino never went back to Auschwitz.'

'What happened?'

'Luchino made himself indispensable to Pfaffenroth – and Dr
Frank. But early in 1945, with the Russians coming in from the
east, the war was going to be over soon. Frank had looted paintings and other priceless objects and needed to move them all out,
somewhere safe, and where he and Pfaffenroth could get at them
after the war. But where to? Luchino told Pfaffenroth how he
could get all this looted art out to a really safe place, where they
could get at it easily after the war as well.'

'Exactly. Hidden in the Contini Carrara quarries up there in
the mountains.' I said. She nodded. 'And where the paintings could
be shipped out later to Dublin, hidden in crated slabs of marble.'

'Yes.'

'And the man who helped my father ship it out after the war
was Roberto Battaglia, your husband, manager of the Contini
quarries here.'

'How do you know all this?'

'I've been working it out these last weeks. But why did my father tell you all about it? He didn't have to.'

'Luchino told me because he had to tell me. They caught Hans Frank and executed him, but Pfaffenroth – he'd escaped from a US army camp after the war. He turned up in our house in Carrara, a few months after Luchino arrived here. He was on the run. Luchino hid him in the cellars – with Roberto's knowledge – since by then he was in on the whole business. I knew nothing of this. Until one day – I'd been in Livorno – I came back to the house earlier than usual and I found this man talking to Luchino and Roberto in the salon.'

'But they needn't have told you exactly who he was.'

'They didn't. Luchino just said he was an Austrian client, wanting to buy marble. Luchino hadn't told me anything at that point about what had happened to him in Auschwitz and Krakow, and nothing about Pfaffenroth – not until he told me he was going to live in Ireland. But why, I asked, when you've just come home? Then Luchino told me everything – what he'd done in Auschwitz with the architect and in Krakow with this Austrian SS man with Dr Frank, and who he really was, how his real name was Pfaffenroth, and all the terrible things he had done in the war, so he could never be safe anywhere, except perhaps in Ireland, where he'd have a new name, a new life. And Luchino was going to go to Ireland with him as well.'

'Why not let Pfaffenroth go on his own?'

'Pfaffenroth didn't trust him, with the loot nearby. Said he'd expose him if he didn't come to Ireland, and if Luchino exposed Pfaffenroth, he'd be implicated himself. So they both went to Ireland.'

'And they carried on their crooked business from Dublin, selling the looted art secretly to special customers, splitting the profits?'

'Yes.'

'And was the name Pfaffenroth took in Ireland Bergen? Joseph Bergen?'

'Yes, but how could you possibly know that, if your father never told you anything about the whole business and you never met the man?'

'I met his daughter,' I said.

I got up, and walked away round the terrace, came back. 'All the same,' I said, 'Luchino didn't have to tell you the truth. He could have just said he wanted to live abroad.'

'Yes, he could have said that, but he was impetuous like his father Amedeo, emotional. He badly needed to confide, and as his mother I was the only one he could confide in. He knew I wouldn't betray him.'

I nodded. 'Even so, why did he do it? Collaborate that with that Jew murderer Pfaffenroth?'

'You haven't understood, Benjamin, living all your life in the safety of neutral Ireland. But we understood what those camps were like, from the few who came back. I knew it especially from Luchino, who told me. You weren't human there anymore, you became a different species. You'd do anything to survive. Cheat, steal, betray, kill – anything. I understand that.'

'Yes.'

'You only survived through sheer brutal tenacity for life. Nothing and nobody else mattered. And after the war, having survived that camp, Luchino was never going to be freezing or starving or bug-ridden or beaten or waiting for a selection for the gas chambers ever again. He was going to be rich, and put himself as far away as possible from all that pain and horror. At whatever cost to his conscience. I understand that, too. Those camps – they didn't just kill millions at the time, they killed the few who survived as well. Killed them at heart, or in conscience, like Luchino.'

'Yes, literally killed him at heart in the end. He died of a heart attack.'

'He wrote me a letter some weeks before he died. Saying he was having chest pains. Your mother wrote a cold letter saying he'd died.'

'I knew he didn't get on with my mother. Rows, silences, and I never knew why.'

'Why? Because he had told her everything as well, some years after he'd married her – what he'd done, in Auschwitz, and afterwards with the looted art. That need to confide again, like Amadeo. Knowing, as with me, that your mother wouldn't betray him. The scandal. Your mother hated your father for what he'd done.'

'Which is why she didn't like me,' I said, 'the product of her marriage to a Nazi war criminal. And that explains the rows between my parents, and my mother's coldness to me when I was growing up.'

'Yes.'

'It's a terrible story,' I said. 'Difficult to forgive.'

'Yes. But try and understand it. You didn't know your father before he went to Auschwitz. I did. And he wasn't that kind of man at all. He was a good man. But the evil in those camps made men behave in ways they'd never have dreamt of in ordinary life, and some of them carried on in the same way after the war, without a conscience. If the evil didn't kill you in those camps it killed you afterwards, one way or another.'

EIGHTEEN ‹‹‹‹‹‹‹‹‹‹‹‹‹‹‹‹‹‹‹‹‹‹‹‹‹‹‹‹‹‹‹‹‹

I'd wanted to expose Elsa's and my father as Nazi art looters and war criminals. I had that proof now, and I was appalled at what my father had done. And afterwards, how he'd gone to Ireland and lived the great lie, bought a big house, fine furniture, servants, a motor cruiser, and a position as one of Dublin's richest, most respected and charitable citizens.

I certainly wouldn't tell Elsa what I'd found out, that her much-loved father was one of the very worst Nazis, along with Eich-mann and Dr Hans Frank. If I was shocked at finding out what my father had done, how much greater the shock for Elsa if she learnt who her father really was, of his far greater crimes?

When I got back to the hotel I told her how the old lady was indeed the Emelia of the nude painting, how she and Modigliani were my grandparents, and how this had come about, years before. As to the paintings hidden in the Contini quarries – I said how the explosion up on the mountain proved my father a crook, clearly involved with some Nazis in the looted art business, but not her father, since Emelia had told me nothing about him, no 'Joseph Bergen' in my father's life during the war. Simply that my father, having helped a group of Nazis move the looted art from Poland, had turned up in Carrara alone after the war, found her married to the Contini quarry manager, and had gone to Dublin, on his own, to make a new life, where – as we knew – he'd met Joseph Bergen with his antiques shop in Dublin and had later moved the looted paintings out of Carrara and sold the stuff through Bergen in his shop.

'So it seems my father did much worse that yours,' I said. 'He collaborated with the Nazis in Auschwitz and Krakow. Your father was just a fence in Dublin, selling stolen goods.'

'Just a fence? That's bad enough, isn't it?'

'Is it? Remember, we weren't in the war, weren't refugees in a strange country without a penny. War changes people completely. It brings out the ruthless nature, the survival gene. There were millions of black-market fences, in and after the war.'

'Maybe. But my father never seemed that kind of man.'

'People don't. Katie never seemed the sort to kill herself. Few people are what they seem.' We looked at each other.

'At least we should know who we really are,' she went on, some urgency in her voice. 'After all we've been through, the best and the worst, neither of us has anything left to hide now.'

'True,' I said, lying, hiding a truth that might destroy her, and us. I kissed her, and she put her arms around me. Flesh and blood – and lies – was better than the truth.

The chief superintendent came to see me that afternoon. I told him an equally shortened and untrue version of what Emelia had told me, and nothing about Joseph Bergen.

'Well, it must certainly have been her husband, the quarry manager Roberto Battaglia, who helped your father up in the old quarry,' he said.

'Yes, but she wasn't going to tell me that. So I'm sure she wouldn't tell you.'

'No. Anyway, it hardly matters now. She wasn't involved, but others must have been, apart from the manager. Germans, Nazis – your father couldn't have got all the paintings out of Poland alone. Must have been others who got the stuff down to him here.'

'Yes, I suppose so.'

'The authorities in Rome will try to find out. It's going to be a big affair – a priceless hoard of Nazi looted art, mostly Italian masterpieces. There'll be an enquiry, people up from Rome already, the Special Police, Ministry of Culture officials, journalists.'

'Well, the trail is cold, and the loot is locked in there forever now, isn't it?'

'No. We sent men down the rock face this morning. The explosion didn't block the cave entrance. Blew it all open, in fact, and the paintings, and a lot more, are inside.'

'So,' Elsa said later, back in our bedroom. 'It really is all over now. We can go home. To your barn. And maybe us, then,' she added. 'Together, in some place or other?'

I nodded. 'Yes, I hope so. Dear Elsa.' It was the sentence I'd waited five years for Katie to say, which had never come, and now that it had, a whole new life rose in my mind and heart. 'I'll call Harry in Paris, ask him to look after my boat, pay whatever's due, and put it on the market. I don't think I want anything of my father's now. Though I'll have to go back to the house in Killiney, clear up, see the Mullinses. But the Dublin charity can have the house.'

'I'll have to do the same with my father's house. Clear up, put it on the market, then back to New York.'

'But you'll come back with me to the barn first?'

'Of course.' She kissed me, and that was enough. I didn't ask any more questions about what sort of future we might have. After Katie I'd learnt the folly of asking a woman about the future.

A man from Rome, a public prosecutor or some such, came to see me that afternoon, asking me to make a statement, confirming all that I'd told the chief. Some Italian journalists, hanging around the hotel lobby as we were going out to eat, tried to ask me questions. I brushed them off.

'I'll be glad to get out of here,' I said to Elsa, walking quickly away towards the fish restaurant. 'We'll book a flight out to London tomorrow.'

Next morning the carabinieri chief came to see me again. Elsa and I were in the breakfast room, almost finished, sipping coffee. I offered him a seat. He was in a good mood.

He spoke to me in Italian. 'We've been going through the cave overnight, making an inventory of the stuff. We've got the name of the German your father was working with, who must have brought the looted art down here – an SS Major Pfaffenroth, alias "Joseph Bergen" according to your father.'

He had the names out before I could stop him, and Elsa, though her Italian wasn't good, had heard her father's name. She was instantly alarmed.

'Joseph Bergen?' she asked me. 'What does he say about my father?'

'Oh, nothing …'

'Come on! I just heard him say his name.'

It was no use pretending then. I said to the chief. 'How did you find out about this man, that he was Pfaffenroth, alias "Bergen"?'

'It's all here, in a letter from your father. It was in a steel box, beside one of the big paintings.' He produced the letter and handed it to me. It was my father's handwriting. I started to read it to myself, but Elsa insisted I translate. It was dated July 1969, presumably when he and Pfaffenroth had taken out all the paintings he'd wanted, had sold the quarries and booby-trapped the cave.

I write this to say how I was blackmailed into helping get all this looted art out of Poland just before the end of the war, by SS Major Helmuth Pfaffenroth, aide to Dr Hans Frank in Krakow, who afterwards went to Dublin, forcing me to follow him, where he took the name of Joseph Bergen, living in Killiney with an antiques shop in the city where he sold the stolen art over the years.

'Pfaffenroth,' she said. 'The name's familiar.'

'I've not heard of –'

'Wait, wasn't he the man your friend Harry told you about in Paris – a man who worked with Dr Frank in Poland, who'd sent millions of Polish Jews to Auschwitz?'

'No, I don't think so. I don't remember.'

The chief, understanding something of what we were saying, said helpfully, in English, 'Yes signora, the Special Police from Rome confirmed the name this morning: SS Major Helmuth Pfaffenroth – he was the "Joseph Bergen" in the letter.'

Later, upstairs, in our room, Elsa was nervous, haunted, just as she'd been during those first meetings in Dublin. She said 'Ben, there's something wrong. If your father was up to the hilt with Pfaffenroth – with my father in the picture looting business out here in Carrara, then your Grandmother Emelia must have known him.'

'She didn't tell me that.'

'But you said your father told her everything about the looting business. So he must have told her about my father.'

'No.'

'I can see it in your face, you're lying. You just want to protect me.'

'Okay. Yes, she did tell me about your father. And I do want to protect you.'

'You didn't before. That's exactly what you wanted to prove to me, that both our fathers were war criminals – as we know they were now, and my father was one of the worst.' I turned to her. 'And now you want to deny it all, like I wanted to.'

'Yes!' I said vehemently. 'Because no good can come of worrying over the truth of it now.'

'Which is exactly what I used to say. But we have to face it now. Isn't that what we came down here for, to tell the truth?'

'Right! And we've done that.'

'Easier for you than me. Your father didn't send millions of Polish Jews to the ovens.'

'No. But he was a Jew killer by association, since he must have known all about what your father had done.'

I reached across the table and squeezed her hand. 'Dear God, Elsa, forget it. We were no part of it. No part of it at all.' There was a slight squeeze back, but I don't think she'd accepted my message.

'I'm tired, Ben, I'd really like to go home – but with you first, to your barn.'

I had the feeling she was just being loyal to her promise now, going through the motions. 'I'll ask Carlo to book us tickets. Then I'll call on Emilia before we leave. I'm going to give her the Modi nude.'

Emilia was indoors this time. Rain clouds had come over the great view in the late afternoon. She was not with the other elderly people in the humid, gloomy room, but in her wheelchair in a small chapel, which had been adapted from a room at the side of the villa, where it was cool. She was parked at the back, not praying, just sitting.

'So,' she said looking round, 'The news is everywhere about Luchino and Pfaffenroth.'

'Yes, but I told nobody. It was all in an open letter from Luchino they found in the cave up there.' And I told her what he'd written in the letter.

'He could never blame himself,' she said with finality. 'He always had to be right. Can you wheel me about a bit, Benjamin, with your one good arm?'

'Oh, yes. I can nudge you along at least.'

I nudged her out of the chapel, down a side corridor and out into an overgrown garden at the back of the villa, along a weedy marble path, past ruined flower borders that led into an orchard beyond, fruit and olive trees, wild vine groves with big black grapes, a mulberry tree. Pushing underneath the trailing branches of the mulberry, I said, 'Of course I can understand your affair with Amedeo. And marrying Marcello. But after you'd married Roberto, when you discovered the criminal things he was up to with Luchino – forgive me, I wonder why you didn't leave him?'

'I'd loved him, that's why. He was a good man, too, before Luchino dangled millions in front of him, and he took the bait. Loving someone isn't to know how they're going to turn out later.'

'No, but when you found out you could have left him.'

'I thought it's better to stay faithful to the good in people you've loved, not to betray the faith you once had in them. Better that than leaving and denying the love I'd had for him.'

We moved through the dark wood. The clouds had come right down over the hill. I said, 'You're right. Despite the bad things about Luchino and Roberto, you stayed faithful to the good things in both of them. I should do the same about Luchino. After all, he was a good father: he loved me, paid for my art schooling in Dublin and Paris, always encouraged me. He was the making of me.'

'That's good. If you go on thinking the worst of people, even if it's true of them – you come to think even worse of yourself.'

'Yes.'

'Wheel me on, Benjamin.' We came out of the dark wood, to a view over the sea, and to the west a clearing sky, a glimmer of evening light over the distant water.

'Luchino loved you and was generous to you because you were Amedeo's grandson. He knew that, since of course I'd told him, but he couldn't tell you. Yet he wanted you to be as good a painter as Amedeo, and have all the chances Amedeo never gave himself.'

'And maybe that's why he hid the painting of you up in my old attic studio – hoping I'd find it one day, which would lead me back to the truth about him – and to you.'

'And that's even better,' she said reaching her arm up to me. I grasped her hand and squeezed it. 'That's very good.'

When it started to rain, we went back inside, and I retrieved the painting from the chapel and unwrapped it. I said, 'I'll come back soon and paint you, may I?' She nodded, and I went on, 'Meanwhile, this painting is yours much more than mine.'

'No, no! I don't want to be reminded of what I was once like!'

'Well, then sell it. The Sister told me the villa here, all the grounds … they're being sold.'

'The Sisters only have a leasehold and the owners have had an offer, property development people, a lot of awful apartment blocks all over the hill – millions of Lira.'

'The painting is worth more – millions of dollars. Buy the villa and the hill twice over.'

'All right.' She was suddenly pleased, with just the same bright-faced smile as my father when an unexpected happiness had occurred between us. A bounty out of the blue, fair weather after a squall out on the boat in Killiney bay or two complimentary glasses of champagne before lunch from Harry the barman downstairs at the old Hibernian buttery. 'Thank you,' she resumed, 'I think I could survive anywhere, but the other ancients here couldn't. Thank you. Thank you very much.'

'I'll talk to the Sister now, and I'll sell the painting for you when I get back to England, and send the money.'

'No, come back with the money, Benjamin. You're much more important. Come back often – and take whatever you want of the money yourself.'

'All right, I will.'

I bent down, kissed her on the forehead, and went to talk to the Sister. I showed her the picture, explaining who it was by and who it was of. She hadn't heard of the artist, but she saw the likeness in the nude woman.

'The face,' she said firmly, not looking at the nude body. 'Yes, it's certainly Signora Battaglia.'

I said that I was going to sell it, on Signora Battaglia's behalf, so that they could buy the villa and the hill. The Sister was suitably grateful, but in the manner of having received expected news, something that God had in mind for them all along.

It was raining hard. The Sister called me a taxi. Waiting for it, I thought I had all my answers now, except about Katie – and I didn't need any answers about her, now that I had Elsa. I thought of burning Katie's diary and throwing the ashes over the small town where we'd been so happy. But there were no fireplaces in the hotel, so rather than condemn it to the hotel garbage bin, I packed it before we left Carrara for the airport next morning. I wasn't really sorry we weren't going over the mountains into the olive groves. I was going back with Elsa to my old barn. And that was a far better thing, what I'd wanted from the very start – to make a proper story of my life at last, and to make it with Elsa.

It was mid September when we got back to my Cotswold barn. I'd called Margery, my landlord's wife, from the airport and the taxi we'd taken from Kingham station had dropped us off at their farmhouse at the top of the lane. I said to Elsa, 'They're going to think you're Katie. They met her several times, but I'll explain.'

'Some explaining.'

Elsa was right. When we turned up at the door Tom said nothing, expressionless. Margery, on the other hand, looking at Elsa, was startled.

'It's all right, Margery. This is another friend of mine, Elsa – Elsa Bergen.'

'Oh.'

They were puzzled, but welcomed us warmly. We were ushered into the kitchen. They were about to have their tea – ham on the bone, tomatoes, lettuce, pickles, a big chunk of cheddar, and salad cream laid out on the long pine table.

'Yes, it's strange to meet someone who looks so like someone else,' I added.

'It is,' Margery said, in an easier manner, 'but then you're always coming up with surprises, Ben. You'll have tea with us,' she continued. 'There's plenty.'

'Oh, no, we don't want to disturb …'

'Not at all. It's good to see you both – to see you back.'

She busied herself about the kitchen. The kettle was murmuring on the hob, with a big brown teapot next to it. She got out one of her white home-baked crusty loaves from the bread bin. We took our places. Silence.

'You've hurt your arm,' Margery spoke with concern.

'Oh, that's nothing. Climbing the mountains in Italy – we were on holiday. I slipped. You got my card?'

'Oh, yes, we got your card. Thank you.'

'Slippery mountains,' Tom said. 'Marble, the card said. They'd be slippery mountains all right.'

They both looked at us, covertly, bemused, the strangeness of this woman, who was both Katie and Elsa, sinking in. Elsa was sitting beside me. Since becoming one-armed, she cut up any difficult food for me. I sat there, disarmed, dependent, almost useless. It was still a new feeling, but it was surely good for me not to be in control for once. I said brightly, 'Second childhood!'

We tucked in and I told them a little of what had happened to us on my 'painting holiday' as I put it, in France and Italy; a barge trip, walking in the Italian mountains where I'd slipped and hurt my arm, and so on. 'And here?' I asked. 'All well here? The weather and the crops?'

'Well, it wasn't that good a summer, too many storms, the winter barley was flattened.' Tom complained a bit more before Margery interrupted him.

'Tom, stop moaning and give them a bit of gin in their tea.'

Tom got the bottle of gin out and doused my tea with it. Elsa showed surprise at this old rural habit, but couldn't refuse. Tom took a good whack for himself. We chatted. Nobody mentioned how alike Elsa and Katie were.

I'd left my car in one of Tom's dry barns. He came with us to see it started.

'But you can't drive it one-armed,' Elsa said.

'Oh yes I can, down the lane at least.'

The car wouldn't start. Battery flat. Tom had to get leads, attached to the battery of his Land Rover. The huge engine murmured into life.

'Logs,' Tom said, 'You'll be coming up for some logs, I expect. They say it'll be a hard winter.'

'Thank you – yes, I'll be up, Tom. Thank you.'

We drove off down the lane, over the fierce bumps, in and out of the ruts, and with half a mug of gin in me I sang the 'Skye Boat Song', loudly. Things seemed to be turning out well at last, but looking at Elsa, my doubts surfaced again. She was staring straight ahead, not unhappy, or happy. Just silent. The huge flax field on either side was just an expanse of dry stubble in the waning evening light. We passed Katie's beech tree, which I didn't point out.

Elsa seemed to like the barn just as much as Katie had. The wide open spaces and the doves were still there, cooing and chuckling in the rafters above my studio, having left quite a snowfall of droppings and feathers on the flagstones below in my absence. This didn't worry Elsa. Even the outdoor privy didn't.

A touch of autumn in the air, so I lit a fire in the huge grate, dry wood, and soon the flames were roaring up the chimney. I went outside and pumped up water into a bucket, and Elsa helped me fill up the big preserving pan I used to heat the water, and we put it on the electric plate of the old cooker. When it was warm we poured it into the old porcelain sink and Elsa tidied up, washing the plates and glasses and putting away the bottles I'd last used, and emptied, that evening after Katie had died, nearly two months before, when I'd left for Dublin the next morning.

'There's nothing much in the cupboard,' I said. 'We can go shopping tomorrow, buy some anchovies, extra-virgin olive oil and white bread, and maybe a shoulder of Welsh lamb to roast, with potatoes, mint sauce, and a bottle of Rioja Reserva. Can't do better.'

'No. That's true.'

I went to my old music centre, turned it on. I still had my Richard Tauber tape in it: 'Without a Song', the violins tentative at first, gradually finding the theme, then the passionate, high tenor voice. I came back to the sink, grasped her round the waist with my one good arm, and slow-waltzed her round the flagstones.

'God, I'm happy,' I said.

'I know you are.'

We danced. She held me with one arm, the other holding the washing-up brush, both of us one-armed now. We sat on the big divan by the fire. I wanted to make love, but I sensed she didn't. So I didn't suggest it. I waltzed her back to the sink.

While she finished the washing up I climbed the open wooden staircase to the studio. There was the partly completed clay sculpture of Katie in the corner. I covered it with a sheet and made sure all the paintings of her were turned to the wall. I was starting a new life, wasn't I?

She said when I came back, looking at me steadily, 'Incurable romantic.'

'Who wouldn't be, with you around?'

'Thank you.' She stopped, indecisive, as if she'd been about to voice the same feeling for me. She didn't. 'But thank you,' she continued, 'for thinking that way.' She smiled.

We made love that night, in the big divan by the dying embers of the fire, but it was somehow an inconclusive engagement. It was warm again the next morning, a fine autumn day. I asked if I could paint her. I didn't say nude, just to paint her. And she agreed, though I had the feeling that again she was simply keeping a promise.

We went upstairs, and she helped me get my paints ready – oil, turps, cleaning my brushes, getting a fresh primed canvas out, two by four, setting it up on the easel. One-handed and even with her help, my progress was slow and awkward, and I cursed myself. Later she came up in her shorts and T-shirt and together we worked out the best place for her to pose. I had an old chaise longue, picked up from the dump, on which I'd painted Katie. I moved it away from the direct light from one of the skylights. I had no longer expected, or even wanted, to paint her nude. But then, as if it were part of another commitment to me, like a paid model, she got undressed, sat down, raised her legs and propped herself up against the back of the chaise longue.

I asked her to get comfortable. She moved about until she found a position she liked. Half on her side, so that her legs were firmly closed, one arm partly covering her breasts, the other casually hiding her sex, face turned away in half-profile. A shy position, covert, hiding something. Like Katie when I'd painted her in the last years. Like Emilia in the Modi nude.

And gazing at Elsa, I thought to abandon the whole painting, for I was looking at all I had lost with Katie – the same build, sharp cut of cheekbones, chin. I was gazing at the same shapes and contours, colours and shadows of Katie – of all that was dead. Perhaps I was tempting fate to paint Elsa nude.

Dropping the stick of charcoal I said, 'Maybe it's not a good idea painting you like this.'

'Oh go on!' she said, bright now, almost provocative. Indeed provocative, for she changed position, taking her arms away from between her legs and her breasts, and let her legs relax, thighs slightly open.

Now I wanted to paint her.

I moved the easel towards the end and to the side of the chaise longue, so that I was looking down along her body at an angle, and started to line in her shapes with the charcoal stick. Quickly, getting the crucial flow of her body and the angles right – the slightly risen leg, the torso, the arm lines, how her hands would have to go. What the right balances were. Back and head propped up, her face slightly turned away from me.

Her face. Elsa's face, which so recently I had seen with every sort of vivid expression. Anger, terror, laughter, her bemused smile. That bright, tense, abandoned face, when we'd first made love the night before O'Higgins had arrived. Now her expression was mute.

Finally I had the lines right, and the first quick washes of paint. I painted fast, a broad brush filling in a light-umber background, a medium brush, peachy white, on the body. Sweeps of colour, but the light was too bright. I stopped and pulled the curtain over one of the skylights above me. I needed more subdued tones. Softer peach on her stomach, a paler lemon on her thighs. And the umber of the chaise longue was too severe. I clothed out a lot, diluted, softened the paints, worked rapidly. I painted fast again. Her face now.

Her face. Of course it wasn't that mute. It said something. Harry always said that was my gift, that I could display better than most painters the secrets in a person's face. So what did Elsa's expression hide now? The fact that she was slipping away from me. So that after another ten minutes I said I'd done enough and we stopped, and I said, 'Let's go to a pub I know, have lunch in the sun. I'll show you how to drive the Bentley. It's not difficult.'

She drove the big car well. I wondered – should I ask her what was wrong? But I knew what her problem was, the knowledge she had now of her father, one of the worst Nazi war criminals and murderers. But we'd talked that out, I hoped. Meanwhile, it was time just to be happy – to make her happy.

So at the Plough Inn, and for the next few days at the barn as I painted her, I talked of what was happy there and then, in front of us – the crystal autumn weather, golden views over the corn stubble, of present moments lost in the Wolds, of my work, and hers, her book on olives and olive oil. But she seemed to have lost interest in all this, despite my encouragements, so I spoke of the chance of my doing good work again and the purely material gains that beckoned me.

'The *Sorrento*,' I told her that evening. 'I'll go over and see Harry in Paris soon, put the boat on the market, get some cash so I can have plumbing put in here, and a phone. And then there's the Modi nude. Have it auctioned. Maybe ten or fifteen million dollars. Well, I'll take 10 per cent, the rest to Emelia and the sisters, so I could maybe buy the barn from Tom and do it up properly.'

'Yes,' she said, but not to any of my implicit invitations for her to share in these changes with me, for she went on immediately, 'You have a future there.' Oh, yes, a future beckoned everywhere, yet Elsa gave no sign that she wanted to share it.

Up at the Phillips' farmhouse I called Angela in Yorkshire and spoke to our daughters, Molly and Beatty, who happened to be in the cottage with her. They'd received my innocent postcards from Carrara. I talked briefly of the long painting holiday I'd taken. Molly was thriving at university in Edinburgh, and Beattie had done well on her A levels and had applied to do French and Art History at St Andrews. They were both keen on the Scottish connection. I said I'd see them soon, we'd make a date, up in Yorkshire or down with me in the Cotswolds.

I called Harry that evening, with a more truthful account of things. I asked him if he'd check my boat out and pay the dues, and said I'd be over in a week or so when I'd tell him all. Harry could wait.

What couldn't wait was Elsa. I had to get her out of her dumps, that empty expression, which I didn't want to paint. There had to be some present happiness for her, if there was to be a decent painting, let alone a future for us.

Happiness between two people can be silence, of course, but silence can hardly be sustained on a twenty-four-hour basis, with the two of us alone in the barn, sleeping together. One has to speak of something. Especially during the hour or so every morning when I was painting her.

So next morning, when she was comfortable again on the chaise longue, I said, 'I wonder, if I was a writer, if I'd write about our last six weeks together – rather than painting you?'

'It would take much longer.'

'Well, I, we – we have the time now.'

'You wouldn't need me in the way you need me now, as a sitter. You could do it from memory.'

'Yes, I know, but the painting won't take long, a day or two more, and I can fill in the rest from memory.'

I saw now how my position was the reverse of Penelope's, unravelling her weaving at night to keep her suitors at bay. I could only keep Elsa here in the barn as long as I was painting her. I hadn't much time to set her to rights.

I said, trying to lighten things, 'I'd call the book *The Two Musketeers*.'

'No. Only one musketeer.'

'Oh, no. You were a musketeer as well. That headscarf woman – when you bashed her with that Roman broadsword in the museum: completely musketeerish.'

'I wasn't swashbuckling though. I was running away all the time, you know that.'

'No. You did some swashbuckling, too. And you didn't run away in the end.'

'I did. I have.'

We were on dangerous ground. 'No you didn't, you haven't,' I said emphatically.

'You're a tough, true, marvellously attractive good woman. I'll tell you what,' I went on quickly, 'When I go to the hospital to get the wound dressed, we could go on afterwards – the Welsh National Opera are doing *Un Ballo in Maschera.*'

'Yes, all right. Of course, you are an opera fan.'

'Oh, yes. Verdi especially. I'd love to paint like Verdi: that lavish musical colour, extremes of mood, the body's sex and death – but the life force, the need to win! He gets it all together, every damned thing on heaven and earth. No footling around, everyone goes for bust. Honesty of emotion. Opera, like sex, is as salvation. All the voices in the world are there.'

'The need to win?'

'Yes, to spite death and win against all the odds. Look at Ricardo, in *Ballo*, in the graveyard scene when he spits death in the face.'

She nodded. 'Yes, like you. You've done quite a bit of going for bust and spitting death in the face these last six weeks.'

'Only because I had to.'

'No, it's you. You're quieter now. But the life force, going for it against all the odds, spitting at death – that's the real you.'

She seemed to hold this against me. I changed my brush and the paint. I was doing her feet, always difficult, like hands, but I wanted to be sure of the right colour first. Peachy white? Something in that direction. I mixed the paints, tried it out first on an old canvas on the table beside me.

She said, 'If that wasn't the real you you'd not have saved our lives. Several times. Of course you could have had us killed just as often.'

She seemed to hold this against me, too.

That afternoon we drove to the Cotswold Wildlife Park and looked at the animals, and had cream teas in Ye Olde Tea Shoppe in Burford, and she bought me a Barbour waterproof jacket in one of the trendy shops afterwards. 'For the winter,' she said. 'It rains all winter in the Cotswolds, doesn't it? So you'll need something really good for your winter walks.'

I didn't want to be reminded of the coming winter, at least not if I was to spend it alone in the barn, and she seemed to be hinting this would be the case. But I held my tongue, except to say, 'Why didn't you get one as well?'

She said, 'I wouldn't need it in New York.'

Next morning I resumed painting again, but found myself working almost by rote now, without enthusiasm. Oh, the painting was all right: the body was good, the pose, the background. But the face – there was nothing there. And it's the face that confirms the body in a nude painting. Elsa's face gave nothing to her body. It was just a body, flesh, not attached to her mind.

We went to the hospital in Oxford the next afternoon. The wound was healing well. Afterwards Elsa went into a travel agent to book a flight to New York. I thought of staying outside, and so not knowing whether she was booking a single or a return, but I couldn't resist going in with her, hovering, and I heard her say quite clearly to the agent, 'An open return, please.'

'That's twice the price,' I said lightly, back in the street.

'I don't know exactly when I'll be back. And I have money now. The Killiney house is worth a million or more, I'm sure.'

Since money was no object, had she had made a neat move in buying an open return just to reassure me? She might return. She might not. She hadn't reassured me at all. I tried not to show my worries and we went to the covered market where she bought provisions for the meal she'd promised to cook for us before she left. Then she suggested we have an early supper at the Randolph Hotel.

I said 'It's rather pricey.'

She shrugged. 'Doesn't matter. It's a treat.'

We had smoked salmon and a half-bottle of champagne.

She had bought the best seats at the opera. It was well done, vibrant, passionate, tragic. I forgot my own problems until the graveyard scene, Ricardo spitting at death, when I remembered there were real deaths in the midst of life.

The next evening she cooked her promised meal, a Georgian mountain recipe: strips of venison marinated in dry white wine, a touch of crushed garlic, lemon and wild honey, black pepper but no salt, all sealed quickly in a sizzling pan of extra virgin, then into a casserole with sun-dried tomatoes, shallots and red peppers, cooked slowly in a casserole for an hour. A bottle of Rioja Reserva.

We ate outside, on a rough table, behind the barn. It was still warm. I said easily, halfway through the meal, 'Well, there you are, off tomorrow. I'd drive you to the airport, but the arm ...'

'No, of course not. I'll take a taxi to the train.'

'But I'll come with you on the train.'

'No, there's no need.'

'Of course there's need. I'm not doing anything else. And for God's sake, Elsa, why wouldn't I come with you?'

'I don't know. I mean ...'

'Elsa, I love you. We love each other.'

'Yes,' she said in a tone that I couldn't identify as being one of confirmation, regret or falsehood.

'So there'll be – some kind of future.'

'Yes. There's always some kind of future,' she said, and this seemed as good answer as I was going to get, so I left it at that, apart from repeating that of course I'd come to the airport with her.

'It's not that I wouldn't want that, just that I'm bad at goodbyes, airports, trains. Really. See me off in a taxi here. Please. I promise you ...' She stopped.

'What?'

'Of course I'll come back, when I've settled things in New York. I've got an open return ticket to come back to England. You saw me buy it.'

'We'll keep in touch in any case, won't we?'

'Of course we will,' she said, and again I heard the placatory tone in her voice. No certainty.

Twilight closed over the great beech tree by the privy, and pinprick stars came out in the clear velvet sky, and now there was a chill in the air.

I lit the fire when we got in, and later we went to bed, naked on the sheet, no need of anything over us in the heat, and seeing her limbs move – red and yellow and ochre in the dancing shadows of the fire – we made love, she made love, with such abandon, such vehement pleasure, as if there was no tomorrow. So that afterwards I thought happily we cannot but be together, in all our tomorrows.

Almost as soon as Elsa left in the taxi early next morning, driving along the track between the flax stubble and past Katie's tree, I wanted to follow her in the car. I wanted to follow her to the airport, fly with her to New York – anything to be with her. I would have done that if I could have driven, or had any money. As it was I only had a few hundred pounds she'd given me from her AmEx card to tide me over until I came into my own money with Harry. Still, I'd call her that night from the Phillips' house, to see that she'd got home safely.

I spent the day on tenterhooks, and up at the farmhouse much later that evening I called her in New York. No reply. Only the answer phone – 'I am not available at the moment. Please leave a message.'

I left an encouraging message. 'Dear Elsa,' I said. 'I hope you got home okay. I'll call you later. I love you.' I stayed on with the

Phillips' to watch the late evening news, I hadn't followed the news since getting back.

And there it was, ten minutes in, the latest on what had clearly been a big story over the last week from Italy – the Carrara story. The discovery of a huge hoard of Nazi looted art in a cave up the mountains. There were clips of the quarry cave and of the paintings and gold chalices and jewelled reliquaries, and the identification of two of the perpetrators of this vast wartime theft, SS Major Helmuth Pfaffenroth, alias 'Joseph Bergen', responsible, with Dr Hans Frank, for the death of several million Polish Jews, and an Italian marble-quarry owner, Luchino Contini. Both men had gone undercover in Dublin after the war and were now dead. But it had been discovered that 'Joseph Bergen' had a daughter, the well-known cookbook writer Elsa Bergen – there were shots of her from the dust jacket of one of her books.

Tom Phillips had dozed off on the sofa and so saw nothing. Margery had seen it. I was about to make some explanation when she put a finger to her lips, looking over at Tom. Neither of us made any further comment.

Afterwards I went into the kitchen and called Elsa in New York again. Still just the answer phone. I drove home, the boot filled with winter logs, opened a bottle of the Rioja, and tried to distract myself with *Pinafore*. I slept very badly that night.

I drove the car, practically one-handed, to Chipping Norton the next morning, I bought three or four papers and took them to The Chequers, the pub on the market square. They were full of the Carrara find: and there was a photograph of Elsa arriving at Kennedy airport, trying to hide her frightened, horrified face with her arm, among a jostle of pushy photographers and journalists, with the caption 'Famous Cookbook Daughter of Nazi Jew Killer Arrives Home', and another old photograph beside it, of Pfaffenroth in his SS uniform. Shit, I thought.

'Shit,' I said out loud.

I left the pub, bought a phone card at the post office, and called Elsa again. The same answer-phone message. I left a message, saying I'd read the papers, that I was coming over to New York at once. I drove home. Turning into the lane by the Phillips' farmhouse, Tom was in the yard. He flagged me down.

'There's been a message for you, Ben.'

I went into the kitchen. Margery handed me a piece of paper. 'A woman phoned from New York, about half an hour ago. Asked if you'd call back.' My heart leapt. It could have only been Elsa.

It wasn't. It was Martha, Elsa's old girlfriend. What could she want? I called the number, prepared to hear her admit they were lovers once more, but by the time the edgy, brittle voice answered, I knew I was about to hear the worst.

Elsa was dead. 'I'm sorry,' she said. 'I'm truly sorry. There was a note beside her in her apartment, giving my name and phone number, and yours in England. Asking whoever found her to call us. I found her.'

I barely took in the rest, but I got the gist of it. Martha, seeing the morning TV news in New York and the clips of Elsa's arrival among the media crowd at the airport the previous day, had phoned her at once, several times, that same morning. Just the answer-phone message, each time. So she'd gone to her apartment. No answer from the buzzer. She'd called the police. Broke the door down. Elsa was lying on the kitchen floor, her sanctum; an empty bottle of pills and the two messages, to Martha and me, on the kitchen table.

'Was there nothing else to the message?' I asked.

'No,' Martha said, 'Nothing.'

'I'll call you back,' I said.

I wept.

NINETEEN〈〈〈〈〈〈〈〈〈〈〈〈〈〈〈〈〈〈〈〈〈〈〈〈〈〈〈〈〈〈

Since I was the only person who knew what Elsa had heard about her father in Carrara, I was the only one who could have prevented her suicide. I'd seen the depression she had been slipping into, and failed her by not insisting on accompanying her back to New York.

And then again I never should have goaded her into this Nazi hunting in the first place, never have encouraged her on our trip across Europe, in search of our fathers, to Dachau, to that end in the Michelangelo Hotel. I was responsible for Elsa's death.

I had murdered her with this drive for truth and honesty. My 'principles' had killed her. I'd thought it was a joint battle we were fighting, against the liars, the smug, the hypocrites, the crooks and Nazis. She and I, birds of a feather – it had seemed natural that we should fight this battle together.

But I should have seen how there were exceptions in this fight for truth and principles. In some circumstances you should throw them away. Even Elsa had told me how she would have given up her principles in return for holding Martha again.

But for Elsa to discover who her father really was, and the terrible things he'd done in the war, together with the ghoulish publicity in the media on her return to New York, had been too much for her.

Truth and principles? I'd followed mine to the end and lost Elsa by them. And when I saw Katie's diary on the shelf where I'd left it, I picked it up to throw it on the fire. The truth, whatever Katie had hidden from me, had killed her as well, I was sure.

I didn't throw it on the fire. Before I could, several sheets of paper fell out; they had been roughly taped in between the pages and had come adrift. I'd never seen them before. On the first was a map, drawn in what must have been her father's hand, with writing on the top.

> *Here is the Glastonbury and Avebury area map I've made, and you can clearly see how Glastonbury Tor was the Sacred Mount Tabor, the 'Hill of God' and the scene of the Transfiguration, and what the other places were called by the original Britons. And I've put notes about it all on the back of the page.*

The map showed two different place names in each case. Avebury was the 'Egyptian Abaris', Hackpen Hill was the 'Mountains of Abraham', Silbury Hill was 'Shiloh', Marlborough was 'The Pyramid Mound'. And so on.

I turned the map over. On the back, in his small neat hand-writing, was a continuation of earlier notes he'd sent her.

> *So you see, from my previous notes and our trips to the long barrows and hill forts all round here, how Britain was civilized from the earliest times, and was undoubtedly the cradle, the earth mother, of our civilization. And that the drowned island-continent of Plato's Atlantis was not myth, but a fact – and that Atlantis was the British Isles, drowned in a catastrophic flood (Noah's flood), but not permanently submerged, that these islands rose again after the flood to become the Happy Isles, the real Hesperides, inhabited from*

the earliest Palaeolithic times by the sons of Adam, who were the Titans of classic fame, as well as being the Atlantians of Plato. So the research I've been doing all these years shows conclusively that the British were the original master race, the 'onlie begetters' as it were of our whole civilization. The master race, where you can trace their subsequent civilizing journeys all over the world, into the Middle East, which became the Holy Land of Abraham, where the Britons were one of the two lost tribes of Israel, the British Israelites, and from there elsewhere – as the Persian Aryans, for example, into India and so on. The British race, from whom all intelligent races stemmed and the others depended on. It's a wonderful story, full of what seems myth and legend but which are in fact truths.

These myths are truths. The very roots of our being. That's the whole point. Myth is vision, holiness, wholeness. And without these we perish. As we very nearly have in this century, where, apart from some German thinkers and leaders we've come to see these Nordic myth-truths as nonsense, or as evil and malignant. Whereas they are the true well-spring, the real life force. And those who see this are our real masters. As the British race once was, because they first expressed this vision, this life force.

So here at last, in this confused farrago of master-race rubbish, was the answer to the Katie mysteries. Here was the matter that had so attracted Katie to her father on his return and had taken her away from me. I read her diary now, on the page opposite where the map had been taped in.

That trip we made, picnicking at the Avebury Circle – Pa and I talked so well of the far distant origins of these circles, and the myths behind them, which we think of as fairy tales but which are truths …

I stopped. I was shaking. What I'd thought were innocent archaeological trips hadn't been innocent. He'd been seducing her with his pre-history, master-race fantasies.

Katie had been taken in. I wouldn't have been, which was why she had never mentioned this shared interest of theirs to me. In her next paragraph she gave her reasons for this.

One of the problems with Ben is I can't talk to him about these things. He hasn't an interest in the past, in myths as truths, in the wholeness and holiness to be found in legend and myth. For him it's always the here and now. He's so literal. 'The touch of a woman's body is the only true loss,' he once said to me. He lacks the spiritual dimension, and of course he doesn't have the archaeological and linguistic knowledge that Pa has, his skill in linking them up, sorting out the mistakes of history, setting history to rights. And I need that real heart of excitement. I feel that so much with Pa – the search for the truth and the ideal, and there isn't a future with Ben in that way. Pa's historical creativity appeals to me, as Ben's painting doesn't, in that I'm not involved, just the obsessive subject of it. And besides, Pa needs me for his work, as a helpmeet and sounding board, and Ben doesn't. There's nothing I can share with him in his painting. With Pa I have real involvement. I feel I'm necessary to his work, that I have some control in what he's doing.

Indeed, I thought – control over him, as she sensed she could never have with me.

I feel all this now, since Pa has returned, the company and stimulation I have from him. Ben's life, his love for me – it's the body love, not me the spirit. We could never be soul mates as I am with Pa. Ben cuts corners, lacks true principles. Pa has them, and sticks to them against every criticism and setback.

Well, here it all was, the real reason why Katie had dropped me: she had found a reciprocated love with her father. Though she was right about me in one way. I was a here-and-now man, a believer in the visible. That was where I found the wholeness and holiness.

And most of all I'd found this with Katie. And to have dropped fidelity to me for the sake of a philandering madman who believed the British were the children of Adam and Atlantis – this was madness indeed. There was more in this part of his notes, mostly along the same lines – Katie setting her father's inspired sleuthing against my limited mind.

I couldn't read any more. Whatever the confusions in it for Katie, the message for me was clear. I'd banked everything on her, and lost. Like her father I was always one to defy reason. The big difference was that I did this with life in hand, not with crazy dreams of a British master race and myths of Atlantis. I suppose, in biblical terms that her father would no doubt have acknowledged, Katie had 'risen to the Father'. Her suicide was her way of joining him.

But why in the living Christ, dear Katie, did you not rise with me? I'm not the grail you sought and thought you'd found with the return of your father. Better the urgent sex in fields of flax and clover than the dry bones in hill forts and long barrows. Better the naked sinner than a crazy knight in shining armour.

I opened a bottle of the Rioja Reserva.

Always take long odds on a woman, or set her on a canvas in a splash of colour – the body was the ultimate honesty. This had saved me – as Katie's crazy confusions had condemned her, just as Elsa's conscience, faced with the horrifying truth about her father, had killed her. They'd still be alive if they could have taken just a leaf or two out of my corner-cutting book – the book of laughter and the half-litre.

More practically, if I wasn't to sink in the swamps of drink and muddy self-justifications, there were things to do. I had to keep occupied. I called Martha in New York the next day. She hadn't much more to tell me, she said, only adding by way of rather sour comment here, 'I'm sure you must know about Elsa and me already.'

'Yes, she told me quite a bit about you,' I said, returning the sourness in my voice.

But her next words and tones were conciliatory. 'I'm sorry. It's just her death ... I feel somehow responsible.'

'Maybe. But I was much more responsible. It was more finding out about her father that killed her. And you know all about that now.'

'I'd no idea about who her father really was.'

'I did. And I shouldn't have driven her to finding out about him, as I did.' And I gave her a précis about the Modi nude and about our trip through Europe. But I didn't want to go on with it over the phone. 'Maybe another time,' I said to her, 'I can tell you things in more detail.'

'Yes. I'd like that.'

'What about the other details with Elsa? She had no family. The funeral, her apartment, her estate – and she had this big house in Dublin.'

'I know about the house. I can see to everything. She made me executor in her will, some time back. I'm an attorney.'

'She told me.'

'Do you want to come over? The funeral is at the crematorium in Brooklyn.' She was literal, business-like, the sort of person Elsa had unhappily described to me, a woman with chilly undertones, an eye for tidiness and survival, as much in practical affairs as those of the heart.

'I don't think so. Maybe one ex-lover's enough,' I added, unable to keep the bitterness out of my voice again. There was jealousy beyond death. Elsa had loved Martha better.

'I understand,' she said. 'Her death, it's very difficult ...'

I stifled the urge to scream 'But no! She's not dead!' Just as it had been with Katie, when I couldn't believe that she had incinerated herself in the oven of the flaming car, so I couldn't accept

Elsa's death – that this whole life, this body that I had loved was soon to be ash in the wind.

And then I understood – that which you loved most you were going to lose twice over, as I had lost each of them, the good in one, the faults in the other. I'd loved Katie's flaws just as much as I'd loved Elsa's virtues. Jekyll and Hyde were the same person after all.

There was a charged silence on the phone, as if Martha and I both had a lot more to say, as indeed we had. But we didn't. It wasn't the moment.

'We'll be in touch,' I said at last, not believing this.

'Yes, we'll be in touch,' she said, in a tone that didn't make me believe she meant it either. No doubt she was jealous of me as well.

My God, with this sort of thought starting to haunt me, I have to keep busy, I thought: make plans, see Harry in Paris. I needed a future more than ever. I knew I certainly couldn't face another winter in the barn alone. I had enough of Elsa's money left to get to Paris, and Harry would advance me some real cash on the strength of selling the boat. I called him at once, took an early train to London next morning and got a Eurostar standby ticket over to Paris at midday, taking the Modi nude with me.

It was crisp and sunny that afternoon rolling down the boulevards to the Marais, a day between seasons, a stillness in the weather, when a long time of heat is over and winter is no more than a hint on the calendar. Bright with a fine sharpness, a little crackle in the air of an Indian summer.

Harry opened the door, taking me into the large salon looking over the neat little square.

'Well, home is the hero,' he said, laconic as ever. 'From the wars, I see,' he added, looking at my arm, still in a sling. I could now use it to eat with, at least. He noticed the bubble-wrapped picture under my arm. 'One of yours – or Modi's?' he asked.

'His,' I said.

'Good. You managed to hold onto it through your adventures.' He gestured to a pile of newspapers on the sofa. 'It's been everywhere, your Carrara story.'

'Yes. More's the pity.'

'What d'ya mean? Wasn't that what you wanted? To prove your father a crook? And you nailed his partner, too – that guy Pfaffenroth, the real war criminal.'

'Yes, I nailed them all.'

'So what's the problem?'

'Pfaffenroth turned out to be the father of the girl I was with, who looked so like Katie – Elsa Bergen. When she found out who her father really was she killed herself. Didn't you read that in the papers, too?'

'Yes. But I didn't think … I never met her. I didn't associate her with the girl who was with you here, when you came to see me that morning. Christ, I'm sorry.'

'You were right. I shouldn't have turned over old stones.'

I rolled a cigarette. He said, 'Sit down, Ben, have some coffee, or a vodka, and start from the beginning.'

And I did, telling him the whole story of our trip across Europe.

'A journey I should never had made. Elsa would still be alive if I hadn't. What possessed me?' I was shaken.

'That's very tough, Ben. Let's have a shot.'

'And you certainly told me not to,' I went on. 'Offered me ten million bucks for the picture, in effect not to go on with it.'

'Yes, I did that.'

'You didn't want those old art-looting stones turned over either, did you?'

He stopped halfway to the kitchen. 'No, I didn't.'

I left it at that. I'd exposed enough damn truths and secrets. He returned from the kitchen with a bottle of chilled Polish vodka and two shot glasses. We moved over to the window.

'Ben, it's a damn sorry story, but if it's any consolation let me tell you now you were right about that Modi painting, and I was wrong when we last met that morning. "All that is necessary for the triumph of evil is that good men do nothing." But good men sometimes have to say nothing – for the success of happiness.' He raised his glass.

'Yes.' I raised mine. We drank.

'Tell you what,' he said. 'Talking of provenance – that Modi of yours, selling it and giving the proceeds to Emelia and the nuns – well, your being Modi's grandson and the woman herself still alive, and the dedication, gives the painting superb provenance, adds another couple of million to it at least.'

'You think?'

'Sure I do. I can get you – I'll give you – ten, fifteen million bucks for it. Whatever it's valued at.'

'What do you mean?'

'I mean I love it, Ben. I can have it valued here and buy it myself. Full value. You'll lose twenty, maybe thirty per cent of it – two or three million – at auction, remember.'

'You? You have fifteen million dollars to hand?'

'I have plenty of dollars, don't worry. And if I need any more, I can sell that Renoir nude, or the Soutine – each one around ten million alone, and I've seen plenty of them. I'd prefer to look at your grandmother for the rest of my life.'

'Yes. Yes, okay. Then I can look at her, too.'

'Right! Let's celebrate – lunch at La Tourelle?'

I nodded. Harry and I were back where we'd started, twenty-five years before, when he'd bought two of my early canvasses and he'd taken me to celebrate at the same little restaurant.

We walked out into the sunshine, across the square, down to the quays, towards the Pont Neuf. The way I'd gone with Elsa two months before, and before that with Katie, making for the same restaurant. And as if he sensed my thoughts, he took my arm, and said, 'I'm sorry, Ben – giving you hell about all your women that morning.'

'Yes, I wondered why.'

'Because you think too much about women, Ben. And maybe you're right. I'm not a painter. So you see, I don't know the processes, whatever it takes, the inspiration. And if it's women – any woman, prim and prude or naked under fur coats riding circus horses – why, that's the best possible inspiration, and certainly a hell of a lot better than pickled sharks and tins of Campbell's soup.'

'Yes, those frauds made a real meal of that.'

'But listen,' he turned to me, taking my arm again. 'The great thing is that you've survived. So the work must survive. You've got to get back to it, Ben.'

'Yes, I know.' I wasn't very convincing. We walked on, crossed the river and entered the restaurant.

'I'll tell you what,' he said, after Madame had greeted us and led us to a corner table, and we'd ordered the coarse pâté and the plat du jour, the *lapin à la moutarde* they had on that day, and a bottle of Beaujolais. 'You know I have a share in that gallery round the corner. Get a dozen or so canvasses together, whatever's good in your barn and some new stuff, and I'll organize an exhibition for you. But we'll need some new material. Right?'

'You're sure?'

'Course I am. You're a damn good painter. Told you that last time we met, when I said some of your nudes were like Modi reincarnate. Well, as you're his grandson, it turns out I was right about that at least.' He smiled.

'I'll get some work together. Thank you, Harry.'

We drank the Beaujolais and chattered of other things, among all the other local chatterers, all squashed in together, the heady fumes of food and wine going nicely to my head.

And that was it, I thought. Paris, a new beginning. A week later, back in the barn when I had a letter from Harry saying that 'Emelia' had been valued at between fifteen and twenty million dollars, and that he'd buy it, I realized I could take a flat in Paris with my ten per cent, for that winter and the next. Paris was for painters, as well as lovers. I'd lost the latter. I could concentrate on the former.

What an autumn it was when I got back to my barn, days on end, still and gold and warm. Each morning was like the start of summer, except for the leaves of the chestnut tree and the beech above the privy, turning yellow, orange, ochre. My arm healed and a week later the sling and bandages came off. Harry had advanced me ten thousand dollars cash in Paris against selling the boat and the picture, so I had a phone installed, paid Tom three months' rent, had the Bentley serviced and drove up to Yorkshire to see Angela and our daughters.

The girls were excited by their own young lives, and it was exciting for me that they were happy and doing well. They listened to my Carrara story, bemused. Not that Molly and Beatty didn't want to know of my adventures, looking for the truth behind the painting and of Modigliani himself, their great-grandfather, and of Luchino, their grandfather, and hearing of what the latter had done in Auschwitz and afterwards. But it asked from them an understanding of which they were not yet capable. I didn't speak more of the story. The two of them were perfectly aware, at least, that it was, in fact, unspeakable. So there was silence at the end of my telling.

As for meeting Angela again – that was rather speechless, too. I told her I was coming into some money and that if she needed any that wouldn't be a problem now. She declined politely. She was a woman of principle too – albeit that she maintained this at the expense of deceiving her lover's wife, and living mostly on his money.

I had brought two thousand pounds in cash to split between Molly and Beatty. They accepted their share with some surprise, and grace. Molly said she'd use it to take her apprentice forester boyfriend to a holiday cottage near Loch Lomond, and the more prudent Beatty said she'd put it into her building society savings account.

When I left, driving down the rough track, waving furiously at the three of them standing outside the cottage, I felt a bad tug of familial sadness.

Back at the barn, with the ready money I had now – cash that I kept under the mattress – I stocked up on new paints and canvases for my Paris exhibition, a new music centre, new Verdi CDs, and some decent château wines. I went to Oxford and bought a few expensive art books from Blackwell's, and visited my favourite pictures in the Ashmolean gallery – Pissarro's *The Tuileries Gardens in Rain* and one of Cézanne's views of Mont Sainte-Victoire, and gave myself another treat – a formal, donnish lunch alone at the Elizabeth restaurant.

I spoke to Tom and Margery the next Sunday, telling them of the money I was coming into. Would they be interested in selling me the barn? They would. They were both getting on, wanted to retire, and were thinking of selling the entire farm in any case. I could buy the barn first.

'Thank you,' I said. And Tom got out the gin bottle, dispensing a good whack of it in our tea mugs. We raised our mugs, and on the way home, driving down the lane, I sang 'The Skye Boat Song', loudly.

I tidied up my studio, sorting out possible pictures for the exhibition and finding old ones that I could work on again. I turned the nude of Elsa to the wall, along with the others of Katie. All over. Finished. For the first time since Elsa had died I was almost happy.

It didn't last. I fiddled about with some old paintings – one of Tom and Margery, a trial for a portrait I'd given them several years before, and thought again with what I might start afresh. But what was there that could genuinely excite me, without a sitter, a model, a woman?

I thought of putting an ad in the local paper. 'Model wanted, to work nude, for local painter.' In our rural area such a request might have been misinterpreted. Or I could advertise as a portrait painter, looking for a commission, and perhaps, as a result, some wonderful new woman would swim into my ken, as Katie had. I doubted it. I might have set my brush to paintings of old horses, pet dogs, cats and prize porkers. There was a market these days for that.

The fact was I hadn't any enthusiasm for painting pigs or for models or for strangers in my studio, nude or not. I was depressed. So much had happened in the last months, so much activity, danger, emotion and loss, that I was drained of any kind of response. The juices had gone, leaving me stranded on a dry shore, facing a cold winter alone.

One evening, after a week messing around pointlessly in the studio, I gave it all up. Instead I uncovered some of the old nudes of Katie and the reclining nude of Elsa. I brought the paintings downstairs, put them in semicircle by the big fire so that the peachy flesh tones, the lemon of thighs and ochre shadows between their legs glimmered memorably in the yellow flickering light. Unable now to distinguish between the women, they seemed as one – limbs moving, inviting, alive in sensuous delight. I gazed at them. I put on my new Tebaldi and Domingo *Traviata* CD and opened a bottle of the Rioja Reserva. And another.

It was early evening, a week later. I was outside the barn trying to start the Bentley. I hadn't driven it in a while, and it had been damp and humid the last few days, which was why the bugger wouldn't start. Thunder grumbled distantly in the air. I heard the sound of a motor coming up the lane. I looked round and a smart new red Peugeot drew up in front of me. A woman got out.

She was in her late thirties, smallish, with a delicate, rather plain face, two swathes of reddish hair to either side of a central parting, rather formally, unfashionably dressed in a black wool skirt, cream silk blouse with a cameo brooch and brown buckled shoes. Fragile and dainty, an air of reticence, but in control.

'Hello.' She stood there in the darkening air, both of us now uncertain. 'I'm sorry – I left a message with your farmer friends up the lane.' The voice was old-fashioned American. The words clearly enunciated. New England, I thought.

'I've not been out for a while,' I said sourly. I was in no mood to entertain strangers. She looked at me, a trapped look. 'I don't think I know …'

We were both trapped now, standing gazing at each other, until she broke away.

'I'm sorry. I'm Martha. Martha McGowan. Elsa's friend. I'm over here in Oxford at a legal conference, Association of the American Bar. So I thought I'd call on you.'

'Of course – Martha.' We shook hands. I gestured to my car. 'Damn car won't start,' I said.

'Oh. Can I take you someplace?'

'I was going shopping,' I said. 'I've run out of booze.'

'Oh,' she said again, nervously looking up at the sky and the approaching storm. 'I got some – at Kennedy on the way over.' She turned, rootled about in the car, and took out a bottle of Jack Daniels.

I was surprised. 'Elsa said you were teetotal.'

'Did she? Well, I'm not.' She looked at her watch. 'Not after six o'clock anyway.' Then she glanced up at the threatening sky again.

The vast flash of sheet lightning dazzled me, the crack of thunder like the pit of doom opening. She ducked, holding her hands over her head. 'Oh my God!' she said. Now she was different: panicky, eyes darting, as if the approaching storm was about to hurl itself upon us and sweep her up into the raging skies. She was adolescent, naïve, frightened, and this appealed to me. Besides, any woman with a bottle of Jack Daniels in her hand couldn't be all bad.

'It's all right,' I said. 'You'll be better off inside.'

'I'm sorry. I'm terrified of thunder and lightning. It's childish.'

'Nothing to be ashamed of. Joyce was terrified of it, too.'

'Joyce?'

'James Joyce, the writer. You wanted to write too, didn't you?'

'Elsa told you a lot about me.'

We were in the barn now. The place was in some chaos, the result of a week's dejection. I turned on the gilded papier-mâché chandelier. Another flash and another crack. The lights flickered and went out. It was almost completely dark in the long space.

I said, 'Sorry about the lights. The power lines are a bit wonky up the lane. I'm pretty isolated.'

'Oh no, I like it. I love this sort of place.'

'I'll get some light.'

There was no other light but the fire, which I lit. The wood was dry, so that soon the flames were storming up the chimney, a yellow flickering light illuminating the room.

'I hope the chimney won't go on fire,' she said.

'No. The chimney wall is at least to two feet thick.'

'It's not the stone that goes on fire, it's the soot, and the birds' nests.'

I was annoyed at this correction. 'I didn't know you had birds' nests and chimneys in New York.'

'We don't, but we do in my parents' farm up in New Hampshire.' She was immediately enthusiastic, eyes gleaming in the firelight, looking at me. 'I was brought up there. An old farm and stone barn, quite like this. My mother still lives in the farmhouse, and I made over the barn as a weekend place for me. All in the middle of nowhere, just like here.'

'Elsa told me nothing of this about you,' I said. 'She gave me the impression you were a hard-nosed New York attorney. Never mentioned you were a country girl.'

'Well, I am.'

'Said you were shrewish.'

'Only in court. I hope.'

'That you had dark, not red hair.'

'Well, reddish. My father's family is Irish. From the North.'

'A red-headed Irish girl – that's not at all how Elsa made you out to be.'

She laughed. 'People have to see you the way they want to see you, don't they?' She wandered about the room, looking at things, finding security in the long, thick-walled space, until there was another flash and a fearful crack, right above the roof. She put her hands on her head again, came back quickly to the hearth.

Before we sat down I said, 'There's no plumbing – no tap water and only an outside privy. If you're in need of that.'

'I think I'm all right,' she said primly.

'I have enough water for the whisky.'

'Does one need it?'

She wasn't that prim. I poured us each a good tot of neat Jack Daniels, and we sat down in the two old armchairs with the stuffing coming out, some distance from the roaring fire.

'Your health,' I said.

'And yours.' She only half-raised her glass.

I had the feeling that neither of us really meant it. Turning her head to the fire, she smoothed her hair back. A fine profile, straight brow and a nose that angled out smartly.

'You have a lot of paintings on the walls. Nudes. Are they yours?' she asked.

'Yes, though I do portraits as well, when I try to paint the real person.'

'You don't seem to have managed that with Elsa.'

'No, and you're not giving me the truth. She gave me a very different picture of you.'

'What?'

'She said that you became difficult with her,' I said. 'For no good reason. That you dropped her to write a crime novel, trying to get one up on her in the writing game.'

'Not at all,' she said quickly. 'It was her idea that I write a crime novel. She encouraged me, but I never wrote it.'

I was surprised. 'Well, she had this idea that you thought her a maverick, that her cookbook work was frivolous.'

'Yes, she was unconventional. I'm not. And as for her work – she'd made a big success with her cookbooks. She was famous.

How could I ever have thought that frivolous, or tried to better her in writing?'

'No. I suppose not.'

'People like to rewrite history,' she said evenly. 'Especially when they think you've behaved badly to them.'

'She thought you left her because you were frightened by what the big noises in your law office would say if they found out you were living with a woman.'

'That's certainly not true. One of the big noises in my law office – a vice-president – has been living with another woman for twenty years.'

'I see.' I didn't see. 'You've contradicted almost everything Elsa told me about you.'

'Yes, but …'

She didn't finish. There was another flash of lightning, another crack right over our heads – the flames storming up the chimney, blazing like hellfire in the big grate. She cowered in the other chair. I gave us both another shot of whisky.

'I suppose I'm really wondering why you came here,' I went on. 'To run Elsa down?'

'No!'

'One of you must be wrong about the other,' I said tartly. 'I knew Elsa better than I know you. So I tend to take her view of you.'

Another flash and a fierce crack. She ducked again. 'Why should I want to do that?'

'Because you feel guilty?' I said briskly. I was annoyed that I hadn't made any impact on her, and the drink gave me confidence now.

'Why should I?'

'Well, because you left her only the mushy bits of an apricot and meringue tart she made one Sunday evening for a little dinner party when she was late back.'

'My God! She told you everything, didn't she? Next it'll be my not washing up the dishes that evening.'

'It's true then?'

'Yes, but it wasn't intended,' she added quickly, defensive for the first time.

'It never is.' Silence. 'And what of your asking her if she'd slept with other women while she was away on her trips?' She didn't reply. 'Did you ask her if she slept around?'

'I did! And what damn business is it of yours anyway?' There was fire in her voice. She was rattled. 'Anyway,' she took up her cudgels again, 'if anyone's guilty, it's you. And that's why you're attacking me. It's you who took her Nazi hunting round Europe. If you hadn't she'd never have found out about her father. She'd still be alive.'

'Exactly, and I certainly feel the guilt. But I'm not attacking you for that. What I'm really wondering about is the truth – why did you leave her, for example?'

'Does it matter now?'

'It mattered plenty to Elsa, because you wouldn't tell her.'

'So? It hardly matters to her now.'

'No? Can you sit on a bad conscience forever? Don't you and I owe Elsa the truth? – now just as much as when she was alive?' I was roused. 'Listen,' I said, 'I swore I'd never go truth hunting again, because that's what killed Elsa. But maybe I was wrong. Maybe, if I look at it coldly, I was right to uncover the dirt on her father, even though it killed her. Because don't we owe the truth to the two million Polish Jews her father sent to the ovens? Who speaks for the dead there? Well, maybe I did, by finally identifying the man who sent them there.'

'You're arguing that you sacrificed Elsa to a good cause.'

'Yes, if I'm being honest. So why can't you be honest?'

Silence. I got up and offered her another tot of whisky.

'No thank you.' She stood up. 'Is this trial over?'

'As you like.'

'I'll tell you one truth,' she said bitterly. 'I was curious to see who Elsa had taken up with.'

'And you're surprised it was a boozy tosspot – and a man to boot.'

'Yes.'

'No accounting for it.'

'There is. There must be. Elsa was an intelligent woman.'

'Exactly. Which is why we were happy together. I was the same sort of man, in better times.'

'Well, everyone has their own way of getting over bad times.'

She glanced at the bottle.

'What's yours?'

'Work,' she said shortly.

'And love?'

'I've put that behind me.'

She was about to leave, but there was another flash and a receding crack, and she had second thoughts. She hovered.

'Oh,' I said, 'That's a pity.'

'You think you – I – can just take up with someone else when you feel like it?'

'No. You're right.' I stood up myself, kicking a log back onto the fire in a shower of sparks. 'I'm sorry,' I said. 'I don't just feel guilty for Elsa's death. I miss her badly.'

'So do I. And maybe that's why I came all this way to see you, and if you weren't just a boozy tosspot you might see that.'

The storm passed. She left, and that was that, I thought. She had her view of me, and I of her, but this hadn't brought us any closer to the truth about each other or Elsa.

Martha had her head in the sand. She would face any crime in court and expose it, but wouldn't face the crime in her own heart, about what she'd done to Elsa. She had left the bottle of Jack Daniels. I poured another one, settled the logs on the fire, and put on *Traviata*.

Next morning I realized I'd behaved badly and called her first thing at the Randolph Hotel. 'I'm sorry,' I said. 'I was rude. No excuse.'

'You have a good excuse. Elsa. And two million Jews in the ovens.'

Her voice was cold. In a moment she'd put the phone down and we'd never speak again.

So I said very quickly, 'Look, let's not leave it this way. Will you have dinner with me tonight? I'll pick you up at the hotel. There's a pub I know not far from Oxford, they do very good fish.'

I was sure she'd say no, but she replied 'Yes. Yes, thank you. That would be lovely.' Her tone was almost warm.

I picked her up at the Randolph that evening. We went to a country pub I knew, beyond Woodstock. A back room, pine tables, not trendy, good cooking. I gave her the menu. She put on a pair of neat gold-rimmed spectacles to look at the dishes. I asked if she'd like red or white wine. 'White,' she said at once, very definite, unlike Katie, who hated to commit herself, even to a choice of wine. Would I tell Martha how Elsa had so resembled Katie, and how much Katie had meant to me? There was no point. I hardly knew Martha and once we'd made things up I was unlikely to see her again. She lived in New York. She liked women.

I looked across at her. In the good light I saw her properly. The face neat and composed, seemly. It was difficult to think of this woman being passionate with Elsa.

'The haddock pie here is very good,' I said. 'Homemade.'

'I'd like that.'

She got up to go to the Ladies. I saw her figure properly now: slim all over but thinner in the middle, like an hour glass. Her skirt came down to below her knees, and her calves were – how can I describe them? – were scimitar-shaped beneath the folds. Yet I realized I didn't want to paint her. I went up to the bar and ordered our food, with a bottle of seemly white.

She said later, 'About last night ... you were right, I was avoiding the issue of me and Elsa. And you're right to want to examine why things go wrong between people.' She put down her glass. 'Maybe I can give you some real truths now. She was the person I really wanted to spend my life with. But –' She stopped. 'I don't know, after a year or two I got to feel we weren't on the same wavelength, and never would be.'

'She told me that, but you wouldn't tell her why.'

'No. Because I didn't know why. I knew something was wrong between us, so that one day one or other of us was going to have to give it up. And when it came to it, I did and she wouldn't.'

'Why weren't you on the same wavelength?'

'I wasn't right for her.' She screwed up her eyes, frustrated.

'No?'

'She was going against her real nature, and you and she are the proof of that.'

She was stalling again. 'Maybe it would be simpler to say you just fell out of love with her?'

She considered this, as a piece of crucial courtroom evidence that might save her. 'Yes.' She paused. 'But it wasn't quite as simple as that. I didn't fall out of love with her. She only had to be near me, and I loved her, and then I got to wonder if it wasn't just sex.'

'All right, but why did everything else go wrong for you?'

'She overwhelmed me with her love and I couldn't give it back, and this made her vulnerable, gave me power over her. I used that power. I wanted to hurt her because I didn't really love her, and the more she needed me, the less I needed her. And the more I behaved coldly to her, the more she warmed to me, and so the worse I behaved. Trapped in that awful equation. I should have got out before the cruelty started.'

Silence, so that I went on quickly. 'Point is, though, you still haven't said what it was in her character that put you off her.'

'You should be a lawyer.'

'Don't you owe it to her?'

'To you, you mean.' She let her shoulders slump, looked down, then up at me. 'All right – she was so confident, especially in her unwavering loving, so absolutely right and complete about it. And this began to annoy me. I couldn't match her fine loving character, knew that the only control I was ever likely to have was in hurting her. There, I've told you the truth. And I don't feel any better for it.'

'No.'

'And even that's not the whole truth. You see ...' She paused, as if this time she really had to get it right. 'We're back to one reason why Elsa killed herself. It wasn't just because you took her round Europe Nazi hunting, and she found out about her father. It was just as much because I wouldn't give her the life she so much wanted with me. That was cruel of me, denying her what I could perfectly well have given her, if I hadn't always been counting the possible cost to myself. Just selfish. If I'd simply accepted the marvellous things we did have, we could have built a lifetime together on those.'

'But ...'

'You see,' she went on, fiery again, 'What was wrong was that I started thinking it wouldn't work out with us. So it didn't. The thought created the fact.' Silence again. And then in a quieter tone: 'I think if I'm quite cold about it all, I know I did the right thing in leaving her. It wouldn't have worked out. There'd have been worse things if I'd stayed, awful rows, hatred. And you did the right thing too, in nailing her father. But then Elsa was doing the right thing as well, for her, in loving me the way she did.'

'Exactly. I loved Elsa that way too, which is why she and I would have been a real house on fire together.'

'Yes. I didn't have her blind guts in loving. Or yours. I wish I had.'

The haddock pie came, and it was damn good, and we felt better about each other. Later, still unsatisfied, I said 'All the same – my God, Martha, why did she do it?'

'We know why. She couldn't face the knowledge of what her father had done in the war. That was the final nail in her coffin.'

'The final nail?'

'Well, we both could have stopped her killing herself. If I hadn't left her she'd never have gone off Nazi hunting with you. She'd have stayed in New York with me. And later you could have stopped her if you'd gone back to New York with her.'

I nearly wept again.

We didn't say anything more, looking down at the pine table, fiddling with the cutlery. A silence that might have lasted forever, so that I felt I had to say something. 'Dear Elsa,' I said.

Martha looked up. 'Yes,' she said. 'Dear Elsa.'

'Look,' she said later, 'I'm at a disadvantage – you know so much about me from Elsa, and I know nothing about you. I'd like to know what Elsa might have told me about you.'

'She'd probably have said I was a bounder.'

'A what?'

'A chancer, and a drinker.'

'Are you?'

'Sometimes. And I've blown things that way with women, along with my high-hatted loving.'

'Your what?'

'You know – red roses, too much singing and dancing.'

She was puzzled. 'Let me play the lawyer – it's dishonourable not to be absolutely full-hearted in loving. And I wasn't with Elsa.

As for being a "bounder", or whatever, those are misdemeanours. The grand-jury trial is surely for a lack of loving, and that doesn't seem to have been your crime. You seem to have been a real copper-bottomed lover.'

She paused again, looking up over my shoulder. 'So, members of the jury? Your Honour?' She nodded, then looked back at me, smiled. 'Not guilty, case dismissed.'

'Sounds like special pleading to me.'

'What did you think lawyers were for?'

I drew back in my chair. 'You're funny. I hadn't suspected that.'

'Not all the time. And you seemed just a boozy bounder at first, but you're not. Where it matters you're sober as a judge.'

'We're not the people we seem.'

'No, and it's just great luck if the real person coincides with the other real person in love.'

'And if they can go on seeing the real person that way,' I said.

'Ah, yes. There's the rub.'

'That's the risk you have to take in love. "Better a day as a lion than a lifetime as a lamb".'

She considered this. Then she said, in her definite way, 'Yes, that'd be quite something.' She paused again, smiled. 'I'd like to get to wear that high-hatted lion-lover's hat of yours!'

We talked effortlessly then. You can tell when there's a lucky coincidence, that flash of lightning between two people, when the talk is easy, always on the brink of laughter. I gave her my phone number and drove her back to the hotel. 'We'll be in touch before you go back.' I said.

'Yes, I hope so.'

But when she disappeared into the lobby of the Randolph, I didn't know if either of us meant it. It might all have been the wine, the good haddock pie, the release of coming to terms with each other, and with someone we'd both loved, lost or betrayed.

She phoned next day at lunchtime. 'I have a break in the conference,' she said. 'It's all rather heavy going. Some British lawyer: "The Law of Tort in Property Conveyancing".'

'My God.'

'And worse, there's an even more weighty address tonight before dinner: "Estate Law: Disposable and Non-Disposable Assets, as between the Quick and the Dead".'

'You're joking.'

'Not really. Anyway, I don't want to go. I feel among the quick. Can I return your favour and buy you a meal in Oxford tonight?'

'How will you get out of the dinner?'

'I'll say I have a headache.'

'That's rather bounderish.'

'Yes,' she said. 'Exactly.'

We ate at a Greek restaurant I knew on the Banbury Road and took up effortlessly where we'd left off the previous night. The red Demestica was good but the kebabs were tough.

'You need to grill them very hot and quickly,' I said. 'Over wood, with really good lamb, not the cheap cuts. I do them on my big fire in the barn in winter.'

'What – on a spit?'

'No. I have an old metal half-gate, and chicken wire over that. Got it from Tom, my farmer landlord up the lane – had it as part of his sheep fencing.'

She laughed.

I said to her, 'I'm happy.'

'So am I.'

'Unhappiness makes one monstrous.'

'Shall we have another half bottle?'

I nodded and we looked at each other, before she broke the silence. 'Ben' she said, 'It wouldn't work, with you and me. It worked with you and Elsa, because I think that's how she really was. But I know I'm really like I am.'

'Yes,' I said, and there was a stab of sadness.

'Though I wish …'

She stopped, looking at me, trapped in each other's gaze, as we'd been that first time we'd met outside the barn in the coming storm. Then her eyes broke away, and we chatted of other things, before I drove her back to the Randolph.

We kissed by the entrance, a kiss just short of our lips. 'We'll be in touch,' I said.

'Yes, we will. And will you come to New York?'

'Yes. And you – back here sometime?'

'Certainly.'

A smile and she walked up the steps without another word, but inside the door she turned back and waved, as if to confirm a further promise of something, I knew not what. But that didn't matter now. Loving and truth-hunting with women – I was going to have to put that aside for the moment. I'd tried, and found you could plumb to the depths of any human heart without finding the truth there. What mattered now was that Martha had seen some virtue in my trying. And more than that she'd brought back hope, and I felt that small thrill in the pit of the stomach that comes when you know you can do good work again, where in my painting, at least, I could display, in a portrait or a nude, the real truths of another, where their secrets could emerge in a dazzle of light and colour, on an incorruptible canvas. Martha had already given me as much as any lover. I could paint again.

It had been cloudy most of the day, but the sky cleared as I drove home, and there were pinprick stars all over. Very softly, I started to sing 'The Skye Boat Song'.